This book is for Eileen Rendahl,
who gave me laughter and love and a winery tour
when the stress monster was crushing me.
I couldn't have survived this move to Japan without you.

And to Michelle Cunnah,
who packed up her notebook and pencils,
investigated the Tower of London for me,
and even asked one of the Beefeaters how to steal
the jewels and make a quick getaway.
Now *that's* friendship!

And, always, to Judd.
Marrying you is the best thing I've ever done—
here's to our new adventure.

continued . . .

ATLANTIS UNLEASHED

"This character-driven tale will grab the reader's imagination from page one . . . An epic thrill ride that should not be missed."
—*Romance Reviews Today*

"A terrific romantic fantasy thriller."   —*Midwest Book Review*

ATLANTIS AWAKENING

"Alyssa Day's Atlantis is flat-out amazing—her sexy and heroic characters make me want to beg for more! I love the complex world she's created!"
—Alexis Morgan, national bestselling author

"Superb writing, fascinating characters, and edge-of-your-seat story bring the legend of Atlantis to life."
—Colby Hodge, award-winning author

ATLANTIS RISING

"Alyssa Day creates an amazing and astonishing world in *Atlantis Rising* you'll want to visit again and again. *Atlantis Rising* is romantic, sexy, and utterly compelling. I loved it!"
—Christine Feehan, *New York Times* bestselling author

"The Poseidon Warriors are HOT!! Can I have one?"
—Kerrelyn Sparks, *New York Times* bestselling author

ATLANTIS BETRAYED

A Warriors of Poseidon Novel

ALYSSA DAY

BERKLEY SENSATION, NEW YORK

THE BERKLEY PUBLISHING GROUP
Published by the Penguin Group
Penguin Group (USA) Inc.
375 Hudson Street, New York, New York 10014, USA
Penguin Group (Canada), 90 Eglinton Avenue East, Suite 700, Toronto, Ontario M4P 2Y3, Canada
(a division of Pearson Penguin Canada Inc.)
Penguin Books Ltd., 80 Strand, London WC2R 0RL, England
Penguin Group Ireland, 25 St. Stephen's Green, Dublin 2, Ireland (a division of Penguin Books Ltd.)
Penguin Group (Australia), 250 Camberwell Road, Camberwell, Victoria 3124, Australia
(a division of Pearson Australia Group Pty. Ltd.)
Penguin Books India Pvt. Ltd., 11 Community Centre, Panchsheel Park, New Delhi—110 017, India
Penguin Group (NZ), 67 Apollo Drive, Rosedale, North Shore 0632, New Zealand
(a division of Pearson New Zealand Ltd.)
Penguin Books (South Africa) (Pty.) Ltd., 24 Sturdee Avenue, Rosebank, Johannesburg 2196,
South Africa

Penguin Books Ltd., Registered Offices: 80 Strand, London WC2R 0RL, England

This is a work of fiction. Names, characters, places, and incidents either are the product of the author's imagination or are used fictitiously, and any resemblance to actual persons, living or dead, business establishments, events, or locales is entirely coincidental. The publisher does not have any control over and does not assume any responsibility for author or third-party websites or their content.

ATLANTIS BETRAYED

A Berkley Sensation Book / published by arrangement with the author

PRINTING HISTORY
Berkley Sensation mass-market edition / September 2010

ISBN: 978-0-425-23810-3

BERKLEY® SENSATION
Berkley Sensation Books are published by The Berkley Publishing Group,
a division of Penguin Group (USA) Inc.,
375 Hudson Street, New York, New York 10014.
BERKLEY® SENSATION and the "B" design are trademarks of Penguin Group (USA) Inc.

PRINTED IN THE UNITED STATES OF AMERICA

10 9 8 7 6 5 4 3 2 1

Acknowledgments

Books are like pancakes. They're okay alone, but only truly spectacular when covered with butter, syrup, berries, and whipped cream. So this book is for the folks who are the strawberries: Cindy Hwang—calm, brilliant, and insightful—who quite probably leaps tall buildings in her spare time; Leslie Gelbman, Leis Pederson, and everybody at Berkley for working so hard for me and my books; Shelley Kay, who made my website so very cool; and finally, the funny and fabulous werearmadillos—Barb, Cindy, Eileen, Marianne, Michelle, and Serena. You're all rock stars.

And a big thank-you to reader Arantza Cazalis Ruano, for the werewolf pub name The Melting Moon, to Judd for the vampire club name Daybreak, and to all my friends on Twitter and Facebook who help me out with odd research questions in the middle of the night. How did insomniac authors ever survive without you?

Dear Readers,

I hope you'll love Christophe and Fiona's story as much as I loved writing it, and as always, thank you from the bottom of my heart for spending some time with me and the Warriors of Poseidon.

As usual, a few apologies for taking liberties with the real world: First to the Yeoman Warders who protect the Crown Jewels. It is highly unlikely that any of that honorable group, founded in 1485, were actually shape-shifters. Also, Vanquish, the sword William the Conqueror first wielded and that figures so prominently in this book, is entirely a creation of my slightly twisted mind. It sounds like a sword old William would have carried, though, doesn't it?

Hugs,
Alyssa

The Warrior's Creed

We will wait. And watch. And protect.
And serve as first warning on the eve of humanity's
   destruction.
Then, and only then, Atlantis will rise.
For we are the Warriors of Poseidon, and the mark
   of the Trident we bear serves as witness to our
   sacred duty to safeguard mankind.

Chapter 1

Present day; London, England

Jack the Ripper must have been a vampire.

Christophe sat on the tiny ledge underneath the minute hand on Big Ben's western face—twenty-five past midnight—thinking random thoughts and surveying the moonlight-drenched city that had always been like a second home to him. It was a perch custom-designed for philosophical reflection, with its view of the resilient heart of London spread out before him like one of old King George's feasts.

The clock tower was arguably London's most recognizable landmark. Perching on it, nearly three hundred feet off the ground, Christophe felt spurred to an unfamiliar longing to peer into the blood-drenched darkness of England's past. Not so long ago, these modern sophisticates had fought war after war over territory, possessions, and how to worship which god. War bred its own evil shadow; reflected its black soul onto even the innocent. Or were there any innocent? Ever? Were all the so-called pure simply on an earlier stage of the descent into wickedness, hatred, and vice?

Christophe laughed out loud, startling a nearby pigeon into raising its head. "Sorry, buddy," he told the bright-eyed bird. "Something about this damn place sends my mind to strange places every time I'm here. Jack the Ripper. The Scarlet Ninja, although at least he doesn't hurt anybody. What a town."

He shook his head. "Of course, now I'm talking to a bird, so clearly I'm also insane."

He leaned back against the familiar gilt lettering, "DOMINE SALVAM FAC REGINAM NOSTRAM VICTORIAM PRIMAM," and wondered if Queen Victoria the First had been honored to have each of Big Ben's four giant clock faces proclaim that her people called out to their god to keep her safe.

Another, far more bitter, laugh escaped him at the idea that Poseidon would ever worry about keeping *him* safe. Centuries of fighting had taught Christophe the bloody and painful lesson that the sea god didn't care much about keeping his Atlantean warriors anything but honed for battle. Throwing them to the wolves and the other shape-shifters, sure. Using them as cannon fodder against the vampires, no problem. Eleven thousand years after the original pact, the current members of the elite Atlantean fighting force were still fulfilling their sacred duty to protect humanity.

Humanity should protect its own damn self.

Not that it could, or had ever been able to, against the dark and ugly that crawled out of the night. Since the monsters had revealed themselves—more than a decade ago—to be more than the fictional fodder of nightmares and bad movies, the stupid humans had done more and more to offer themselves up on the proverbial silver platter, like the sheep the vamps called them. Christophe had suggested a few times that the warriors change their mission from protecting humans to rounding them up, stuffing apples in their mouths, and then jamming sticks up their asses.

Human-kabobs. Simple, easy, and everybody goes home happy.

The high prince wasn't exactly down with the idea. Christophe "wasn't a team player." "Had a chip on his shoulder." *Insert psychobabble here.* Conlan's new human wife had the prince by the balls, and Princess Riley the former social worker was all about kindness and understanding.

Which sucked.

Christophe would have preferred that Conlan just haul off and punch him in the face, like the prince used to do in the old days when somebody pissed him off. It would have been far less painful.

"Less painful than smelling your stench, for example," he said to the vampire who was silently floating up the side of the tower, trying to surprise him. Probably thinking he'd found a midnight snack of the liquid variety.

"Interesting place to hang out, mate." The vamp levitated up until he was eye level with Christophe. "Got a death wish?"

Christophe scanned the vamp, his gaze raking it from spiky purple hair to steel-toed boots. He blamed London's punk rock scene. Bunch of lame-ass wannabes who were still trying to re-create the days of the Sex Pistols.

Like this bloodsucker.

Christophe put a hand on the hilt of a dagger but didn't bother to draw it. "You threatening me?"

The vamp shrugged. "Just pointing out that you're pretty far up for a breakable human."

Christophe bared his teeth in what passed for a smile with him these days, and the vamp flinched a little. "Not human. Not breakable."

Holding his hands up in a placating gesture, Punk Boy floated back and away from him. "Got no beef with you. Just surprised to see somebody in my spot."

"You're Queen Victoria, then?"

The vampire laughed and, surprisingly, seemed to be genuinely amused. "Know your Latin, do you?"

It was Christophe's turn to shrug. "I get by." But then an inconvenient twinge of duty nagged at him, and he sighed. "You planning to kill any humanity tonight?"

"Any humanity?" The vamp floated a little closer, but carefully still out of reach, his pierced eyebrows drawing together as he studied Christophe. "What are you talking about?"

Christophe slid the dagger from its sheath and studied its

liquid silver gleam of reflected moonlight, not raising his gaze to the vamp. "Duty, sacred oath, blah blah blah. If you're planning to kill any humans, I need to end you."

"I'd be stupid to say yes, then, wouldn't I?" The vamp's voice held genuine curiosity, and not a little wariness.

"Stupid. Vampire." Christophe shrugged again. "Yeah, those words have gone together a time or two."

"No."

"No?"

The vamp eyed the dagger. "No, I'm not planning to kill anybody tonight. Or ever, for that matter. Who needs all the trauma, with synth blood and donors?"

Christophe judged the vamp to be sincere enough. He considered killing him with a thrown dagger anyway, just for something to do, but didn't really feel like chasing his dagger all that way down after it sliced the vamp's head off. Especially since his night wasn't over—he still had to go steal one of the Crown Jewels from the Tower of London.

He slid the blade into its sheath and shot a considering stare at the bloodsucker. "So. Here's a question. Was Jack the Ripper a vampire?"

∾──⊱

Campbell Manor, Coggeshall, Essex

Fiona pulled the scarlet leggings up, then the trousers, tying them at the waist, knees, and ankles, and fastened her belt over her jacket. Technically, it wasn't ninja gear, but it was so important to have the right accessories these days, although no fashion magazine would ever feature her hand-worked leather tool belt with its many compartments on an Up-and-Coming Trends page. A memory flashed into her mind, though, as her fingers checked the snap on one tiny pocket that held her backup switchblade, and she laughed. Her assistant Madeleine had rushed into Fiona's office just last week waving a glossy magazine in the air. *Vogue UK* had done a spread on the new color for spring: a gleaming scarlet. The red of a slash of bold lipstick—of freshly spilled blood.

The red on Fiona's calling cards, which the entire world had seen by now. TV presenters delighted in spouting breathless and inane theories as to her identity while showing the cards in their full silver-and-scarlet glory.

The Scarlet Ninja was setting fashion trends, even though everyone thought *she* was a *he.*

"Sorry, Dad," she murmured, glancing out the window into the uncharacteristically clear night sky, as if he might be looking down at her from heaven. Spring weather was wet, wet, and more wet, but she'd planned this little outing for the one night this week that the meteorologists had promised would be dry. So unpleasant to plan impossible heists in the pouring rain, after all.

The expected knock came, and she heaved a sigh. "I'm not decent, Hopkins, please go away."

The door opened and the man who was the nearest thing to a grandfather she'd ever had walked in, carrying a tray. "I prefer indecency in both women and foreign films. Chocolate?"

Fiona sighed again and tried not to grit her teeth at the sight of his perfectly combed silver hair and his perfectly proper black suit. It was after midnight, for heaven's sake. "I don't have time for chocolate. And I'm not a little girl anymore, whom you must coddle out of her nightmares. You should be in bed, wearing your lovely pajamas that Madeleine gave you for your birthday. You look like a butler, Hopkins."

"I am a butler, Lady Fiona," he responded, exactly as he had a billion or so times since they'd started this verbal dance more than twenty years ago, when her father died. "I was your father's butler, may he rest in peace, and before that your grandfather's butler, may God rot his vicious soul."

"You're not supposed to speak ill of the dead."

"I said far worse when he was still alive," he said dryly, raising one silver eyebrow. He whipped the cover off the silver pot of chocolate, and the aroma teased her senses. "Furthermore, should you ever catch me wearing silk pajamas decorated with tiny barnyard animals, please feel free to commit me to a home for the senile."

"They're sheep, Hopkins." She clamped her lips together

to keep the laugh from escaping. "You know, for counting sheep? It's a sort of joke. Also, when will you drop the 'Lady' and start calling me Fiona?"

"Undoubtedly at the same time I begin wearing the barn-yard animal nightclothes." He poured the rich chocolate into a delicate china cup and handed it to her.

Fiona took the chocolate. It was just easier to go along on the little things. "She means well."

"Faint praise, indeed," he pointed out. His brilliantly blue eyes sparkled with amusement, though, and she wasn't fooled. She'd caught him bringing chocolate to Madeleine just that morning.

"Down to business, Lady Fiona. Do you have your un-traceable phone?"

"Always."

"Is it charged? When you broke into the British Museum—"

"How long are you going to hold that against me? I came out of that with an entire collection of jade figurines, includ-ing Tlaloc." She pulled out the top drawer of the Louis XIV bureau until the faint depression in the wood bottom of the drawer was in sight. A muffled click signaled the opening of the hidden compartment, and she removed one of her scarlet hooded masks and a single glossy silver card.

"Yes, Tlaloc. The rain god. The wettest autumn in re-corded history after you brought that home, if I recall. Thank you *so* much. We certainly needed more rain on our prop-erty," Hopkins managed to say with a straight face. "A clean handkerchief?"

She froze, slowly turning her head to stare at him. "A clean handkerchief? Are you actually making a joke, Hopkins?"

He carefully folded her unused cloth napkin, its white linen folds as spotless as the gloves he still insisted on wearing, before he looked up and met her gaze. "I never joke. If an employer of mine is planning to steal one of the most famous gems in history from the Tower of London itself—which is, mind you, absolutely burglar-proof—then by queen and coun-try she *will* have a clean handkerchief."

Fiona stared at the spots of color flaming on his cheek-bones and realized she'd been a fool. She'd spent all of her time worrying about the logistics of the job and no time at all concerned with the people who cared about her. She dropped her mask and the card next to the chocolate on the table and walked over to him.

"I'm not stealing anything tonight. This is just an exploratory expedition, you daft old thing. Now, give me a hug."

She thought for a moment that he was actually going to refuse, but finally he sighed and embraced her, patting her back like he'd done when she was a child restless with the burdens of position and, later, tragedy.

He quickly released her and handed her the mask, which she tucked into her belt, and then the card.

"Do you really want to leave your calling card before you take the Siren? They'll throw everything they have at the Tower to prevent you coming back, after you made Scotland Yard and Interpol look like fools the last time."

She shrugged, glancing down at the silver gilt card with the tiny figure of a scarlet ninja embossed in its exact center. "It's only sporting, isn't it? Besides, they'll think I'm taking the entire sword. Perhaps that will mean different security measures."

"Sporting might get you killed. Or sent to prison for a very long time."

"Not tonight. This is just a scouting trip." She shouldered her small pack and grinned up at him.

"After all, how dangerous can it be?"

Chapter 2

Christophe soared through the air in mist form, circling the Tower of London as he had many times before, but this time with the goal of finding a way inside, instead of admiring the exterior. He recognized the irony of planning to steal William the Conqueror's sword, famously and prophetically named Vanquish, from the tower whose construction old Will had first begun. Technically, he didn't need the sword, and Prince Conlan probably wouldn't like it if he took it—interfering with sovereign possessions and so forth—but just taking the Siren from the sword's jeweled hilt seemed like a waste of opportunity.

Not that he had much need for what rumor claimed was a ceremonial-only, badly balanced sword. His own, left in Atlantis this trip, was utilitarian, simple, and deadly; undecorated except for the single emerald on its pommel. A line from an old nursery tale flitted through his mind, though perhaps in a different form than he'd heard as a child.

The better to fight evil with, my dear.

But, after all, why not? Calculating the ways and means of how he might remove the entire sword from one of the most fortified locations in the world made for an amusing way to pass the time. An endeavor that didn't bore him.

Passing over the main gate and the long-unused moat, he floated over the bridge where millions of tourists crossed into the Tower grounds every year. He could have taken the easy route and made his way in as a tourist during the day, except first, he didn't like crowds of smelly humans, and second, when had he ever done things the easy way? Not to mention that asking himself rhetorical questions was probably one of the unpaved steps on the road to insanity. Not far up from talking to pigeons.

The pale yellow brick glowed in the night air, resonating with the quiet dignity of walls that had stood sentinel, indifferent and stoic, as the tempests of humans had ebbed and flowed over the centuries. If walls could talk, as the old saying went, these would offer a history lesson on power—or a cautionary tale for those in search of it.

Somewhat like the ancient tales of Atlantis herself.

Floating over the spot where the Duke of Wellington's statue had been before somebody decided to banish it to the Royal Arsenal at Woolwich—*ha, the fleeting nature of fame, Duke, old boy*—he examined the exterior windows of the Waterloo Barracks, opposite to the scaffolding and white stone of the White Tower. A flicker of light glinted off a gargoyle as it . . . moved.

Damn. Either imagination or adrenaline was working overtime, because Christophe was sure that the gargoyle had moved an inch or two. He approached it, still suspended as mist, only to find exactly what he should have expected: there was no way the gargoyle had moved since somebody put its butt-ugly self there in the first place.

He must be having hallucinations.

It was adrenaline. The excitement of doing something different for a change, instead of the same old same old. He'd had enough of killing vampires and smiting shape-shifters to last a lifetime. And Atlantis was no better. It was getting crowded in the palace, with all of his fellow warriors finding women. Not temporary women, either. No, these were *keeper* women, the long-term, asphyxiate-a-guy kind of women.

No, thank you. Not for him. He was going to steal the Siren, the enormous aquamarine that graced Vanquish's hilt, and take it back to Atlantis so it could be reattached to Poseidon's Trident, where it belonged. Hand that sucker straight over to Alaric. Or better yet, instead of to the high priest in person, to one of his minions, so there would be no repeat of Alaric's most recent lecture: *Why Christophe Was Wasting His Magical Abilities by Refusing to Join the Priesthood, Part 784*.

He didn't want to be a priest. He wanted some fun. Like this job. It was a heist, pure and simple. Fun.

The jewels were housed on the first floor, with nobody but the Tower Guard, various electronic devices, and the Yeomen Warders to protect them. Of the three, only the Yeomen Warders concerned him at all. The shape-shifters in that group were rumored to be pretty damn tough, and no few of them claimed to be descended from the shape-shifters who'd been among the original Warders back in 1485.

Of course, back then, shifters weren't roaming around in broad daylight, with everybody knowing who and what they were. Vamps, either, for that matter, but the past decade-plus had brought big changes to the world.

Mostly for the worse.

The Tower Guard was part of the Queen's Guard, according to the handy tour guide a tourist had conveniently left on a bench for Christophe to find. They didn't live in the Tower, but the Warders still did, unfortunately. If only everybody trusted their electronics these days. Atlantean magic wreaked holy *hells* on electricity.

The thought of powerful Brennan, locked in that electric cage with Tiernan, flashed through his mind, and his mood soured. Sometimes the electricity won.

Christophe eyed a tiny crack in the casement of a third-floor window on the tower, just to the left of the main doors. Not even a large insect could fit through that crack.

Mist, however, could get in just fine.

Fiona had timed out the midnight-to-eight A.M. shift patterns of the Tower Guard and the Yeoman Warders on multiple occasions over the past several weeks. One thing was certain: the men and women, human and shifter alike, who guarded the Jewel House, were serious, dedicated professionals. No mere thief would get anywhere *near* those jewels.

Good thing she was no *mere* thief. She was world class.

Stealing onto the grounds had been child's play, but breaching the Waterloo Barracks and the Jewel House would be a little trickier. She knew her . . . *talent* would keep them from seeing her, but shadowing only completely fooled living eyes and cameras. Motion detectors made for trickier adventures.

From her position leaning against a tree in the courtyard at an angle to the main doors, she saw the team of two stride around the corner of the building exactly on time. Two A.M. on the dot; one could set her clock on the punctuality of the guards. These were two enormous, burly men, probably shifters, having a lovely conversation about rugby or something else vital to England's national stature.

She slowly leaned farther back into the rough bark of the tree, concentrating fiercely. Shifters were tougher to hide from than humans—she'd have to bend air as well as light, and the shifters' minds were not as easily amenable to clouding.

Ribbons of silken moonlight danced through the air surrounding Fiona and the tree, circling her with nearly imperceptible shadings of dappled light. A spill of liquid darkness spread over her—*through* her—so gradually that only the keenest observer would have felt even a tingle of awareness. Light and the very air itself bent to her will as Fiona focused on dispersing her scent and disappearing from view.

The shorter of the guards stopped suddenly, his body tensing and leaning forward in the unmistakable sign of alert. He held up a hand, and his partner whirled to face the direction from which they'd come and settled into the same wary crouch. Precision back-to-back stance; these were no decorative guards put in place to amuse and delight tourists with their furry hats. These were the guardians of the dark hours between dusk and dawn, and their honor stood guard with them. For a shifter to lose face over the theft of a jewel under his care would be a gut-wrenching, soul-deadening failure.

For an instant sympathy encouraged hesitation in her mind, but she forced herself to visualize the rebuilding of Wolf Hall as a headquarters for the United Kingdom shifters. More than *one hundred million euros* of public money had been thrown into the project thus far, with much more to come. Now that the family of Jane Seymour, the third wife of Henry VIII, were rumored to have been shifters, the press were tantalized, and even Hollywood had come to call. Anyone who questioned the extravagant expenditure was drowned out in the usual British religion of celeb worship.

Shape-shifters with ties to royalty: the new rock stars.

Fiona clamped down on her mental wanderings when indignation made her focus waver for a split second. The taller guard lifted his nose into the wind and leaned forward, staring into the shadows around her tree. His sense of smell wouldn't be nearly as keen in this form as when he was a wolf, but still better than that of any human.

Deeper. She sent her mental command arrowing ever more deeply into her own brain, until she felt the almost audible click that signaled total control of her Gift. Air and light bent to her will in the space surrounding her. The scent of her body dispersed into the vestigial odors of the millions of tourists who crossed this courtyard. Her image vanished, hidden by the shadows caressing her. Even the sound of her heartbeat and breath floated away, broken up and scattered with the obedient winds. To any of the guards' five senses, she simply did not exist, so long as she didn't get close enough to touch.

Damn the luck, though. Her Gift had no control over the sixth. Intuition. Hunches. The peripheral senses of shifters who trusted their own instincts—they'd come near to unveiling her more than once in the past. Her lips quirked at the idea of how unhappy Hopkins would be if her outrageous streak of good fortune chose now to desert her.

She caught her breath and tightened her hand on the grip of her tranq gun as the shifter took a step toward her. There was no possible way she could outrun a wolf, not even one in human guise. It was the matter of a moment, anyway, for the more powerful shifters to transform, and these looked anything but weak.

The guard with his back to her glanced over his shoulder at his partner. "What is it?"

"I don't know," the one with the nose said. "Nothing. Something. Maybe."

The first one snorted out a laugh. "Thanks for clearing *that* up."

"I don't *know*. But whatever it is—"

The sharp sound of pebbles clattering to the ground interrupted him, and Fiona and the guards all turned their attention to the sky. Or, more specifically, to the roof of the building, from where the pebble shower had originated.

"Maybe a bird?"

"That was no bird." The guard lowered his gaze and aimed one long last stare at the tree where Fiona stood—perfectly still, perfectly silent—with her gun at the ready. "But maybe what I thought I sensed over by the tree was."

"Or maybe we've got vamps playing games," the other one snarled, as he turned sharply on his heel and started running back the way they'd come. "I warned those freaks the last time they tried to hang out here—"

"Bloodsuckers don't listen to warnings."

Neither do ninjas, Fiona added silently, as the pair vanished behind the building, presumably making for the particular side door that was the guards' preferred entrance. But with just a bit of luck, they'd call in for replacements who might choose a different door. The main entrance not thirty feet away from her, for example.

It took her fewer than ten seconds to make her way to the side of the double wooden doors and plaster her body up against the wall. Another ten seconds and the sound of pounding feet approached, and the doors swung open, spilling out a new pair of guards. This time, they were both human, but their reflexes were almost shifter-quick.

Fiona wasted no time in ducking under the arm of one guard to enter the building, seconds before he yanked the door closed. Still shadowed, she slowly stood, careful not to move until she'd scanned the area for further guards, either human or shifter. Glowing carriage lamps with modern bulbs lit up the dark hallway, their illumination dimmed for night but still bright enough for their light to pounce on any unwanted visitor.

It was a familiar sight and one she'd toured often enough, usually with guests from elsewhere. A left turn would take her to the Hall of Monarchs with its various and sundry thrones and coats of arms. Glorious, but not really what she was after tonight. Nor was the cinema room with its video of Elizabeth II's coronation, or Processional Way, with its walls of shining maces, or even the Temporal Sword of Justice. No, Fiona wanted a jewel from a quite different sword and it was in the Treasury. The *jewel* part of the Crown Jewels.

One jewel in particular.

And all she had to do was liberate William the Conqueror's sword to take it.

No worries.

Chapter 3

The Summer Lands, in the forest not far from the Unseelie Court palace

Prince Gideon na Feransel stared at Maeve and wondered, not for the first or tenth or even the hundredth time, how the smartest, most powerful Unseelie Court Fae prince in recorded history—himself, naturally—had been saddled with an idiot for a sister.

"Maeve, if you'd quit playing with your hair and listen for a single minute, I'd explain this in words even you could understand."

Maeve continued brushing her silky blue-black hair and rolled her eyes at him. Which he hated—which she knew.

Damn Fae princesses were astonishingly arrogant.

"We tell the humans we're cousins, because the closer relationship of brother and sister would involve certain expectations we don't wish to entangle us."

She handed her hairbrush to one of the fawning males who always surrounded her. "Such as?"

"We'd have to pretend to like each other."

Her delicate features screwed up in a tiny moue of distaste. As Fae, she could never be truly ugly, but Gideon privately thought this expression came close. Of course, his taste ran to paler beauty. A certain blonde had caught his eye.

"You're wrong, in any case, *brother*," she said. "I know many human siblings who despise each other."

"This is all beside the point, Maeve. Now if you don't mind, please send your entourage away so we might speak privately."

She shot a speculative glance at him, reminding him anew that vanity was not a signal of lack of intelligence. Anyone who underestimated Maeve na Feransel was a fool, and Gideon was many things, but never, ever a fool.

"Go," she said, waving a slender arm. The various men—lesser Fae and human both—all bowed and fled, obeying her order with an alacrity that underscored his reason for the conversation with his sister.

He leaned against the trunk of a winged elm tree and inhaled deeply, comforted by the scent of all things green and growing. The soil beneath his boots was a touch dry, but he knew rain would soon arrive to soothe and nourish the forest. The connection with the earth and all things growing was so much a part of Fae nature that he sometimes wondered how humans survived without it. Perhaps it was how they could destroy nature with so little concern or remorse.

Perhaps he was a fool to try to save any of them, but then again, he did occasionally need them. All of that chaotic life-force energy was so delicious.

"I've put out the word that a very wealthy buyer will pay top money for the sword Vanquish," he said. "I've also told Telios, but that fool vampire is more interested in murder and destruction than anything else, so I doubt he'll be able to come up with a coherent plan to steal it."

"Why don't you just steal it yourself?" Maeve turned away from him and bent to admire a profusion of wild orchids tangled around the base of a jasmine bush. "I know you're only after the Siren and what it can do. The power to enthrall shifters on a large scale? Why would you possibly care about that?"

"Power held is never useless. Far more important, though, is power *withheld* from others. If the vampires were to learn what the Siren can do, their misguided attempt to take over the entire world would be one step closer to its realization. Even you should realize that this would be utter annihilation for the Fae."

"You do know that Rhys na Garanwyn is working with the Atlanteans toward the same end? Why not join forces?"

Rage flared inside him with sudden, sharp intensity. He forced it to recede. The time would come for him to unleash his fury. Not now. Not yet.

"I will consider all options," he managed to say calmly. "For now, if you see your little human friend, encourage her to steal the sword for me."

"Friend? What are you talking about?"

He started laughing at her so-obvious attempt at deception. "Don't bother to deny it. I know that your friend Lady Fiona is a thief. The Scarlet Ninja, isn't that what they call her?"

She whirled around, and he saw her shock before she masked her emotional response.

"I don't know what you're talking about. She—"

"Don't bother," he repeated, folding his arms over his chest. He was enjoying this. "I targeted her, specifically, by making sure her contacts got the word. She has Fae in her, you know."

This time, his beloved, wicked, deceitful sister could not hide her shock. "How did you know?"

"The way you were drawn to her from the first, when you attended that human school. Don't you think we noticed? Do you really believe we would allow you, a Fae princess, to mingle in the human world without constant surveillance?"

She shook her head. "No. I would have known. I watched for anyone. There were no guards."

"There were dozens of guards, you fool," he said, enjoying the way her lovely white skin paled even further. "Always. The first time we caught her shadowing, we backtracked her heritage. We're almost certain she's of Fae blood. Probably Seelie Court, and quite possibly royalty."

"You leave her alone," Maeve said hotly. "She's mine."

"Yours? I thought your tastes ran only to the male of the various species." He swept his gaze over her luscious curves.

Too bad she was his sister. He was in the mood for a little bed play.

"Not like that. She's my friend. You hurt her and you will answer to me." Her voice was quiet as she said it, but somehow deadly. For just an instant, a chill of apprehension slid over him, but then he came to his senses. She was so far below him in the hierarchy of power as to be entirely unimportant.

"You aren't threatening me, are you, little sister?" He strode over to her, crossing the distance between them with slow, deliberate intent. "Never forget who holds the power of Feransel. I could crush you with a thought."

She paled again but said nothing. Just bowed her head.

"Permission to return to my rooms, Lord Feransel?" This time, her voice held nothing but submission and a tinge of bitterness.

Better.

"Yes, go. But have a care. If Telios approaches you, be sure to emphasize how important that sword is to me, but make no mention of the jewel on its hilt. I'd steal it myself if William's witch hadn't ensorcelled it to destroy any Fae who touched it when not freely given." He laughed. "William the Conqueror, indeed. How did they never wonder how he became such a conqueror? A powerful witch on his side for all those years, and none suspected."

"You knew," she pointed out.

"Yes, but what care did I have for human affairs at that time? There were more than enough of them and the vampires still hid in the dark. Now, things are different. I want that gem. A perfect aquamarine, or so I hear."

She bit her lip but said nothing. Probably thinking about her next bed partner. Useless female. He made a go-away gesture with his hand and she all but ran off down the path toward the palace.

"The Siren and Lady Fiona. I'll have them both. Quite lovely prizes for one who seeks to rule both courts, don't you think?" he asked the empty air.

Only the trees heard his laughter.

Chapter 4

Damn crumbly centuries-old stone.

Christophe had known as soon as the coalesced mist of his magic-held shape displaced the tiny shards of stone that the shifters patrolling beneath the window would hear it. What he hadn't expected was how fast they could make it up to the third floor. He found himself hovering in the center of the room, wondering how in the nine hells the guards were going to miss a miniature rain cloud floating in the middle of a storage room that was basically an overgrown broom closet.

England was famous for its rain, but this was ridiculous. Time to bail and try again another night, maybe. It's what a *reasonable* man would do. The thought was enough to jolt him into motion.

"Reasonable, my ass," he said under his breath as he transformed back into his body, a fierce grin spreading across his face. "May as well be dead as reasonable."

Booted feet pounded down the hallway and he could hear the sound of doors opening one by one, sequentially. They'd reach him soon. He scanned the room for something—anything— and found it in the least likely, humblest of objects.

Seconds later, the door swung open and one of the shifters stepped into the room, not even breathing hard. "Storage room looks clear."

This one smelled like wolf. Angry wolf. Hopefully he wouldn't start pissing on the walls to mark his territory. Christophe wished he could see what the guard was doing, but curiosity wasn't worth risking his disguise.

Footsteps rang out, crossing the floor toward him, and Christophe tensed, holding his magical form and crushing his every maddening instinct that screamed at him to call to power and *attack*. The footsteps paused, no more than a handful of inches from him, and then passed by. The muffled sound of the wolf shifting boxes and shoving the heavy wooden table by the window to one side preceded a loud crash. The guard let loose with a blistering string of profanity so creative and descriptive that even Christophe had to admire the man's resourcefulness.

More footsteps. A different voice, as a second guard arrived at the doorway.

"Find anything?"

"No. I knocked the damn box of copy paper on my foot."

The new guard laughed. Not much sympathy there. "Did he hurt his wee footsie?"

"Shut up, you moron. It's the same foot I broke last week and it's still a trifle tender, even after shifting five different times." The first guard walked past Christophe again, this time with the definite suggestion of a limp. "There's nothing in here anyway. Must have been a bird after all. We need to get the cleaning crew to do a better job, by the way. Why is this bucket sitting here full of water? Should we dump it out?"

"I'm not dumping it out. Not my job. And maybe it was a bird, or maybe it was a vamp," the other said darkly. "Or who knows what else? I'll feel a lot better when we get those magic detectors up and running."

"Right. You count on that. Sure, and the witches are going to figure out a way to detect all of the hundreds of different kinds of magic. In your dreams."

Christophe heard the faint squeak of hinges that were just

on the cusp of needing to be oiled, and as the door shut, the second guard put in the final word.

"I heard the prime minister herself say that there's not a form of magic on this earth that the new detectors won't catch."

Christophe rose up in one silvery ribbon of water from the bucket in which he'd hidden and promptly changed back into the shape of a very amused Atlantean warrior.

Exactly. Not on this earth. Bet your witches aren't ready for magic that comes from under its oceans.

Now, let's have a look at that sword.

He took a deep breath and cleansed himself of the last traces of plastic and the faint bitter tang of cleaning fluid, shaking his hands to fling the droplets of water from his skin. He'd held mist shape too long this night, and it was tiring—a drain of magical resources—on the best of nights. Nights that did *not* involve hiding in buckets. But it would make for a good story, and surely Ven or one of the other warriors would stand him a mug of ale for the laugh.

He pushed his focus deep within, calling to the power that waited, tantalizing, always ready to seduce him. Formed the link in his mind that gave up the very atoms of his body to the universe; traded for the water magic that belonged uniquely to Poseidon and his people.

Soaring through the room, he performed a celebratory twirl of silvery liquid power before dispersing enough to slide smoothly under the door. The hallway was empty, the guards gone searching birds or ghosts or shadows. He followed the hall to the stairs and, careful to stay in the dark shadows masking the ceiling, he descended to the ground floor right over the heads of the guards pounding up, presumably to join their colleagues in a futile search.

Radios crackled with "all clear" and "headed for the roof access" messages, and as Christophe passed overhead, the headset of the guard directly beneath him sizzled with a loud crackling sound.

The man snapped out a guttural curse. "Damn radios. This one just shorted out in my ear."

Christophe increased his pace. If he was already shorting out the electronics, stealing the actual sword might be a problem. He snapped an even tighter leash on his control. Atlantean magic and electricity didn't get along, and he didn't want to send the place into lockdown because the security system suddenly crashed.

One of the shifter guards paused and cast a sharp glance up at the ceiling, his keen gaze examining the area directly where Christophe passed overhead in the shadows. There was absolutely nothing to be seen, even to shifter eyes, since his form was so dispersed among the shadows, but the man's instincts were good. Shifter instincts generally were. It was a good enough reason to have at least a few of them on Atlantis's side.

◆───◆

Gaining the ground floor, he turned the corner and headed for the Treasury. Tonight was just for scouting. He wanted a look at the sword when there were no crowds, no moving walkways. He'd come back another night to take it.

No rush, after all. The quicker he achieved this goal, the quicker he'd be forced to return to Atlantis. More missions to the surface for vampire slaying. Cut off their heads, stake them in the hearts, jump back to avoid goop on the boots as they turned to nasty acidic slime. Same old same old.

He wanted something different. A challenge. *Excitement.*

Rounding the final corner, he stopped moving, dispersing his mist form even more, and hovered as close to the ceiling's shadows as possible. The five guards clustered in front of the open security door to the Treasury spoke in low tones, but their body language didn't display any particular tension.

One of the guards, a shifter whose enormous arm muscles strained the seams of his uniform shirt, made a dismissive motion with his hand. "Probably a bird taking off and displacing a few pebbles. Certainly there's nothing in here."

Another one, a human, tapped his fingers restlessly against the wall. "As soon as Lefty gets out here, we'll lock up tight and resume regular rounds."

The others nodded and made varying noises of assent.

Christophe, still hidden in mist form, automatically cataloged the guards in his memory, but a whisper of unease shivered through him that had nothing to do with the handful of Tower Guards. Something—*someone*—was playing with magic, and he or she was doing so in this very room. Very near the door. In fact, not six paces away from where the guards clustered around the door to the Treasury.

The biting chill of magic broadcasting from the corner tasted nothing like the sea and salt of Atlantean power. No, this was of the earth. The tang of freshly turned garden soil and the faint scent of ripe apples in the fall. An earth witch? Seelie Fae?

How strong, he couldn't tell. The faint ripples were as subtle as his own, which meant either a practitioner with very little power to project or one with enough power to be able to hide it from both Christophe and the shifters, who normally had some sensitivity to magic. It definitely wasn't one of the guards. The light and shadows around that crowd broke normally, following accepted laws of physics.

But in the corner the shadows were . . . different. Just a whisper of a touch of difference, nothing that would alarm even the keenest non-magical observer, but to Christophe it was a beacon. A flare at sea from a drowning ship.

A sixth guard appeared in the doorway from the Treasury and nodded once, sharply. "All clear."

"Thanks, Lefty. Better safe than sorry," one of the older guards said, probably a familiar refrain from him, considering the carefully averted rolled eyes of a couple of the others.

As the guards began to disperse, heading in different directions, Lefty carefully slid an innocuous-looking information plaque on the wall to the left, revealing a digital keypad. He rapidly pressed buttons in a long sequence of numbers, pausing twice, either as part of the sequence or to think of what came next, and the security door began slowly to close. Christophe, soaring silently and quickly, traveled across the ceiling and into the room with seconds to spare before the door closed behind him with a muffled clanging sound. Several clicking noises sounded directly beneath and in front of where he hung, suspended, startling him, and he turned his attention downward.

Toward the . . . *ninja*.

Which startled him enough that he released his mist form, plummeted down from the ceiling, and landed on his ass. "What in the nine hells—"

The figure in scarlet whirled around and Christophe was treated to two more surprises: the shiny, deadly looking gun and the lovely curve of scarlet-covered breasts and hips.

The Scarlet Ninja was a woman—and she was armed.

～～

"Who the bloody hell are you and where did you come from?" Fiona glared at the intruder, her gaze traveling up and up as he slowly stood, holding his hands out in front of him. He was a few inches over six feet of tall, dark, and sinfully gorgeous, and he had no right to be here in the middle of her scouting trip, never mind those astonishingly muscled shoulders and the dark waves of hair framing the most beautiful green eyes, sculpted cheekbones, and deliciously masculine face she had ever seen on a living, breathing man. Her breathing sped up, and her heart, which had already been racing faster than the lead car in the Birmingham Super Prix, thundered so hard it surely would pound its way out of her chest any moment.

She was a thief, standing in the middle of one of the most priceless collections of gems in the entire world, and yet she wasn't tempted to look anywhere but at him.

Oh, yes. He was trouble.

Trouble blinked; long, dark lashes closing over emerald-green eyes so gorgeous they had to be illegal in most of Europe. Then he threw back his head and laughed, and shivers traced a delicate pattern down her spine. His deep, rich laugh was dark chocolate and champagne and silk sheets all presented in one wickedly mouthwatering package.

Oh, damn, it had been far too long since she'd had sex.

Her watch beeped. Glancing down, she saw that she had

twelve minutes. Declan had hacked into the security cameras and put them on a circular repeating pattern or something equally complex and brilliant, but he'd warned her a dozen times that she had exactly fifteen minutes and not a second more.

She raised the tranq gun and used her best frosty, lady-of-the-manor voice. "I repeat, who the bloody hell are you?"

"You're Scottish," he said, quite unnecessarily.

"Give the man a gold ring. You have ten seconds to tell me who you are and why you're here before I shoot you." She raised the gun, hoping the first time she had to shoot a man while looking him in the eyes wouldn't haunt her dreams for months to come. But needs must and, well, the Siren was waiting, no matter how mouthwateringly delicious this man might be.

"The Scarlet Ninja is a woman. A Scottish woman," he said, his gaze sweeping over her from head to toe, blistering every inch of skin under her garments, as if the heat in his eyes were a palpable touch.

Of course, the negative here was that he appeared to be a blithering idiot.

"Yes. Ninja. Woman. Scottish. Do you have something against Scotland?"

Her watch beeped. Eleven minutes.

"Ninja," he repeated, taking a step toward her. "*Nin. Ja.* Have you ever cracked a history book? Scotland. Ninjas. No."

Fiona's watch crackled. Declan checking in, and he was going to go mad if she didn't respond soon. She raised her wrist and spoke softly. "Bit of a problem. Don't worry. I'll handle it."

The luscious bit of man candy had the nerve to flash a devilish grin at her. "You can handle me anytime. I like to play dress-up games, too. You can be the ninja, and I'll be the pirate."

"Lovely. A thief *and* a boorish lout," she snapped. Declan squawked from her wrist, but she lowered her hand and ignored her overprotective brother for the moment.

Ten minutes.

"Thief, huh. Pot, kettle? I guess we all know *why* you're here, but a better question is what kind of magic were you throwing around out there?"

"I don't know what you're talking about," she lied, careful not to let her shock show in her eyes.

"Fine. Another question, then." He took another step toward her, all leashed power and hard-bodied male. She felt like a particularly scrumptious piece of catnip caught in the path of a tiger. "Scarlet Ninja. Today's answer to Robin Hood. What are *you* here for? Not that it matters." He waved an arm at the glass boxes filled with crowns, scepters, swords, and sundry. "Luckily, there's plenty for both of us."

It was her turn to blink, but she was out of time for small talk. "You'll never succeed. But I'm only here for one thing, so feel free to look around."

He smiled, and she wondered dizzily if the devil himself had a smile as seductive. "I think I'll stick with you. I'd like to see under that mask. That lovely skin and those blue eyes are making me wonder what the rest of you looks like, not that those scarlet silks are hiding much. A man would give much to get his hands on those curves."

The blunt words packed a sensual punch, maybe due to the sheer honesty of the admiration on his face and in his tone. She had to clench her thighs together against the heat.

"No time for this," she said, inexplicably both glad she wore the mask and regretting it. "Step closer and I'll shoot you."

He bowed, a study in grace and elegance, and she had the oddest feeling that the courtly gesture came naturally to him, as if he'd done it many times before.

Her watch ticked over again. Nine minutes.

Still keeping one wary eye on him, she turned toward the shatterproof glass case on the far wall, crossing the electronic walkway to view the sword in its solitary state.

"Vanquish stands apart, doesn't it?" he murmured next to her ear. He was too close; he was suddenly right next to her. She couldn't contain the startled gasp. Nobody but vampires could move that fast. He clearly wasn't *that*, though; her senses could recognize a vampire at twenty paces. But what?

She backed away, aiming the tranq gun carefully, although he didn't seem the least bit afraid of it. He also didn't seem to be trying to scare her.

Not that he could. She was tough and brave, right?

Mostly?

"Isolated from the rest of the room, and even from the remainder of the sword collection," he continued, as if unaware of her reaction. "Proud and unbending, like its owner."

She dismissed his flight of fancy. "A conqueror. A predator."

He turned to face her, the heat from his body radiating through the inches separating them until she felt herself beginning to lean forward into him. She stumbled back a step and raised the gun, aiming it at his heart.

He didn't pay the slightest attention to it. Those green eyes lasered into her as he tilted his head. "And you don't care for predators? You, who yourself live your life in search of prey? Dressed like a *ninja*?"

"My prey doesn't breathe."

"Doesn't it? The treasures of a society are not the living, breathing representations of its history?"

Not an idiot, then. In spite of those cheekbones and sculpted lips. The pretty boy had a mind.

Click. Eight minutes.

"Bit fancy for a predator, isn't it? I'd imagine predators use more practical blades."

His attention snapped back to her, that piercing focus almost palpable. "Funny. I was thinking something similar earlier tonight."

"Why were you thinking about Vanquish?"

"I plan to steal it."

A jolt of sheer adrenaline raced through her, chasing chills down her spine, and she whirled around to face him straight on. "No. You can't. It's mine."

Chapter 5

Christophe's mental warning system for critical danger had stood him in good stead for many long years and saved his ass, not to mention his life, on too many occasions to count. Right now warnings were flashing through his brain on high alert. This woman was clearly dangerous. She was definitely trouble. He should be wary and on his guard.

Instead, he was elated.

She was a little bit of a thing, maybe five and a half feet tall, but she seemed bigger because pure attitude added a few inches. And those ice blue eyes—well, even without the husky, sexy purr of her voice, he would ignore more than a little warning flare for the chance to see her face. The silk of her loose garments couldn't hide her ripe, curvy body, and a wicked corner of his mind kept picturing what she might look like in his bed, wearing nothing but that scarlet mask.

His cock hardened at the thought of it, and it was almost enough to distract him from what she'd said. *Almost.* Vanquish was hers? He thought not, lovely ass or no.

"What's yours?" He schooled his voice to calm, silken menace and allowed power to glow in his eyes and resonate

through his words. Grown men—humans, shifters, and vamps alike—had all trembled at the sound of that voice.

She laughed.

"Ooh, scary glowy eyes. Do you try that trick on everyone, or just the odd ninja you meet when you're planning a heist?" She glanced at her watch and, in spite of the casual amusement in her voice, he could tell her anxiety level was ratcheting up. Whatever she was up to, it looked like she was running out of time.

"You didn't answer my question." He stepped closer, taking two quick strides, until he was so close to her that the barrel of her gun pressed into his chest and the scent of her tantalized him.

She didn't have it in her to shoot him.

He was almost sure.

"Back away, big boy," she told him, pressing her body weight, such that it was, into the warning until the gun dug into his skin beneath his shirt. "Don't make me shoot you. It would be messy, and who needs that?"

"What are you trying to steal?" he repeated, ignoring the gun and the banter, because it was pretty obvious exactly what she'd meant.

She sighed and stepped back, then lowered her gun and flicked something small and silvery at the base of the glass case. "More than twenty-three thousand gems in this collection, and we're both after the Siren. Too bad, you really are extremely luscious, but that gem is mine."

Before he could think of a response, she tucked her gun into a holster on her leather belt and stepped closer to him. Her scent teased him again, swamping his senses with the light fragrance of jasmine underneath a spring rain.

"Perhaps just a taste? As a sort of good-bye?" she murmured, maybe to herself, and then she rose up on her tiptoes and pulled his head down to hers with one hand. With the other, she lifted her mask a little and pressed a soft, gentle caress of a kiss against his lips. Utter shock kept him motionless just long enough for her to drop her mask, step back, and press something hard into his abdomen.

"Lovely. I really do regret this," she said.

And then she shot him.

"You *shot* me—" he blurted out, but looking down, it wasn't the expected bright red of his blood flowing out of his body that he saw, but bright red . . . feathers? A dart. It was a *dart*.

And feathers. Dancing feathers, and the room spun around them. Magical feathers? Oh. Oh, no. Not magic . . .

Drugs . . .

As he hit the floor, his Atlantean metabolism instantly began to push the drugs out of his system. But instantly wasn't quick enough, if the way the floor was trying to suck him into it was any clue.

She bent down, and his senses reeled at the sight of her features all gone topsy-turvy, until his drug-hazed mind realized that he was looking at her upside down. Her mask had dropped down a little to show the wry curve of luscious lips. Even after she'd shot him, he still wanted to taste that mouth again.

"I really am sorry, you know. Hopefully since you haven't actually stolen anything yet, they won't imprison you for too very long," she said, with what sounded like sincere regret. "Best of luck to you."

She said something else, but by then the drug had temporarily—at least, he *hoped* it was only temporarily—overwhelmed his body's efforts to push it out, and the gray pushing at the edges of his vision swarmed in to take over his conscious mind. The last thing he saw before the blackness claimed him was the small rectangle of paper, with its tiny scarlet image, that she'd dropped on the ground.

"Ninja," he managed.

Her unexpected peal of laughter echoed in the swirling dark.

~~~~~~

Fiona clapped a hand over her mouth, stifling the laughter. Fool. She was out of time and had nearly been out of luck. What was she *thinking* to kiss that man? He could have grabbed her and ripped her mask off or, worse, held her for the authorities. He was certainly big enough to have over-whelmed her and done hideous things to her with his hard-muscled body.

Lovely, dirty things. Or at least naked things.

She stifled another laugh. Clearly panic and adrenaline had combined to drive her mad. The man was a *thief*, she reminded herself, acknowledging and then proceeding to ignore the obvious irony.

She could almost hear Hopkins's voice in her head. Lady Fiona Campbell did not kiss common criminals.

She allowed her gaze to travel the length of his hard, muscled, and quite decidedly *male* body. Well. She shouldn't kiss *un*common criminals, either.

Declan's tinny voice squawked from her wrist, and she tapped the button to silence it. Time was up. She gathered the shadows around herself and stepped into the corner behind the door. The guards would be joining them any moment. Unfortunate, that. She rather hoped the man didn't face too much trouble, but the stakes were too high to let him interfere with her plans.

This job was too dear. The Siren was on the auction block; that absolutely flawless and enormous square-cut aquamarine centered on Vanquish's hilt was meant to be hers. The anonymous buyer who'd put the word out had also said those magic words: *Money is not an object.*

There was no possible way to even cost it out. The sword itself was priceless and the Siren was as well known as Vanquish. According to history, William had always claimed it came from his own many-times-great-grandmother, and she was an actual siren. The kind who sang sailors to their deaths. Apparently old Grandma the Conqueror had kept at least one sailor alive long enough to get a little frisky with him.

Fiona figured she'd start high and negotiate her way down. She wasn't planning to steal the sword, after all. She wasn't irretrievably destroying a national treasure. Just defacing it a little. They could put a different jewel in the hilt. A paste one. Fakes were brilliant these days; nobody would even be able to tell without a jeweler's eye.

Guilt whimpered and tried to raise its ugly little head in her conscience, but she firmly pushed it back down. Vampires didn't feel guilty, so why should she?

The man on the floor—the man she'd just *shot*, for Saint George's sake—stirred and groaned. Guilt didn't just whimper, this time. It jumped up and down and sang an aria. She'd never shot anyone before. She didn't want to ever shoot anyone again. She was *not* her grandfather's child.

The warning gong clanged as the security door began to rise, and she swung her attention to the glimmer of light that slowly widened between the floor and the bottom of the steel door. Right on schedule. Time to make her way home and decide what to do next. She focused with all of her concentration on shadowing her presence—sight, sound, and scent—from even the shifters and their ultrasensitive noses and ears, then cast one last regretful glance over her shoulder at the ever-so-gallant thief.

It was quite fortunate that her shadows dispersed the sound of her gasp even as it left her mouth, because the floor was empty.

The man was gone.

~~~~~

Christophe made it as far as the roof of the White Tower before he collapsed out of mist form and fell heavily to the stone. The drug had left him weak, barely able to reach for and channel the magic that had helped him escape before the Tower Guard found him lying helpless as a mewling babe on the floor.

Wicked little wench. She was going to be very, very sorry she'd ever shot an Atlantean warrior. He might have to tie her up and take a considerable amount of time teaching her a lesson.

With his lips.

And his cock.

The thought of her warm, willing body underneath his flashed a sizzle of heat through him that got him up and moving. Now was not the time to be caught on the grounds. He'd come back for the Siren; he'd seen enough to know she hadn't taken it. Not yet.

Now he wanted to find her. Needed to find her. The Scarlet Ninja was suddenly the only mission he cared about. He'd wanted a challenge, hadn't he? She was definitely that. How had a woman he hadn't really even seen aroused him more with a brief brush of her lips than any tumble in the sheets had done in decades?

He pulled himself up and, from a crouching position so as not to shout his presence to the world, scanned the grounds for the uniquely bending shadows that had signaled her presence inside the Tower. It took several long seconds, but he found her. She was running, and she was still shadowed. There was nothing magical or preternatural about her running speed, however, and he would easily catch up.

Wouldn't she be surprised at what she found when she finally stepped outside her magical shadows? He laughed and, channeling the power of Poseidon once again, threw himself off the roof and into the rain. This would have to be his last effort to travel as mist until he'd had rest and food. Exhaustion was pulling at him, amplified by the remnants of the drug still working itself out of his system. The transformation itself should help remove the drug, though, balancing out the drain on his magic as he changed forms yet again.

He focused on the way the curving shadows moved through the grounds and toward the gate, barely perceptible in the drizzling rain. She moved so gracefully, almost dancing between one raindrop and the next. It couldn't be just the light she was bending with her magic. Shifters had extremely powerful noses, and she'd been within scenting range. But clearly they hadn't caught so much as a whiff—or the sound of her heartbeat, either. If he hadn't known better, he might have thought she was a vampire.

He did know better, though. More than two centuries spent fighting vamps had taught him how to recognize a vampire when he confronted one. She had a magic he hadn't seen before, that was all. Maybe Fae, but even as he thought it denial rose to counter it. Not Fae, please not Fae.

He hated the Fae.

There. She'd veered away from the loose grouping of guards near the gate and circled around, slipping through behind them even as Christophe watched. That easily, and she was gone.

He wondered if it was always that simple for her. Decided it must be. After all, she was the Scarlet Ninja, celebrated throughout the United Kingdom. People in every pub he'd entered during the past few days had happily and drunkenly embellished rumors about this phantom who'd stolen millions of euros' worth of jewelry and art, but never been caught or so much as seen. People were speculating that *he*—and wouldn't they be surprised to see just how much the Scarlet Ninja was *not* a man—was a descendant of the legendary Robin Hood. He gave an amount worth exactly half of every take to various charities and causes, accompanied only by his calling card: a shiny silver card embossed with the scarlet silhouette of a ninja.

Distraction. If he kept thinking about her, he might forget to realize how much he was hurting. Exhaustion took on the form of physical pain, even for an Atlantean warrior, when he'd been living on pints and very little else, not even sleep, for days, and then overused his magic in pursuit of a phantom. Alaric would be furious. The thought cheered him up enough to keep him going for a little farther, just a bit . . . *there.*

He'd caught her. The long, dark car pulled smoothly away from London's hideous traffic and up to the curb just long enough for the back door to be opened ever so briefly, seemingly by whoever sat inside behind those dark-tinted windows. And if Christophe hadn't been watching very, very closely, he never would have seen the flash of scarlet silk materialize before the door slammed shut and the car pulled back out into traffic. Not a chance the traffic cameras had caught a bit of her, either. Just another anonymous dark car in a city filled with them. Even the license plates were mud-splashed and unreadable.

As he soared down toward the car and its mysterious passenger, Christophe spared a flash of grim amusement at the thought of how very surprised his Scottish ninja was going to be when she reached her destination.

Chapter 6

Waterloo Barracks

Telios returned to his perch near the gargoyle and puzzled over what he'd seen. A flash of a man who could turn into water? It wasn't a Fae talent he'd ever heard of, but the Fae kept their secrets close and their enemies closer. He'd be a fool to believe that Prince Gideon na Feransel truly wanted him as an ally. More likely the Fae planned to use him and discard him. Or kill him. Until he knew the truth, he couldn't trust any of the new members of his vampire coalition. They'd watch for which way the wind shifted and be as likely to try to kill Telios themselves as to assist him.

Telios's fangs extended and he danced a little capering jig. Far more powerful beings than a minor Unseelie prince had tried to kill him before. None of them still walked the earth in their precious Summer Lands. Or anywhere else, for that matter.

The water man was no concern of Telios's, anyway. If he'd been carrying the sword, Telios would have seen it when the man had lurched off the roof. Time to move on to part two of the plan and go inside, find out what the uproar his vampire hearing had detected was about, and get a little help from one of the dogs. He so loved making shifters obey.

Telios flew down to the front of the building, timing it perfectly for the guards' circuit. He focused every ounce of his power and stared them down, enthralling the human first and then the shifter before either could so much as draw a weapon.

"We need to go see the Jewel House," he said.

"We need to go see the Jewel House," the human responded, eyes glazed over and blank.

"Make sure Vanquish is safe," Telios prompted.

"We must make sure Vanquish is safe," the shifter said. His face was a blank mask like the human's, but a tiny bit of twitching ran through his muscles. Shifters were always harder to completely enthrall, and he'd never yet managed to put more than one of them under at a time.

He shrugged. He'd make do with what he had, as usual. He'd been doing just that since 1888. "You'll kill anyone who tries to stop us."

"We'll kill anyone who tries to stop us," they both repeated.

He stood aside and pointed. "Lead the way."

∼⌒⌒∽

Telios had expected the guards to discover him every step of the way: through the employee entrance, down the twisting corridors, and even while they stood, exposed, as the shifter punched in the code that opened the security door to the Jewel House. Naturally, since he was prepared for every contingency of attack, none happened. Now they stood guard, his two minions, as he admired the lovely jewels on display.

Not as many as he'd expected, to be sure. Perhaps the queen and her offspring were prancing around somewhere at some state dinner, all bejeweled and crowned. Did they even do that anymore? It was so hard to keep track of current traditions as the decades passed, faster and faster. The closest he'd come to a spark of interest in years had been when that American author came to London to try to discover his real identity. She'd failed, of course—they all failed. But then again, that had been before they knew vampires existed. Perhaps now was the time to unleash his alter ego again.

Whitechapel and its residents had missed him for far too long.

A sound from the hallway interrupted his reveries of flesh and blood and death, and he crossed to the case that held his prize. Vanquish, sparkling like a whore who'd robbed a jeweler. Gaudy and over adorned. The question crossed his mind yet again—why did the Fae want this particular sword so very, very much?

Voices in the hallway sounded, closer, and he had no time for questions. He pulled on his favorite leather gloves, punched a hole in the glass, and removed the sword with both hands. Even through the gloves, a tingle of power zapped him with an almost electrical shock, but it wasn't his left hand that felt the jolt. It was his right—the hand that held Vanquish's hilt.

The jewel on that hilt glowed with the fierce blue of the ocean dazzled by sunlight. He'd never seen a more beautiful gem, but it wasn't only the beauty that captured his interest. This aquamarine was magical, somehow. No wonder the Fae wanted it. Perhaps Telios would keep it for himself for a while and try to discover its secrets. Always better to know the things that others tried to hide. Especially the nasty secrets of Unseelie Fae.

The voices changed, from conversational to aggressive, and he realized his presence had been discovered. By the time he whirled around to face them, his two enthralled guards were fighting like madmen to keep their colleagues from entering the room. Three lay dead or dying on the floor already. Telios knew he could take on the remaining five by himself if he had to do so, but there was no need.

"Guard me as I leave," he commanded, and his two guards immediately fell back to protect him.

But they were protecting him from no one. The other guards weren't attacking. They weren't rushing his two guards or even trying to attack Telios. Every single one of them had turned, backs to Telios, weapons held in the air at a readiness position.

Telios tried to understand this new trick. How was this strategy supposed to work? Before he could puzzle out even a possible answer, all seven guards—the two he'd enthralled and the five others—spoke as one.

"We guard you as you leave, Master."

Telios's mouth fell open and his fangs retracted involuntarily from pure shock. He stared around the room at the guards. Each face held the same expressionless blankness. The same readiness to serve him. The gem in the hilt of the sword pulsed once in his hand, flaring a brighter blue than before, and he slowly bent his head to look at it.

"It's you, isn't it, my beautiful bit of rock?" He whispered the words, almost not daring to believe them. "No wonder the Fae prince wants you so very badly. The sword was a distraction. What he really wants is you and your power."

He raised his head and felt the triumphant grin spread across his face, stretching long-unused facial muscles. It had been a very long time since he'd had reason to smile. "Let's all dance," he told the guards, and he laughed his very rusty laugh as they waltzed all the way to the door.

Chapter 7

Fiona finished changing into her jeans and shirt, toweled off her damp hair, and pressed the button to lower the privacy glass so she could talk to Sean.

"I'm still not sure hiring you was such a good idea," she said, uncapping a bottle of water and taking a long drink as they prowled through the dark and light of London at night. "I don't know how much good 'getaway driver' is going to do you on your résumé. Not to mention the unfortunate and very real possibility of prison."

He grinned at her in the rearview mirror, still looking far too young to even be allowed to drive, let alone be the chauffeur of a hardened criminal like herself. "Funny, that. Just sent out fifty résumés yesterday and I've had forty-nine job offers already. Evidently getaway drivers are in high demand these days."

The grin faded and his eyes narrowed as he swerved around a badly parked car. "Stick your arse end out in the street, and you'll lose it, Mr. Volvo," he muttered.

"Forty-nine offers, hmm? Does that mean you're leaving me to fend for myself?" Fiona rested her head against the back of the seat, suddenly utterly fatigued.

"Not quite yet, Lady Fiona. I was really holding out for that fiftieth outfit." He smoothly rounded a corner and glanced back at her. "Get some rest, why don't you?"

She aimed her sternest glare at the back of his head. "Call me Lady Fiona again and you're fired, my young friend."

"Whatever you say, Lady Fiona."

She growled at him, but he just chuckled and switched on the music, something light and classical that one wouldn't expect a twenty-two-year-old man—boy, really—to enjoy. Although it was true that he had never quite had the chance to be a boy. Not with the way he'd grown up. She'd stepped into the middle of a beating that day, seven years ago, and come out the other side with a broken arm and a fifteen-year-old boy who wouldn't be parted from her, no matter how many times the authorities had tried to find him a suitable home.

So her home had become his home, and the child of a murderer and a whore became the ward of a thief. In her more self-aware moments, she wasn't that sure it was a step up. But the truth was that she needed the help—help she could trust—and the reward was far too great for far too many for her to retire the Scarlet Ninja just yet.

Even though now she was in danger. She'd been seen.

Her thoughts returned to the man from the Tower. She hadn't had the time to ask him how he'd gotten past security, not that he would have answered her anyway. But he knew she was a woman; a Scottish woman. He knew and he had absolutely no reason to protect her identity. She'd shot him with drugs and left him for the Guard.

She'd *shot* the man. *Shot him and kissed him*, her conscience whispered. Bloody hell. She'd shot the one witness who could ruin everything. She was absolutely mad.

"*Should have killed him*," the ghost of her grandfather whispered in her mind, but she shut him down, hard. She'd retire the Scarlet Ninja and go to work cleaning toilets before she'd become anything like *him*.

The soothing music and the exhaustion pulled at her, helping to repress the worry for just a few minutes, and brooding turned to dozing until the car smoothly pulled to a stop and she realized they'd arrived safely in her garage. Sean was out of the car and opening her door before she could do it herself, another gallantry she'd tried to talk him out of many times. He took his chauffeur's role seriously, though, and wouldn't be dissuaded.

"We're safe home," he announced, grasping her arm and helping her out of the car as if she were a ninety-year-old woman with a bad case of the gout.

She bit back the impatient retort that sprang to her lips. It wasn't Sean's fault that she'd botched the job. A simple reconnaissance. "How dangerous can it be?" she'd said to Hopkins. Flippant and carefree. *Foolish.*

How dangerous could it be? She was ruined. That was how dangerous.

"If you're all right, then, I'll say good night," Sean said. He lived in a lovely little apartment over the garage. Hopkins had overseen the decorating himself, though he'd never admit it.

"Fine, thanks. You get some sleep." She put a hand on his arm as he started to walk away. "Sean? You're a wonderful help to me. I know I don't tell you that often enough. Thank you."

His pale face slowly flushed to a glowing pink under the dusting of freckles on his cheeks. "You don't, I mean, I just, we—"

Hopkins's dry voice sounded from the doorway to the laundry. "He means to say 'you're welcome,' don't you, Sean?"

"Exactly!" Sean said a shade too loudly. "Just off to bed now. To sleep, that is. Just sleeping. In bed."

Fiona watched, fascinated, as Sean's face turned a peculiar shade of plum-purple before he made a bizarre squeaking sound and practically ran for the stairs to his apartment.

When the door had closed behind him, she gathered her bag, closed the car door, and turned to Hopkins. "What on earth was that about?"

"That young man has believed since he was fifteen years old that the stars and moon shine for you alone. Didn't you realize that all of his puppy adoration and hero worship would almost certainly turn into something a bit more personal?"

She blinked, trying to force her tired mind to put some sense into his words. "He—oh. Oh, no. He has a crush? On me? I'm far too old for him."

"Oh, yes, all of five whole years. You're ancient. And yes, a crush, as you say. Unrequited love. Quite an astonishingly fierce case. But don't fret, it will pass. In fact, perhaps sooner rather than later, considering how lovely the housekeeper's niece is," Hopkins said, stepping forward to take her bag.

Fiona decided she'd had enough to deal with for one night and chose to put this latest problem aside. Far aside. Perhaps for the next ten years or so, or at least the next few months, until Sean grew out of it or switched his affections to the housekeeper's niece.

"Nice pajamas," she said, managing a grin. He still wore his perfectly creased jacket, shirt, and trousers. "Do you sleep in that outfit?"

A shadow crossed his face, probably at her pathetic attempt to force a bit of lightness into her voice. "Well, then? How did it really go?"

"It could have been better," she admitted. "We have a bit of a problem."

Hopkins narrowed his eyes, but she just shook her head. "Upstairs. When we're in my office."

"I see. That big of a problem," was all he said, before leading the way into the house.

"Oh, my dear Hopkins. You have no idea." As she followed him through the house and up the wide staircase to her second-floor office, she wanted to laugh but clamped her lips shut against it. She was afraid if she started, the edge of wildness racing through her would come out in hysteria, and one thing a lady must never do was succumb to hysteria. Her grandfather had told her that often enough, generally while brandishing his cane through the air and terrifying the servants. Odd that he'd never addressed the issue of a lady going to prison for the rest of her life. That lecture might have come in handy right about now.

As she trudged up the stairs, her thoughts returned to the mystery man. Whatever he was up to, she hoped—quite illogically—that he was safe.

"We're going to have to put something in that space, you know." Hopkins indicated the empty space on the wall where her grandfather's portrait had claimed pride of ownership on the landing.

When she was a little girl, she'd always thought the eyes in the painting followed her around. Frankly, it had felt like that now that she was an adult, as well. That's why she'd finally asked that it be taken down, ostensibly for cleaning. It felt wrong to tell her staff that a painting "creeped her out," as Declan would say. Not very ladylike. It sat in the attic now, draped, where her grandfather's dead, painted eyes couldn't glare down at them all anymore. As far as she was concerned, it could stay there forever.

"Something with tiny kittens and butterflies, perhaps, and a motivational slogan such as 'Hang in there, pussycat,'" Hopkins continued, his voice drier than ever.

She laughed and stumbled, almost missing the step. "What on earth are you talking about?"

"Just checking in to see if you were listening. We do need to hang something, though. The bare space is too dramatic and invites questions. Perhaps another deceased family member with a slightly less dour countenance?"

She shivered. "Not likely. How about you, Hopkins? We'll have your portrait done. You can even wear the sheep pj's."

His un-butler-like snort sounded as it reached the second floor. "Yes. I'll put that in my planner straightaway. Shall we say Tuesday of never?"

She caught up with him and put a hand on his arm. "I'll tell you more, later. But with Declan, I'm going to . . . play it down, shall we say."

He stopped walking and stared at her in silence for a long moment, then finally inclined his head. "As you say. He'll never be off to university if he thinks his big sister is in danger. He's quite protective of you, you know."

"He's not the only one," she said, flashing a sudden grin.

She started off again, but this time he caught her arm. "*Are* you in danger?"

Fiona bit her lip, thinking about how to respond. Finally she went with truth. Always easiest to remember. "I might be. This time, I really might be."

The door to the last room on the right of the warmly lit hallway opened, and her brother popped his head out. His hair stood straight up, a sign that he'd been at his beloved computers most of the night, and he instantly launched into an excited swarm of questions.

"Oh, boy, that was close. Did you set off the alarm? Guards swarmed the room for quite a while after you left, and who was that bloke on the floor? Where did he go? They put the cameras and computers in emergency lockdown mode right after that, so I got kicked out, and Fee, I think they knew I was in there. They've got somebody top-notch. It would have to be somebody really, really good to know I was there and find out it was actually me, you know? Not in an arrogant way, but you know. What did you think of the Siren? Did you get a really good look? It's absolutely gorgeous, but I've always been moved along by the guards when I try to—"

She finally stopped him, dazzled by the sheer volume of words. "What did I tell you about caffeine after midnight? Slow down, let me in, and we'll talk about it. I don't really care to discuss this in the hall."

Not that the hall housed anyone but herself and Declan; those few of the staff who didn't return to their own homes at night had the other wing, but it never hurt to be careful. She took a step toward the combined office and computer room she thought of as her brother's private nerve center, but this time Hopkins clamped a hand on her arm with the tensile strength of a cast-iron manacle.

She glanced up at him, and her question died in her mouth at the sight of the flames practically shooting out of his eyes.

"There was a *bloke*?" he said, enunciating very, very precisely, always a bad sign. "A *bloke* on the *floor*?"

"Inside. Let's get out of the hallway and I'll tell all," she repeated. "But let me warn you now: you're not going to like it."

~~~~~

Christophe opened his eyes to total darkness, and just for a moment, that instant between conscious and not conscious, terror swept through him. *Not again, not now, not the box, I'll be good, please no.* Before he could smash his fists into whatever hard surface he lay on, however, or howl his fear to the menacing dark, realization dawned. The present reality snapped back into focus with the power of a moon-pulled wave crashing around his head in high surf.

He was safe. He was in the trunk of the car—the ninja's car. It was no longer moving, so hopefully they'd arrived at her home base or headquarters. Unless they'd stolen the car and then dumped it, in which case he was screwed. Yet again.

Funny, he hadn't considered that it might be a stolen car until now that it was too late. He was better than that, when he wasn't drugged and chasing a silk-covered ninja. He closed his eyes and forced his heartbeat to slow.

Calm. Serene. He was one of Poseidon's elite, not that little boy. Never again that pathetic boy. Never again helpless.

He was also feeling stronger. The sleep must have allowed his body to metabolize the rest of the drug out of his system and recharge Atlantean magic that had been far too frequently channeled this night.

Stretching out his arms, he carefully felt in the usual places for any type of release mechanism. Ven, the car enthusiast, had told them all about that after Christophe had wanted to put an uncooperative shifter in the trunk of one of Ven's cars once. Newer cars generally had release levers, Ven had said; a protection for children who might accidentally lock themselves in the trunk.

Accidentally. Lock *themselves* in the trunk. The words themselves mocked him. Mocked his helplessness, all those years ago. The word "trunk" then meant a heavy wooden thing, not part of a vehicle. Cars had been a thing of the far-distant future back then.

No. Not accidental at all. When they'd locked a terrified little boy in that trunk. *Demon-borne*, they'd said. Hours and hours in that trunk, but what came later had been even worse.

No. He shook his head and took a deep breath to escape the memories. His trembling fingers found the release lever, and he paused to listen carefully for the sound of anyone in the area who might be surprised to see a man climb out of the trunk of a car. Surprise sometimes equaled guns shooting at his head. Or worse: *vampires'* kind of surprise.

He hated surprise.

But there was nothing. Not road noise, either, so the car was inside a garage or parking structure, or else he'd been asleep for long enough for the car to travel far beyond London's busy streets. He couldn't be sure, but it didn't feel like the latter. He didn't feel rested enough for that.

"Enough delaying, already," he whispered into the dark, just so he could hear the sound of a voice. Even his own. The technique had helped in the past. Not that he needed any help now. Dark was just dark. A trunk was merely a storage space, not a prison.

There were almost certainly no exorcists in the immediate area.

The thought snapped him out of his memories, and taking a deep breath, he pulled the release lever. The trunk popped open smoothly, with not a hint of squeak, and he immediately sat up and scanned the area, his dagger held at the ready. Ceiling lights set to low provided illumination enough for him to see that the garage—for it was clearly that—was empty, however. He climbed out of the car and whirled around to face the other half of the room, searching its dimly lit corners for any dangers.

Nothing. Tools, workbench, a second car, and two very hot motorcycles filled the clean and tidy space, which smelled of gasoline, oil, and polish and, underneath it all, the faintest hint of jasmine. Of *her.* Somebody took very good care of this garage, which didn't feel at all like a hideout for desperate criminals. It felt like a garage attached to somebody's home.

Her home?

Only one way to find out. He closed the trunk and headed for the door in the back corner. Time to find out who the Scarlet Ninja was when she was at home.

Chapter 8

Fiona held up her hands to stop both Declan's flow of words and Hopkins's silent but potent urgings to get on with it and dish, already. Not that Hopkins would ever say or even think "dish." Exhaustion swamped her, the aftershock of adrenaline and, to be honest if only with herself, sexual attraction, pumping through her body. The dull thud of an impending headache pounded at the edges of her skull and she wanted nothing more than to curl up in bed with a cup of that chocolate she'd run out on earlier.

Instead, she was going to face an interrogation. She scanned the room as if looking for answers in its familiar warm blue and cream furnishings, and then nearly fell into an overstuffed chair as a hideous thought occurred.

"Declan? Did you, um, see anything during those fifteen minutes?" *Like your big sis kissing a total stranger, perhaps?*

He rolled his lovely chocolate-brown eyes, identical to their father's. So unfair that he'd won the long, lush eyelash lottery of the two of them. She tried never to go without mascara to compensate for her mother's English rose genes: blue eyes, pale blond hair and lashes. And how tired was she, to be thinking of eyelashes at a time like this?

"Fee, I've told you a thousand times, when I'm looping the cameras on a high-tech system like that, I can't see you, either. I see what I've got *them* seeing, unless we start fitting you out with a buttonhole camera. I only caught a glimpse of the room where they stopped the loop." He flashed a guilty glance at Hopkins. "You'd stepped out, and I didn't want to worry you. But, Fee, you have to understand, it's the—"

"Stop. Okay. I get it. Please, for the love of Saint George, no more technical discussions of wavelengths or pixels or whatever. My brain can't take it." Her gaze automatically went to the priceless oil-on-wood painting of Saint George slaying the dragon, in its place of honor across from her desk. Every time she glanced up from her work, the visual reminder that she, too, could slay dragons, reinforced her mission. Or vampires, as the case may be. The curators in the Louvre might even still believe they had the original, although last she'd checked, the website had listed Raphael's *Saint George and the Dragon* as "not on display."

Not exactly true. It was on display, of course, just not in the museum. It's not like a self-respecting ninja master thief could hang a *reproduction* in her home. The painting represented her entire life's work, after all.

She leaned her head back on the chair and closed her eyes, sighing. So good to be home. So awful to have to share her news.

The scent of rich chocolate wafted under her nose and her eyes snapped open. Hopkins stood next to the chair, still stern and frowning, but holding a cup of freshly poured aromatic heaven out to her.

"Drink it, and then tell us everything, if you please," he said.

So she did, leaving out the flirting part and the kissing part. But what she did disclose was bad enough, judging by the expression on her butler's face and the apparent inability of her baby brother to make actual words, since sputtering noises kept coming from his general direction.

"You let a common criminal get close enough to you that he could have harmed you? He could have ripped off your mask? He could have murdered you and left you lying in a pool of your own blood in the middle of the Jewel House?" Hopkins bit off each word as precisely as a cutter following the shape of an octahedral raw diamond crystal.

Bloody damn precisely, in other words.

Fiona sighed, but before she could respond, the air in the room changed and flames chased ice through her in a blaze of sensation that brought her up and out of her chair so fast she knocked the cup of chocolate to the floor. She whipped around to face the door, and it was him.

Her mystery man.

In her office, leaning against the door frame, arms crossed on that amazing chest and a cocky grin on that gorgeous face.

"Hey, I take exception to that remark," he said. "I'm not at all common."

～～～～

Christophe couldn't believe it. She was freaking gorgeous. Even in faded jeans and an ordinary top, her hair simple and mostly pulled back from her face, she was as beautiful as the priceless art that adorned every wall in the room.

More beautiful. Paintings couldn't blush, after all, and the faint staining of pink on those porcelain cheeks made him think of strawberry jam, Atlantean blushberry tarts, and other luscious, delectable treats.

"Common or not, you are a trespasser, sir," said the well-dressed elderly man with the very large gun. He was dressed like a butler or an undertaker, and yet he held that gun with the relaxed ease of a man who knew exactly what he was doing. Majordomo via MI6, perhaps? Where James Bond types went when they retired?

"Oh, no, I was invited," Christophe replied. "Ask the ninja."

She moved suddenly, shaking her silky white-blond hair out of her face in what he was sure was a deliberate distraction, since she now stood exactly in his line of sight to the younger man in the room. Shielding him from the intruder.

Good instincts. He spared a moment to wonder why it made him want to growl. She was protecting another man from him, and he didn't like it, for some reason that didn't come from his brain but from a more primal part of himself.

Christophe didn't like that either, nor the possible implications of his not liking it.

"I am sure I have no idea what you're talking about, sir, but let's just call the authorities and sort this all out, shall we?" Her Scottish accent was still there but blurred, as if she were attempting to hide it from him. She crossed to the desk and picked up her phone.

He smiled again, showing his teeth. "Yes, why don't we? That should be a fun conversation. Especially the part where I tell them you're the Scarlet Ninja."

The boy—he could see now that it was a boy, not a man, which calmed him down for some reason—behind her gasped.

"Fee! He knows? Is this him? The man from the Jewel House?"

She sighed and her shoulders slumped, which did very interesting things to the generous curve of her breasts, and Christophe's body hardened in sudden, aggressive readiness. Ninjas apparently aroused him, something he'd not known before. He laughed out loud.

The sound of the gun's hammer cocking back tempered his amusement. The dangerous-looking man still held the gun trained on him.

"Did something strike you as funny, sir? Your impending demise, perhaps?" The dry tone only underscored the promise of death in the man's eyes. This one was a warrior, too, underneath that fancy suit.

"Are you going to shoot me? It would be the second time tonight, which isn't my record, but it would serve to piss me off," Christophe said, letting all emotion drain out of his face until he knew that what they saw was nothing more than a cold, deadly killer. "I'd prefer a more friendly solution."

He turned to the ninja, who still held the phone in one hand, forgotten. "We're after the same thing. Why not partner up?"

She dropped the phone and then fumbled it onto the cradle,

those huge eyes of hers widening even further. "Are you mad?"

"Nope." He paused to give the question more serious consideration, given that he'd just followed a ninja home. "Not usually," he amended.

She narrowed those gorgeous blue eyes at him. "I work alone."

"Right. I can see that. You, James Bond over there, and the kid. What's one more partner?"

"I don't even know who you are," she said.

"If you're quite done, may I kill him now?" the old guy asked, still polite, but steel underlay those proper British manners.

The ninja made a sound of frustration that made Christophe wonder what other sounds she might make. Like, for example, when he licked her neck. Or explored those lovely breasts with his hands and mouth. His cock twitched in his pants, and he forcibly yanked his mind away from visions of a very naked ninja.

"Look, I can't keep calling you the ninja," Christophe pointed out. "My name is Christophe. And you are?"

"Christophe? Just one name? Like Madonna?" the kid said, grinning. He didn't seem to have an ounce of self-preservation in his body. Christophe found himself grinning right back at him.

"No, I can't sing a note. And you are?"

The kid took a step forward, hand extended as if to shake, years of breeding and manners clearly coming to the fore. "Declan Campbell, nice to meet— Oh." Declan stopped dead and shot a red-faced glance at the ninja. "*Crap.* Sorry, Fee. Oh. Sorry again!"

The ninja—Fee?—sighed and shook her head. "Don't worry about it, Declan. If he's in our house, it would be easy enough for him to figure out who we are."

She tilted her head and considered Christophe for a moment, then shrugged. "Fiona Campbell. My brother Declan. And the overprotective one is Hopkins."

Christophe grinned at Hopkins. "Just the one name? Like Madonna?"

Hopkins never moved a single muscle, just stood there in a shooter's stance with that damn gun still trained on the space between Christophe's eyes. "This is a mistake, Lady Fiona," he bit off. "You have put years and years' worth of work in jeopardy in a single evening. Congratulations."

"*Lady* Fiona?" Christophe watched, fascinated, as a rosy flush swept up her neck and face. "You're aristocracy *and* a cat burglar?"

"I assure you, I never, ever steal cats," she said, a glimmer of humor underneath the frost in her voice.

"No, just dragons." He flicked a glance at Raphael's depiction of Saint George, then back at her. "That's the original, isn't it?"

"I don't know what you—"

"You're not just good," he said, ignoring Hopkins and his gun and crossing over to the painting to study it more closely. "You're scary good."

He glanced over his shoulder at her, almost able to taste the delicious possibilities. "Oh, yes. We're definitely partners."

"No," she said flatly. "Not a chance."

"Are you going to kill me, then? Or have James Bond over there do it? Because I know who you are, and you know I know who you are. So as I see it, we have several different options. One, I'm your partner. Two, you shoot me to keep me from telling the police and the tabloids that you're the Scarlet Ninja."

"And?" Her voice could have flash-frozen half of Atlantis. "And what?"

"You said several options. You named two. What are the others?"

"Oh. I guess I was wrong. Just those two." He couldn't seem to stop grinning for some reason. The situation cheered him up. Hugely.

"I'll be happy to shoot him, Lady Fiona. In fact, I'm quite anxious to do so," Hopkins said.

"She already shot me," Christophe offered helpfully.

The ninja glared at him. "That was a tranq gun. And nobody is shooting anyone. That's . . . that's my grandfather's solution, Hopkins. You know I won't go down that road. Not now, not ever." The ice in her voice was gone, replaced with a white-hot rage that Christophe instinctively knew would sear anything it touched.

So why did he wonder what it would feel like to burn in those flames?

"I guess we have a partner, then," Declan said, grinning.

"I'd much rather shoot him, but if you insist." Hopkins put the gun down but kept it within reach. "So, then, *partner*. Who are you and what exactly do you want?"

Chapter 9

Fiona suddenly found it hard to breathe as her new *partner* stared into her eyes, a wicked grin slowly spreading across his face.

"Who do I want? That's between me and the ninja," he said, his eyes darkening from a pale spring green to a dark leafy color as his gaze practically burned the clothes from her body. Definitely not human. Human eyes didn't do that. Unless he had a kind of magic she'd never seen before hiding behind that bad-boy long hair. The waves brushing his collar looked silken soft. If only she could touch them, she could discover—

Suddenly, the meaning of his words caught up to her fevered mind. "No! He said *what* do you want. What, not *who*." She felt the flush rise up into her cheeks and had to grit her teeth against the embarrassment. "Stop that at once, or I'll take my chances with the police."

"Hey, *you* kissed *me*," he said, still grinning.

He dropped that long, lean body into one of her chairs, and the floral print of the upholstery didn't do a thing to diminish his aggressive maleness. He was a predator, no matter where you put him, and she needed to be very, very cautious, in spite of the part of her that wanted to crawl into his lap and bite his neck.

Hopkins cleared his throat. "You kissed him?"

"I—"

"Wow! Your first kiss in years and it's a criminal? Sis, you're going to have to watch out. You've got a thing for bad boys. Look at Sean."

Her face was on fire. Surely the house sprinkler system would activate itself at any moment. Christophe's avid interest wasn't helping any, nor was the way he kept checking out her body whenever she moved.

"It was *not* my first kiss in years, not that it's any of your business, and I—he—it was a distraction technique!"

"It's true. She distracted me, and then she shot me," Christophe offered. Then he leaned forward, and those amazing green eyes narrowed. "Also, who's Sean?"

"Don't help me," she told him. "I don't have a thing for Sean," she said to her rotten brother.

"You adopted him!" Declan sputtered. "That's what I meant. Not that you have a romantic thing for him. That would be gross. You're so old."

"I'm not old," she gritted out.

"Not compared to me," Christophe said cheerfully, relaxing back into his chair. "So long as you're not kissing Sean, too."

Hopkins picked up the gun again. "Now I'm definitely going to shoot him."

"I'd rather you didn't," Christophe said, but he was either insane or had balls of bloody steel, because there wasn't a hint of fear on his face.

"No shooting! I won't have it," she shouted, smashing her fist down on the desk, which accomplished nothing but hurting her hand. Everyone else in the room ignored her completely. Stupid men.

"Look, man, in all seriousness, if you mess with my sister, you're going to have to face me," Declan said, and he was only shaking the tiniest bit as he faced Christophe, holding one of the ceremonial swords from the display on the wall.

"When did you get that down? How—"

"Later, Fee," Declan said, suddenly looking a lot more grown-up.

Christophe's grin faded and an expression of total seriousness took its place as he slowly rose from the chair, hands held loosely at his side. "Declan, it is both courageous and honorable of you to protect your sister. I swear on my oath as a warrior not to do anything with her that she doesn't want me to do. Does that satisfy your honor?"

Declan nodded uncertainly, and lowered the sword.

Fiona's mouth fell open, and she stepped between the two of them, placed a hand on each of their chests, and shoved. "I. Am. Standing. Right. Here!" she shouted. "Bloody Neanderthals!"

Hopkins put the gun back down on the table. "Perhaps you might lower your voice before the housekeeper and the rest of the staff call the constables or rush down here to investigate?"

Christophe caught her hand in one of his, raised it to his lips, and kissed her palm before she could snatch her hand away. She had to fight herself not to give him the satisfaction of rubbing her hand against her pants to make the tingling feeling go away. His smile told her he knew anyway.

Damn the man.

"Look. Why don't we all calm down? I don't want to hurt anybody," Christophe said. "We both want the Siren. I happen to represent . . . a consortium of very wealthy investors who will be happy to pay. So we steal it together, I get the Siren, I give you the money. Minus a certain finder's fee for myself, of course."

He poured himself a cup of chocolate, bold as brass, while she and Hopkins stared at each other in stunned disbelief. *Disbelief* being the operative word.

"What possible incentive could you have for giving us all the money? We weren't born yesterday," she pointed out.

Christophe put his cup down and flashed that wicked smile at her again. "No, but the gods clearly blessed whatever day you were born. As to incentive? I'm in the mood for a little challenge, and may Poseidon himself strike me down if that's not the truth."

Oddly enough, the man paused and looked to the windows for a moment before continuing. "I don't need money, and clearly you don't, either, from the looks of this place. So we both do this for the fun of it. Why don't we have a little fun together this time?"

The double entendres in every sentence out of his sinfully gorgeous mouth was sending little shock waves through her nerve endings. Have a little fun together, indeed. She'd like to have *naked* fun with him . . . Oh. No. She was doing it again. She clenched her fists and tried to remember all the reasons this was such a bad idea.

"I don't trust you," Hopkins said flatly, aiming his deadliest stare at Christophe. "I wouldn't trust you with the good silver, let alone a priceless jewel from the British royal collection. Certainly not with Lady Fiona."

"Right. Patriotism?" Christophe rolled his eyes. "From the man who was obviously helping her steal the Siren from queen and country in the first place? Try again."

"We're going to do it," Fiona said. "I'll be your partner, for this one time, and one time only."

Hopkins jerked his head to stare at her in disbelief. "But—"

"We have no options. He will promise never to disclose my identity if we do this, correct?"

Christophe tilted his head and considered her for a long moment, then nodded. "Yes. You have my word."

Something changed in the air—a tingle of power washed over Fiona and she shivered. Words had power, and perhaps his words had more power than most.

Hopkins narrowed his eyes, studying Christophe, but then he slowly shook his head. Fiona knew he must be using that extra sense he had—a super-hyped sense of intuition—that let him read people and their intent. "No. I don't care if you believe you won't hurt her. I can't trust—"

In a flash of movement far too quick for her eyes to follow, Christophe was at Hopkins's side, twin daggers raised, one to each side of her butler's throat. "I respect your need to protect Fiona, but do not question my word, or my honor, as I accord you the same."

Before any of them could move, Christophe sheathed his

daggers and bowed to Hopkins. "I give you my sworn oath that I will not cause harm to come to her, nor will I allow any other to harm her."

That sense of power was back, but more than a tingle this time—more of a jolt. Fiona noticed that the hair on Declan's head and arms was standing straight up.

"Perhaps, since we're no longer actually living in the time of William the Conqueror," she said, in case they didn't understand her point, "you might address any promises *about* me *to* me."

Christophe swung around to face her and strode across the space between them with the arrogant confidence of a conqueror himself. "And so I should. I give to you, my ninja, my sworn oath not to lay a single hand on any part of your extremely luscious body."

She blinked. "Well. Right. Then let's—"

"Until you ask me to." He bowed again, to her this time, and she stared down in disbelief at his lowered head and his broad, muscled back. As he straightened, she considered whether or not it was bad form to shoot the man. Again. He had the nerve to grin at her and she dove for her tranq gun.

Declan pulled her back and put his arm around her shoulders, probably sensing her need to do violence. "Should we start planning?" he asked. "I can work on a longer time-out for the cameras, but they're going to be tougher to crack now that they caught us."

"We can discuss plans tomorrow. It is very late, and Lady Fiona must make an appearance in the morning. Preferably without bloodshot eyes from lack of sleep," Hopkins said, taking charge of the room the way he'd done since she was small. "Have you forgotten the Charing Cross Children's Books reading and signing?"

She had. Somehow this infuriating criminal had driven all rational thought from her mind. *Ask* him to put his hands on her. The cheek of the man.

"Of course not," she lied. "The store owner has been lovely to me; she has nearly two hundred copies of *The Forest Fairies* already purchased and ready for me to sign."

"The what?" Christophe leaned against the wall, his powcrful arms folded across that muscular chest, dangerous even at rest. "Did you say forest fairies?" He grinned and some no doubt evil thought lit up his eyes with amusement.

"Fiona's the best author and illustrator of children's books in all of Europe, maybe the entire world," Declan boasted.

Fiona felt her cheeks heat up again, although she'd have thought she was too tired for even embarrassment. "Let's not get carried away. *The Forest Fairies* is my newest book. It's a retelling of a rather grim Scottish fairy tale."

"Aren't most fairy tales grim? If you'd ever met any of the Fae, you'd understand why. Vicious bastards, most of them," Christophe growled. "Especially the Unseelie Court."

Declan laughed. "Unseelie Court? Isn't that a myth?"

"Sure, that's what they'd like you to think," Christophe muttered. "Then they murder you and steal your child."

"You've met Fae?" Fiona found it hard to believe. Certainly, since the vampires and shifters had announced their presence, there had been rumors that other, more publicity-shy supernatural beings existed, but she'd never known anyone who claimed to have met one of them.

Declan piped up: "There's a new course on the Fae in next year's Oxford catalog." When Fiona turned to look at him, surprised by his first mention of Oxford, his cheeks flushed bright pink. "Not that I'm planning to go to university just yet. You need me here."

"I most certainly do not need you here, you idjit. You and that giant brain of yours are going to school. You need to meet girls and go to pubs. Experience the life of a college man," she said firmly.

Christophe grinned, and she shot him a warning glare. Family business was none of his. He raised his hands in an "I surrender" pose and said nothing.

Hopkins, however, was family and had no such restraint. "Ah, yes. The 'pints and birds' lecture given to generations of budding young Oxford men. A model of decorum, he'll be."

Declan's face flushed even hotter, if that were possible. "I'm not—"

"Having this argument now, yes, I agree," Fiona interjected smoothly. "In front of our new *partner*."

"Don't mind me," Christophe said. "I don't have any brothers or sisters, so I'm finding this all pretty interesting."

She put her hands on her hips, ready to give him a piece of her mind, but she noticed that his smile was looking strained around the edges and he'd gone a little pale under his rich golden-brown tan. Guilt raised its head again. She'd shot the man full of drugs only hours ago, for Saint George's sake.

Speaking of which . . .

"How are you walking around? Those are pretty powerful drugs on those tranq darts."

"I have a natural resistance. But don't take that as an invitation to shoot me again. Please."

"Now would be a good time for bed," Hopkins said, smoothly making the pistol disappear in his jacket.

"Oh, I so agree," Christophe said, pinning Fiona in place with his hot gaze. "Where are we sleeping, partner?"

"There is no *we*. Hopkins, please put him in the blue room for tonight and we'll . . . we'll sort this all out in the morning."

"If he doesn't murder us all in our sleep," Hopkins muttered, opening the door and motioning to Christophe to follow him.

As they left the room, Fiona heard Christophe laugh. "So, Hopkins. Where did you say that good silver was?"

Chapter 10

Fiona flipped the covers off her legs and stared down the length of her traitorous body in the moonlight from the open window. She was utterly exhausted—and utterly unable to sleep. Every inch of her body seemed to be on fire with a series of electrical charges, and her skin was tingling. Her mind kept whispering that satisfaction and relief was *just down the hall.*

He was just down the hall.

All that beautiful male power and that big, hard body just waiting for her to strip him bare and lick every inch of him. Of course he would return the favor. She had some parts that really, *really*, needed licking right now. Her nipples were so hard they ached, for example, and other parts of her? Well. Perhaps she could give herself just a little relief and finally be able to fall asleep.

She closed her eyes and slid one hand underneath the top of her silk panties, groaning a little when her finger touched her swollen clitoris. Yes. Just like that. It was his fingers touching her; those long, strong fingers rubbing, gently at first, then a little harder. Oh, yes.

Her breath sped up, and she felt hot wetness spilling from her core. The mere thought of him had her hotter and wetter than she could ever remember being before. She'd probably catch on fire if she ever had him in bed with her for real. She dipped her finger farther into the slick heat and rubbed it back up over just exactly where she needed the pressure and cried out a little at the sensation. Yes, his tongue would feel just like that, oh, God, oh, it would be so good, even better. But he wouldn't stop there. No, he would be voracious. He'd take his other hand and cup her breast. She took the soft weight of it in her hand and pinched her nipple, imagining him sucking her, hard, and her hips bucked up against her hand. Oh, it wasn't going to take much, just the thought of him touching her, saying sexy things to her, was going to rocket her out of the bed any moment. She murmured his name, trying it out on her tongue, and it felt right, so she said it again.

"I'm here, and I can't believe you started without me," he said, and for a moment she thought she'd imagined it, part of the fantasy, and she twisted on the bed, but then his hands grasped hers and his weight settled on the sheets next to her. Her eyes flew open to stare directly into his, which were a burning, glowing emerald fire.

"I'm your partner, remember? And you called my name. That meets the terms of our agreement, doesn't it?" He pulled her wrist up so that one of her hands was above her head on the pillow, and he took the other, the finger that had been inside her, and sucked it into his mouth, licking every inch of it. She moaned at the sensation, too aroused to be embarrassed that he'd caught her pleasuring herself.

"Ah, gods, you taste good, like the finest Atlantean honey," he growled, his voice a rumble in his chest. "I'm going to taste every bit of you before the dawn, my ninja."

She didn't speak—couldn't speak—it had been so long and she wanted—she *needed*—and just one taste of this man couldn't hurt, wouldn't hurt—the justifications tumbled over themselves in her mind so fast she couldn't think.

Didn't want to think.

Only wanted to feel.

"Then kiss me," she whispered, and he made a noise of

sheer masculine triumph and took her mouth, captured it, plundered it like a pirate. He kissed her with skill and heat and something more—almost a desperation—as if he had to taste her *right now*. He made a noise, or she did, and suddenly he was lying fully on top of her, his hips between her thighs and his hard, thick erection pressing against her just exactly where she needed him. She rocked up against him, crying out into his mouth, and he pulled his head away and groaned, loud and long.

"Gods, you're going to make me shoot off like an untried youngling before I even get you naked," he said, his voice husky. "I want to see you."

She bared her teeth at him in something like a smile. "Then get off me and get naked yourself. If I'm going to be bad, I'm going to be very bad, and I don't feel at all like being proper tonight."

She reached down and cupped him though his pants, and he threw back his head and made a guttural sound of need. She was delighted with herself. She was a temptress, suddenly, inexplicably, and she was seducing him.

"Take them off. The trousers. The shirt. All off," she commanded, drunk on her own power. She knelt on the bed and pulled her camisole over her head, so she wore nothing but the silk tap pants.

He inhaled sharply and froze, staring at her breasts with such predatory hunger that she shivered, and a tiny sliver of doubt tried to surface in her mind. Could she really handle this man?

"You are beautiful beyond any dream of the gods," he said, dropping to his knees beside the bed. "I have never been so happy to have been shot by anyone in my life."

He reached out, cupping her breasts in his big hands, and her nipples visibly tightened and hardened even further. He smiled and looked up at her. "They want me to suck on them, don't they?"

She shivered, staring at the deep, glowing pools of his eyes.

"Tell me," he coaxed. "Say the words."

"I can't—I don't—" She stumbled, flustered. "Ladies don't talk dirty."

He laughed, and the rich sound of it sent a wave of heat through her. "Ah, but warriors do, my beautiful ninja. So let me tell you that I'm going to lick and suck and bite those ripe berries until you cry out for me to do the same to your hot, wet cunt. Then I'm going to tease and torture you until you come in my mouth and finally, finally, my ninja, I'm going to plunge my cock in you so hard and so far that you come, screaming, over and over."

She burned bright red at his crude words, but her body strained toward him, wanting every bit of what he'd just offered. "Too much talk," she whispered, and he laughed again, then licked her nipple into his mouth and sucked, hard. She cried out and would have fallen backward if he hadn't caught her with a hand on her bum. He sucked and licked that nipple until she was writhing in want, needing more, clutching his head and all that silky hair, mindlessly murmuring nonsense words of pleasure and longing.

Finally, when she was near to madness, he released her and stood, stripping his clothes off in seconds and then lifting her in one smooth motion as if she weighed nothing and carrying her to the cushioned seat under the open window. He lowered her to the seat and crowded her until her naked back rested against the cold glass pane at the top of the window, with the cool breeze and nothing else against the skin of her lower back. Then he knelt in front of her again and, grabbing fists full of silk on either side of her hips, ripped her panties from her.

She gasped, the combination of his barely restrained violence and the cool air from the open window pushing her to a dangerous edge.

"Shh, ninja," he purred soothingly, in between pressing hot kisses to her breasts and belly. "I won't hurt anything but that bit of silk. I mean to have you now, though."

He grasped her thighs and pushed them apart, then held them still and bent his head to her. At the first touch of his tongue on her swollen clit, she shuddered over the edge of the abyss to a hard, quaking orgasm, almost as if she'd been ready for his touch since she first encountered him on the floor in the Jewel House.

Waves of nearly unbearable pleasure crested and broke over her until she couldn't bear it as his talented tongue dove inside her and swirled around her and then his lips captured her swollen bud and sucked as hard as he had on her nipple. She bucked up under him, crying out, and tried frantically to get away.

"Too much, too much," she gasped, barely able to breathe around the pounding waves of ecstasy sizzling through her. She pulled at his head to try to make him stop, but he simply shook his head, the soft waves of his hair brushing her inner thighs.

"Not too much. Not enough," he growled, and then he fastened his lips and tongue around her again and began rhythmically sucking and licking at her until she writhed helplessly against him, the cool mist from the night rain icy cold against the overheated skin on her back. The contrast added yet more pleasure, and she had to stuff her fist in her mouth to muffle her scream when she came again, over and over, long, sharp spikes of ecstasy stabbing through her in a pleasure so intense it was nearly pain.

He finally raised his head and shot a look of such possessive triumph at her it sent her off again into a shuddering spasm of aftershocks. He stood and lifted her into his arms again. He caught her bum in those big hands and she answered his unspoken request by wrapping her legs around him.

"Yes," he said fiercely. "Now." And he lifted her up, and his enormous erection jutted up between them as if it, too, sought to conquer.

She shook her head, tried to find her powers of speech. "No, you—condom," she managed, but he shook his head.

"I cannot catch or carry any human illness, nor give a child until I petition Poseidon," he said, positioning his penis at her entrance. Everything in her wanted to wrap herself around him and slide down his erection, but sanity surfaced.

"What? Stop, condom. Now," she gasped, struggling. She pointed to the drawer of the table next to the window seat and he groaned, but yanked it open, still holding her with one strong arm, and snatched a foil-wrapped square out of it and handed it to her.

"Do it for me. Please."

The second she had him covered, he drove inside her and she cried out at the sheer size of him. "Oh, oh, oh. So big, too big, you can't fit—"

Christophe groaned at how tightly her hot, wet sheath wrapped around his cock. "Yes, I can. I will. Take me. Take all of me," he murmured in her ear as he worked his way deep inside her. His cock, even inside the damnable covering, was about to explode from the unbelievable pleasure of her wet heat and her tightness.

He pulled back a fraction of an inch, and then pushed his way in again, the silken wetness of her arousal easing the journey. He bent forward, leaning her against the glass of the window again, so the mist from the rain and wind swirled in against her lovely round arse and his balls. The effect of the heat and the cold combined to make every muscle in his body strain and harden. He had never wanted anyone like this; oh, by the gods, he wanted to spend a year or two just fucking her.

She gasped again and he took her mouth, swallowed her gasp, sucked on her tongue and fed from the honey of her mouth as he had from her sweet cunt. She cried out, the sound trapped between their mouths, and then her body tightened impossibly around him and she came again, shattering into pieces against him.

He tried to hold on—to make it last—but his body rode the waves of her orgasm and he fucked her harder and deeper; one, then two more strokes and he came, shuddering against her. He carried her to the bed and gently lay her against her pillows, then yanked off the condom, desperate to remove it as his seed continued to spurt out of him in the fiercest orgasm he'd ever known. She gazed up at him, still trembling and gasping, then lifted a hand and closed it around his cock, which made him cry out as he bucked against her hand and came even harder, spilling his hot come in her hand.

"Oh, my," she whispered. "I—oh. My."

He sucked in a breath and blew it back out, his body still shuddering from his release. "Yeah. I kinda feel the same way."

She let go of him and her arm fell back to the bed, as if she lacked the strength to hold it up any longer. He just stood there and stared at her, almost unable to believe how beautiful she was. Like a nymph in the moonlight—or one of her forest fairies—her perfect skin glowed. The triangle of silky hair between her thighs was a paler shade of moonlight, echoing the silvery blond of her hair. And those breasts. Surely poets would write odes to those round, perfect breasts.

"You're staring at me," she whispered, and he could tell that she was blushing as the moonlight picked up the slightest touch of pink.

"You're beautiful," he said. "I almost can't believe you're even real."

"I'm feeling rather that way myself," she said, still whispering.

He kissed her again. He couldn't help it, even though this was the time when he usually was looking for the nearest exit, after sex. But there was no *usually* about this.

He had never felt anything like this. He thought his mind might actually have exploded by the end of that orgasm. Surely something was broken, or he would be able to do something other than stand and stare at her like a lovesick buffoon.

"I'll just go and freshen up, then," she murmured, and he followed her, crowding her, pressing kisses to the back of her neck and the curve of her shoulders as if he'd been bespelled by a particularly powerful love potion.

Terror ripped through him at the thought. No. Not love potion. Sex potion.

Besottedness potion, the honest part of his mind corrected. *That was more than just sex, and you know it.*

He should run while he still could. Yet instead, after they made use of warm water and towels, he swept her into his arms and carried her to her bed, then tucked them both into it, his arms around her.

"I'm not going to let you go for quite a while, so it's a good thing we're partners," he said, reveling in the feel of her breasts pressed against his chest and one of her legs tucked between his.

"I may agree to that," she said, ever so primly, her cheeks hot again. His seductress had reverted back to Her Ladyship now that she was satisfied, and it delighted him. He'd be perfectly happy for no one but him to ever see the wild side of her.

Ever?

"You just tensed up," she whispered. "What is going on behind those lovely green eyes?"

"Nothing at all. Just sleep. Tomorrow you have books to sign, and we have a national treasure to steal."

He held her and stroked her hair until she slept, and then he lay there, wide awake and simply holding her, until the sun's first rays sent their golden light through the window.

Ever. He'd thought the word "ever" in relationship to a woman. He didn't know whether to laugh—or run. She murmured in her sleep and snuggled closer to him, and he knew he wasn't running anywhere just yet.

Not yet.

He could always run later.

Chapter 11

Atlantis, the warrior training grounds, later that morning

Alaric, sworn in magical service to Poseidon and widely regarded as the most powerful high priest the Seven Isles had ever known, was getting his ass handed to him by his high prince.

He ducked as Conlan swung a particularly vicious overhand strike toward his head, then whirled and parried. The thud as the two wooden training swords collided in midair smashed its recoil through his arm and shoulder.

"Remind me again why I'm doing this," he called out, feinting left. "When I can destroy any attacker with my magic before his sword leaves its sheath?"

"In case your magic goes on the fritz," Princess Riley said, from her seat on a blanket in the grass bordering the hard-packed dirt training ring. She held her son with Conlan, Prince Aidan, the heir to the throne of Atlantis. His Royal Drooliness, she called him. Alaric felt it lacked a certain dignity, but he refrained from pointing it out.

Humans could be so sensitive.

"My magic does not *fritz*," he replied, vanishing from

under the force of Conlan's advance and reappearing behind the prince. He swatted Conlan in the ass with the flat of his sword to emphasize the point.

Conlan whirled around, bending down with that innate grace that had fooled so many opponents into underestimating his ferocity, and swept Alaric's legs out from under him. Alaric's own ass hit the dirt, hard, before he could teleport. His control over the skill was only slowly improving in spite of practice, and trying to use it while under attack was tricky, at best.

Riley burst out laughing. "That looked like a fritz to me. Did that look like a fritz to you, wittle snookums?"

The chubby baby chortled out a gurgling laugh. Probably at Alaric, if Aidan was anything like his parents.

Alaric jumped to his feet and brushed the dirt off his pants. "One hopes you are addressing your son and not me," he said dryly, lowering his sword and bowing to his prince.

Conlan shouted out a laugh and then returned Alaric's bow. A wide-eyed boy, probably shocked to hear his high prince and Poseidon's high priest jesting so casually, ran up and retrieved the practice swords.

"I can't actually see anybody ever calling you wittle snookums," Conlan said, still laughing. "Nobody would dare."

"I'm sure his mother did when he was Aidan's size," Riley said, grinning with mischief. "You weren't always the scary high priest we all know and love, Alaric. Once you were a cute little baby, drooling on yourself and peeing your diaper."

Alaric's lip curled away from his teeth. "Your Highness, did you mean to beat me into submission with the wooden swords or with your bride's conversation?"

Riley laughed again, not in the least offended. As an emotional empath, or *aknasha*, she could probably read his affection for her as easily as he could read Conlan's worry in the lines of the prince's face. They'd been friends for centuries, he and Conlan, and now that Atlantis was finally preparing to take its rightful place on the surface of the world once more, the problems kept coming, as hard and fast as Conlan's attacks in the practice ring.

"Speaking of diapers, as much fun as it is to watch the two of you all sweaty and shirtless, I'm off to change your son's. See you both at breakfast?" Riley leaned up to kiss her husband, and Alaric had to look away from the depth of emotion the two shared. But even he, who had been alone for so long and had little prospect for ever being anything but, could not begrudge his prince and friend the love and happiness he'd found with Riley.

Conlan watched his wife and child as they headed off toward the palace, but then he sighed and turned toward Alaric. "What news?"

"None good, unfortunately. The scientists Brennan and Tiernan stopped in the United States were not the only ones working toward shifter enthrallment. Europe has a great number of underemployed scientists who are working toward the same goal, evidently. Our sources tell us that not only has the continuing vampire enthrallment of shifters spread to Europe, but someone very highly placed in either Interpol or Scotland Yard's new Paranormal Ops division is the ringleader."

Conlan smashed his fist into his palm and swore. "The bad news keeps on coming. What is the European plan?"

Alaric raised his hand, palm up, and a glowing blue-green sphere of energy spread out to form the shape of Europe. He clenched his fist and it disappeared. "The vampire alliances are growing. The rumor is that an international consortium of vampires has formed, and it is planning a concerted strike on all human rebels, using enthralled shifters."

"Quinn and her counterparts have finally hit them hard enough to hurt, have they?"

Alaric was proud that he barely flinched at her name. "Your wife's sister is the rebel leader of all of North America, Conlan." *And the woman Alaric loved. Not that he would ever be able to say the words aloud.*

Conlan looked at him with some sympathy, and Alaric deliberately removed any expression from his face. "Quinn is constantly in touch with other rebels throughout the world. Though the new laws are making rebel offensives more difficult."

In spite of the dangers vampires represented, or perhaps because of them, more and more human nations were passing laws guaranteeing the vampires equal protection under the law. Shifters, as well. Alaric had no problem with that—most shifters were simply trying to live their lives in peace. The few who had gone rogue were the equivalent of the human populace's criminal element.

But if the vampires succeeded in enthralling shifters, when they had never before been able to do so, they would have a ready-made army of warriors far more powerful than any human soldiers. And shifters could create more shifters easily and quickly. At the very least, it would be a bloodbath of apocalyptic proportions.

"Christophe is in London, isn't he?"

"As you well know, having sent him there," Alaric replied, raising one eyebrow. "Your point?"

"Let's let him investigate. He's already there, anyway. We'll send Denal over to help."

"You're worried about Christophe, aren't you?"

Conlan turned toward the palace and started walking, and Alaric fell into step beside him. "Aren't you?" the prince said. "He's close to going over a deadly edge lately—too much power and too little focus. I fear if we don't give him something to concentrate on that he feels is worthwhile, we'll lose him."

"He should have entered the priesthood," Alaric said darkly. "He has far too much magical power to be running around playing at swords."

"Like the rest of us brainless warriors?" Conlan aimed a not-very-amused look at his friend.

"That's not what I meant, and you well know it. If too much magic is left unchanneled and untrained, the wielder may become unstable. Mages have died—or killed—from simply going mad; and many of those had less power than Christophe." Alaric's mood darkened, thinking of one high priest in particular. The elders had banded together to kill Nereus before he could destroy all of Atlantis with his rage and magic, more than eight thousand years ago.

"That's why I sent him to London to retrieve the Siren. It should be an easy job, and he has always been drawn to that part of the world, in spite of what happened to him there."

"Or perhaps because of it," Alaric said. "Akin to worrying a wound until it won't heal."

"Can that kind of childhood trauma ever heal?" Conlan shook his head. "I don't know. You've been inside his head, what do you think?"

Alaric thought about it until they'd reached the palace gardens. Then he stopped, and Conlan halted to face him and listen. "I don't know. Something is wrong—twisted—inside him. What humans did to him when he was such a small boy caused him to hate them all, as a race, with an almost zealous passion. Can that ever change? I simply don't know."

"And yet he protects them," Conlan said. "There must be hope in that."

"He protects them as duty, and as obligation. He fights vampires because he likes killing, not out of any altruism. He hones his magic in forbidden ways, but I cannot catch him at it, so I cannot censure him for it. Something—or someone—will drive him to the edge of reason, and then we will know whether Christophe will either heal and come to find some peace, or be forever destroyed by the bitterness festering inside him."

"When will that happen, do you think? It would be good if we could schedule around it, since we have so many other crises to deal with," Conlan said wryly.

"I'll keep that in mind," Alaric replied, in the same tone. "While we're discussing such pleasant topics, we need to move on to the maidens still held in magical stasis. The elders have warned me that the magic shows signs of deteriorating and we must either release them all or risk their deaths."

Conlan winced. "Riley calls them the frozen virgins, and she told me if I don't free them immediately, I can sleep on the couch for the rest of our marriage."

Alaric shook his head in mock sorrow. "I cannot believe I've lived to see the day when our mighty high prince and fiercest warrior was brought low by the whims of a helpless human female."

"Helpless. Ha! There's a word I'd never apply to Riley, at least not in her hearing, if I were you, my friend. She's small but mighty."

"I consider myself warned. Shall I send Denal to London, then?"

Conlan paused, and then he nodded. "Yes. He has a calming influence on Christophe, in any case, and perhaps with a new mission, Denal will quit mooning around over my wife."

Alaric couldn't suppress the grin. "I believe Riley called it puppy love."

"Yeah, yeah. He'll get over it when he finds a woman of his own. But in the meantime it's damned annoying the way one of my sworn warriors glares at me whenever I kiss my own wife."

"Perhaps it's not glaring so much as the same nausea we all feel at your repulsive love-struck state, my prince."

Conlan threw an elbow, and Alaric just managed to avoid it. "Don't forget I can kick your ass, priest or no, my friend."

"Yes, Your Highness."

Conlan threw up his hands, muttering a suggestion in ancient Atlantean as to Alaric's future activities, some of which were clearly anatomically impossible even for one as powerful with magic as he. Alaric simply laughed and went to find Denal, but his humor faded and vanished as his thoughts returned to Christophe.

Something would have to be done about the warrior, probably sooner rather than later. Given the nature and power of Christophe's magic, Alaric would be the one forced to do it. It wasn't a task he looked forward to. Perhaps this mission in London would finally bring Christophe some measure of peace.

Chapter 12

Campbell Manor

Christophe woke from a fantastic dream where he was in bed with the most gorgeous woman he'd ever met to realize two things: (1) it wasn't a dream, and (2) it was turning into a nightmare.

"What in the nine hells?" he yelled out, reaching for a dagger as the ominous and furious face loomed over the side of the bed. Unfortunately, or fortunately, depending on his perspective, his daggers weren't currently in reach of his hands, which were full of warm, curvy, and definitely naked female.

"I would have preferred you steal the good silver," Hopkins snapped, depositing a tray on Fiona's bedside table.

Fiona squeaked something and yanked the covers over her head, but not before Christophe saw that her cheeks were flaming red.

"I would *prefer* that you didn't come in a room without knocking," Christophe replied, echoing the butler's starched tone.

"As if you have any right to have preferences in this

house," Hopkins muttered, before stalking to the door. He paused before exiting, squaring his shoulders. "I would have hoped I'd raised you better, Lady Fiona."

Then he closed the door quite carefully behind himself.

"Nice parting shot," Christophe said, pulling the quilt away from Fiona's sleep-tousled hair and flushed cheeks. "He's good with the zingers, isn't he?"

"He's right," she snapped. "I do know better. And I don't know you at all, but I . . . we . . . oh. What a—"

"Great night? Best you've ever had?" Christophe suggested.

"Mistake," she said firmly, yanking the quilt out of his hands and wrapping it around herself as she jumped out of bed. Then she paused, a rueful expression crossing her face. "Although, yes, it was rather great, wasn't it?"

A wave of triumph swept through Christophe and on the heels of that, a more confusing and unexpected emotion. Relief? Gratitude?

"I've got to go to the book signing, partner," she said, not quite meeting his eyes. She seemed almost shy, which was a little shocking after her wildness the night before. "You're welcome to stay here or go wherever you nefarious criminal types go during the day."

"Oh, I'm with you, ninja," he said, jumping out of bed and stretching. She stared at him, her eyes widening when she noticed his erection, which hadn't been the least bit discouraged by the butler's interruption. Waking up with an armful of beautiful woman apparently made his cock very happy and Christophe wasn't embarrassed to show her what she did to him.

She hastily lifted her gaze, her cheeks flaming even hotter. "Well, get dressed. And—and put that thing away."

He laughed as she fled into the bathroom, trying and failing to remember the last time he'd woken up in such a wonderful mood. Oh, yes, this day was going to just get better and better.

~~~⁓~~~

London, Charing Cross Children's Books, three hours later

Christophe looked around and wondered if the third level of the nine hells resembled a children's bookshop. Tiny humans in every shape, color, and size ran, walked, crawled, laughed, cried, and shrieked their way through every inch of the place until the walls themselves reverberated with the noise.

He considered pulling his daggers and discovering if he could scare them into shutting up. Bad enough he'd had to put up with the scowls and glares from that punk chauffeur on the drive over. The boy had a bad case of first love for his boss. Fiona had been too distracted to notice the killing looks Sean kept shooting Christophe, who'd considered, then discarded, the notion of dumping the youngling in the middle of the Thames River just to teach him a lesson.

Now that they were finally here, in the middle of all this chaos, Fiona was at least outwardly calm and happy, smiling peacefully as she talked to the shop owner over in the corner, next to a table with what looked like hundreds of books piled on it. The noise faded a little from the forefront of his mind as he drank in the sight of her. She was every inch Lady Fiona today in a soft dress the pale blue of the sky at noon on a clear day. She wore heels with a ribbon thing at the backs, and her pale hair was worn down in silken waves that framed her beautiful face.

His mind stuttered at the sight of her—all rosy cheeks, flushed with pleasure, and huge blue sparkling eyes. Memories of her passion the night before swept through him and he had to focus every ounce of his concentration to keep his cock from swelling in response. Not appropriate here.

But later, when he got her alone, oh, then he'd strip her bare in the sunlight and see how her beauty shone in the daylight as compared to her moonlit perfection. He'd—

"Help me with this?" Declan's voice interrupted Christophe's erotic thoughts about the boy's sister and an unexpected niggle of guilt twinged him. Not exactly respectful to think that kind of thought in front of her little brother.

"Help you with what?" His voice came out brusquer than he'd intended.

Declan shot him a curious glance but only pointed to the folding chairs. Together with some of the bookstore staff, they set up the chairs for the parents and tossed around more of the beanbag chairs for the children as Fiona prepared to give her talk. Christophe looked up to find her smiling at him, and he shot her a grin of purely wicked intent. She blushed a hot pink color, which pleased him so much he caught himself whistling like a fool.

The owner stood up near the table and clapped her hands. She must have had some magic herself, because the overwhelming din quickly settled down into a dull roar and then quieted to almost a hush.

"Thank you all so much for coming out today to hear our favorite guest author. I know she needs no introduction, so without further ado, here is Lady Fiona Campbell, England's beloved author and illustrator, to talk about her book, *The Forest Fairies.*"

The room erupted into whistles and applause, and Fiona's cheeks pinked up again, which fascinated Christophe so much he nearly tripped over one of the younglings near the back of the crowd, where he stood. The tiny girl looked up at him, all big eyes and pigtails, and he tried not to grimace. She scooted nearer to her mum, though, as if she'd seen inside him to the scary monster within. That was one thing about kids, they were perceptive.

He'd known the couple who'd adopted him were zealots past the point of insanity, but nobody in that backward hamlet listened to a four-year-old child. At least not until he'd started crying for his parents and for Atlantis, and his budding magic talent had displayed itself.

Then they'd listened.

"Mister, are you okay?" The small voice caught his attention and snapped him out of dark thoughts. "You look sad."

It was another small girl, this one brave enough to approach the scary man. Before he could answer, she reached out with one tiny hand and patted his arm. "When I'm sad, I read one of Lady Fiona's books and it makes me feel better. Just listen to her read and I bet you feel better, too."

He blinked and stared down at her in utter astonishment. No child had dared approach him in centuries. He'd even wondered sometimes if when Atlantean parents warned children of the things that go bump in the night, they pointed to him as a fearsome example. Now this tiny girl whose curly-haired head barely reached his waist was comforting *him*.

Any moment, a seahorse would sprout wings and fly through the room.

She smiled up at him, her two front teeth missing, and something in his heart, long unused and rusty, lurched a little. "I think you're right," he told her, but then her mother was there, grabbing the girl's hand and snatching her away.

"So sorry if she bothered you," the woman said, but Christophe saw the suspicion in her eyes. She probably thought he was a predator, here to snack on the children.

"No bother at all."

Declan stepped up next to him and grinned at the woman and little girl. "Declan Campbell, Fiona's brother. I see you've met our friend, Christophe."

The woman's suspicion melted away in a genuine smile. "No, but Lily did. She's never known a stranger she doesn't make into a friend in a heartbeat."

"A dangerous trait in a child," Christophe said harshly. "Not all who smile are friends."

Her smile faltered and she took a step back. "Of course. Quite right." As she hurried away with her child, Declan shoved his hands in his pockets and glanced up at Christophe, who had a few inches on him.

"Making friends wherever you go, I see."

Christophe glared at the boy. "Anyone who calls another *friend* too easily is a fool."

Declan shrugged, not intimidated in the least. "And anybody who doesn't is alone. Which is worse?"

Christophe opened his mouth to answer and then decided to ignore the impertinent boy. He turned his attention to Fiona, who was well into her reading. She told the story of a *Gille Dubh*, a lonely and lost dark-haired lad who played and danced in the forest, clothed in moss and leaves, luring unwary children to come and play. Unfortunately, once they danced with the *Gille Dubh*, they were stolen away to the land of the Fae, to play and dance for years and years and years, until their parents and everyone they'd ever known were long dead.

It was a grim tale, the truth behind her made-up story, and only too real. Christophe had no love for the Fae, who played games with humans as easily as though with chess pieces on their carved marble boards. But in Fiona's version, the lad—a spirit, no longer a living child—fell in love with a bonny lass who enticed him back into the sunshine of the fields, which released him from the spell of the Fae, and he became a real boy again.

As in so many modern fairy tales, the children in the tale all lived happily ever after. If only life outside of books were as happy or predictable.

"We need to help now," Declan said, and Christophe realized that everyone was clapping and standing up from their seats. "They'll ask questions and then queue up to get their books signed."

"What do we do?" Christophe asked, bemused that this lad was confident enough in his new *partner* to order him around like an old friend. Hopkins would have been pointing a gun at him, undoubtedly.

"We ask for names, entertain the kids in the line, that sort of thing."

Christophe folded his arms across his chest. "Do I look like the sort of man who would stand around entertaining children?"

Declan blinked. "Actually, I don't know what you look like. You don't seem to exist in any database, civilian or governmental, so I'm guessing Fae. Hopkins has a bit of a talent for reading minds, actually more like reading intent, and he said you believed you'd never harm us, and, well, you rather look a bit like an action film star, but this is what we do, you wanted to be here, soooo . . ."

It took Christophe a moment to work his way through all that. Hopkins could read people, could he? Obviously not in any degree of specificity or the questions that morning would have been a great deal more intense. As to entertaining children? "Absolutely not. I'll be out front, looking for danger, protecting our flank, and that sort of *action film star* thing."

"Whatever, dude. Gotta get busy." Declan strolled off, turning on his not inconsiderable charm, leaving Christophe blinking at the idea that a human man—barely a man, practically a child himself—had just called him *dude* and Christophe hadn't stabbed him for it. Something was very, very wrong.

Maybe the sex had made him soft.

He grabbed one of the books on his way to the front of the store, where he could breathe since the crowd was all centered around Fiona. As he casually opened the book and started flipping through the pages, he slowed, and then returned to the first page to begin the story. Examining each illustration, he realized that Fiona had a true gift. The soft watercolors made her paintings come so alive that he half expected the fairy to dance right off the page. Her imaginative retelling of the tale kept the slightest undercurrent of danger, but the bright, cheerful language and happy ending guaranteed both small children and parents alike would be content to share this book, over and over, at bedtime, with no fear that it might cause nightmares of being stolen by the Fae.

Not that only the Fae stole children. Sometimes humans stole children after the Fae finished murdering their parents in front of them.

He gritted his teeth against the memories that he'd thought safely buried in the dark recesses of his mind so many long years ago. Perhaps being around all these children was doing it. Whatever the cause, he needed it to stop. He needed to focus. Steal the Siren, forget about his worthless childhood, and conquer his obsession with the Scarlet Ninja.

Easy.

No problem at all.

The voice that spoke up behind him was as unexpected as it was unwelcome. "Christophe, we've got a problem."

Chapter 13

Christophe swung around to find Denal standing behind him. The younger warrior was trying to act casual and doing a terrible job of it. In his black clothing, the bones in his face standing out starkly, Denal was as out of place in the children's bookshop as Christophe himself. Looking around, though, Christophe noticed several of the mothers—and a couple of the fathers—giving the two of them more than friendly looks. The Atlantean gene pool working its magic. Christophe scowled, and most of them quickly found something else to do.

"What are you doing here? How did you find me? And what problem?"

Denal grinned. "One question at a time. I'm here because Prince Conlan sent me. I found you because I could feel your presence on the Atlantean mental pathway, even though you weren't answering me, and the problem is something we probably shouldn't discuss in public."

Denal glanced around curiously. "What are you doing here anyway?"

"Browsing," Christophe said dryly. "This fairy book is

great. Fast-paced, lots of suspense. Later I might go for ice cream."

He grabbed Denal's arm and steered him out of the path of the doorway as the crowd began to filter out, signed books clutched in tiny fingers. "Look, it's a long story and I'll have to tell you later. Now you have to leave. Meet me tonight. I'll contact you. In the meantime, go play tourist and find out anything you can about the Scarlet Ninja."

Denal looked like he might protest, but Christophe outranked him, so he finally nodded and left the store. Christophe turned and found Fiona staring at him, her lovely eyes narrowed. Probably suspicious, now that she'd caught him conspiring. Of course, she thought he was a criminal, which was almost funny, coming from the Scarlet Ninja, but there were criminals and then there were *criminals*. He had a feeling she didn't place him in the high-minded category.

But she'd slept with him, so maybe . . . maybe nothing. Maybe she slept with all the criminals she met. A sheet of red-hot rage blurred his vision for a few seconds, and when it passed he stood stock-still, in shock.

Was that jealousy?

Jealousy?

Not possible. Not once in his centuries of existence had he felt such a stupid, worthless emotion. Jealousy was for fools and suckers, and he was neither. She could have sex with anybody she wanted—*and he'd kill any man who touched her.*

The force of the threat—no, the sure certainty—in his mind rocked him back on his heels. She was dangerous. She was setting him off-balance in the worst way and causing him some sort of insane mental illness. Jealousy. Thoughts of brutal, bloody murder for any man who dared to touch her.

He needed to get away from her. Now. Get the Siren and get out of London and never have anything to do with any ninjas for the rest of his life.

"Christophe?" She called his name from the table where she still stood, chatting with a few customers. "Do you have a moment?"

It was now or never. He was closer to the door than to her. He needed to get the hells away from her in case this madness or magic she'd infected him with could somehow become permanent if he stayed near her any longer.

Now or never.

No.

Every fiber of his being rebelled against the idea. He was Christophe of Atlantis, more magically powerful than any in the Seven Isles except for—possibly—the high priest. He could handle one problematic female whose only real magic was bending light—well, unless he counted the enchanting effect of her enormous blue eyes. He took a last, long, rueful glance at the door and then started toward her, wondering if, somewhere, the gods were laughing.

The bell tinkling as the door opened was his only warning before a woman rushed past him into the store, crashing into him so hard he spun halfway around and had automatically started to reach for his daggers, when he realized the elderly, if rather stout, woman posed no obvious threat. He caught her as she teetered and almost fell.

"He's done it," she blurted out, gasping for breath, her face red. "The Scarlet Ninja's gone and robbed the Tower of London."

Christophe released her. Fiona stumbled to a halt in the middle of the shop, staring at the woman as if she had three heads.

"What? Are you sure?" Fiona said.

Christophe caught her gaze almost before the words were out of her mouth, and he shook his head almost imperceptibly. She didn't want to be remembered by anyone in this crowd for asking about the Scarlet Ninja.

On the other hand, what normal person wouldn't? He followed up. "Where did you hear that?"

The woman put her hand over her heart and struck a pose, thrilled to be the center of attention for such dramatic news. "It's in the papers. Not only that, but he stole old William the Conqueror's sword, what was called Vanquish, don't you know, and he killed three guards to do it."

Every person in the room burst out into excited and shocked babbling as Christophe, with as much courtesy as he could muster, cleared a path to Fiona. She simply stood, an island of quiet in the noise, the blood draining from her face. "It's not true," she whispered when he reached her. "You know it's not true."

"I know. I also know we need to find out what *is* true." He took her hand, almost without realizing it, as a sudden and unexpected need to protect her from this and any danger rose hot and deadly inside him. "Somebody has raised the stakes. We need to find out who and where, and then we'll get it back."

Her lips quirked a little in an almost-smile that just as quickly faded. "Oh, that's all, is it? Glad I have you around to point out how easy this all is. But that's not the only problem here."

The woman who'd brought the news wasn't done. "BBC called him Scarlet Ninja the Bloody and said Scotland Yard is making this a top priority."

The words "Scarlet Ninja the Bloody" swept through the room, increasing the excited chatter tenfold in intensity, and Fiona turned even more pale. Christophe scanned the room for a quick way out, and Declan, entering from the back door and looking around the room in surprise, gave him an answer.

"I think this subject is not quite appropriate for the children," Christophe said to the shop owner as she approached.

"Quite right. Quite right." She clapped her hands. "Now, everyone, let's leave the dreadful crime gossip outside the store, shall we? Lady Fiona must be on her way. Shall we give her a warm thank-you?"

"Thank you, Lady Fiona," the children dutifully intoned, and even some of the parents chimed in.

"You're welcome. I've loved being here," Fiona replied, gracious and poised even in the face of what Christophe knew to be severe distress. His admiration of her went up a few notches. She'd make a damn fine warrior, cool under pressure.

Declan took charge and hurried them all out of the store, murmuring things about another engagement, so sorry, must be off, in his charming way, and within minutes they found themselves in the car, once more in the horrible nightmare the Londoners called traffic. Fiona leaned forward to talk to the driver, who'd started glaring at Christophe again the minute they stepped foot in the car.

"Sean, take us to the Tower of London."

"Now? You want to play tourist with *him*?" Sean's eyes narrowed as he stared a threat in the rearview mirror, and Christophe's very limited supply of patience wore out.

He leaned forward and spoke softly, so no one else in the car would hear. "Look, boy, I don't know and I don't care where this attitude is coming from, but Fiona is not in the best of moods, so why don't you shut up and do what you're told? You and I can have it out later."

Sean made a low growling noise in his throat, but after catching sight of Christophe's eyes, which were almost certainly glowing, he swallowed whatever retort he'd planned to make and pointed the car toward the Tower.

"There's been very bad news, Sean," Fiona said. She told him what the woman had said, and Sean immediately flipped on the radio.

The newscaster was in the middle of the story: "—sometime before dawn. The Tower Guard say they have proof the Scarlet Ninja was involved, since he left his trademark calling card at the scene. Officials are refusing to speculate why the Scarlet Ninja would take Vanquish and nothing else. We'll keep you up-to-date as more details are released and we'll be live on the scene in thirty minutes when Lord Fairsby gives a press conference on-site. In other news—"

Sean flipped off the radio. Fiona closed her eyes, her hands clenched into fists on her lap. "This is the end. Everything I've worked for—finished. It's over."

Declan took his sister's hand. "Fee, don't say that. It's just one sword. We can go after something else. Or even give this up altogether. You knew it had to end one day."

Fiona made an anguished noise from deep in her throat, cutting off her brother's flow of words.

"No," Christophe said, his gaze fixed on her too-pale face. "That's not it, Declan. She doesn't care about the sword. At least, not much. It's her reputation—her integrity. The Scarlet Ninja is known for never harming anyone; only helping those in need or want due to the vampires and their unending greed and lust for power. Now they're saying that the Ninja is a murderer. It's one of the worst things that could have happened to your sister, and it's devastating her."

He suddenly blinked, realizing he'd damn near made a speech. Where in the nine hells had *that* come from? He shut up and angled his body to face the window, clenching his jaw shut against more stupid yammering. But a touch made him glance down, and the sight of Fiona's slender fingers on his sleeve caused something hard and painful to catch in his throat.

"How did you know?" she whispered. "How could you know? You've only just met me, and yet . . . and yet you knew exactly how I was feeling."

He had a moment to wonder if a man could drown in her eyes, before the car slammed to a halt.

"We're here, or at least as close as I'm going to get you," Sean snapped.

"You don't have to do this," Christophe told her, ignoring the driver and Declan for the moment. "I can go listen and find out what they know."

She squared her slim shoulders and lifted her chin. "Yes. I do. I'm going with you. Someone murdered those guards and I'm going to find out who did it. Then we'll get the sword back."

She'd said *we. We'll* get the sword back. A flash flood of fierce joy rushed through him, in spite of the circumstances.

"Let's go to a press conference, then."

"I'm going to work the crowd. Find out if anybody knows anything, what the rumors are, and so forth," Declan said, reaching for the door.

"Good, but don't be obvious," Christophe told him. "We don't want you to become a target. Whoever they are, they've almost certainly got men in place in the crowd watching and listening."

Declan nodded and left.

"Why do you think that?" Fiona asked him. "They got what they wanted, why would they be here?"

Before he could answer, help came from an unexpected source.

"He's right," Sean said grudgingly. "That's how I'd have done it, back in the day. Need to keep eyes and ears on the investigation, find out how hot the situation is. You'd best get out now, before I get moved along or ticketed. I'll be circling. Just give me a ring when you need me to swing back in and pick you up. Same spot."

Christophe nodded his thanks and opened the car door. When he and Fiona were on the sidewalk, he watched the car pull away.

"You have a good kid there," he finally admitted. "He'd do anything for you."

"That's what I worry about, especially now. If I put him or Declan or Hopkins in danger, I'd never forgive myself."

"Hopkins? I'd be more worried about anybody trying to face him down. That man is a warrior dressed up in a butler suit."

A true smile appeared for an instant on her face. "Yes, I've often thought that. He will never tell me much about his younger days, but I get the feeling he wasn't always a butler."

"I'd put coin on that," he agreed, taking her hand. "So let's play tourist and go back to the Tower of London."

"We should be thankful they don't behead people there anymore, I guess," she muttered.

"Nobody will touch so much as a hair on your aristocratic head while I'm alive to prevent it," Christophe vowed, all humor vanishing.

She stopped and stared up at him, a curiously vulnerable expression in her eyes. "Why would you care so much? Or want to protect me? Surely not simply because we . . . slept together. You just met me."

Part of him was wondering the same thing, but damned if he'd admit it. "You're my partner. It's just good business," he finally said.

Fiona pulled her hand away from his and a sheet of ice masked her expression. "Right. Of course. How could I forget? And so long as you have blackmail material on me, I'm stuck with you. Come along, then, *partner*. We have a crime to solve."

Regret swept through him as she marched off, not looking back once to see if he followed or not. Crime solving. Right. Christophe and Sherlock Holmes. Conlan was undoubtedly going to have something very unpleasant to say about this. He grinned at the thought, shoved his hands in his pockets, and strode off after his unwilling partner. At least he could piss off the high prince and the high priest all in the course of one mission. The day was looking up.

Chapter 14

Fiona stormed off toward the main gate, berating herself for her foolish moment of softening toward that *criminal*. What had she been thinking, to sleep with him? He was so aggravating. Annoying. Infuriating.

Delicious.

She ran a hand through her hair, suddenly as disgusted with herself as at him. She decided to break her sexual fast and it had to be with a jewel thief. Who just happened to have blackmail as a trump card.

He caught up with her, and she tried not to notice how his closeness made her skin tingle. Dangerous bad boys had never been her type before, but apparently her hormones were up for new things. The memory of him rising over her, hard and urgent in the moonlight, flashed into her mind and she caught her breath.

"Are you okay?" His gaze moved back and forth, scanning the sidewalk, the street, and everyone on both.

"I'm perfectly fine, thank you." She gritted her teeth against the sound of her own voice, which had come out exceedingly prim, proper, and headmistress-ish.

"Okay, Princess," he drawled, grinning at her.

"Don't call me that," she snapped. "And your humor is inappropriate. Those guards died."

"Maybe. Maybe not. We have an unconfirmed report by a hysterical woman, based on a tabloid story. The radio report didn't mention murdered guards. If you believe everything in the London tabloids, then you also know Elton John is supposedly having an alien baby any minute. Should we stake out the hospitals?"

"If you think—" Fiona stopped mid-sentence and took a deep breath. He was right. She was operating purely reactively, which was not only stupid, but dangerous. "You're right. We need to get to that press conference."

"I'm always right. You'll get used to it," he said cheerfully "There's a big group forming over there, just inside the gate."

She followed Christophe through the throng of people clustered around a makeshift podium until they stood roughly in the middle of the crowd. Close enough to see and hear everything, but far enough away so as not to draw too much attention. When the official spokesperson stepped up to the microphone, Fiona ducked partway behind a large man in front of her, out of the spokesman's line of sight.

Christophe raised an eyebrow.

"I know him. Lord Fairsby, formerly of Interpol. Now he's the director of Scotland Yard's new Paranormal Ops division."

"Does he know you?"

"We've met a time or two, at charity events. I doubt the man remembers me."

His green eyes flared hot as he stared down at her. "Oh, he remembers you. Any man who met you even once would remember you."

Her cheeks heated up, and she tried to ignore the warmth sweeping through her from his tone. "Quiet. He's starting."

Lord Fairsby looked out over the crowd and then down at his notes. "As you may have heard, we've had an incident. The villain who calls himself the Scarlet Ninja has struck at the very heart of our nation, leaving behind his calling card as proof positive. The scoundrel made off with one of England's most precious treasures—William the Conqueror's sword, Vanquish."

The crowd surrounding Fiona erupted with excited chatter, but subsided when Fairsby held up his hands for quiet.

"It's far worse than even that, unfortunately. He managed to brutally murder three of our guardsmen. We promise you this fiend will be tracked and captured with all haste. We at Scotland Yard will be working with Interpol, as well, to bring all possible resources to bear."

One of the reporters raised his hand and waved it around. "Lord Fairsby, why are you on the case? Is there reason to believe paranormal forces are involved?"

"We're pursuing all options at this time," Fairsby responded smoothly. "We will keep the public informed as to our progress."

"When swine fly," Christophe muttered. "There's something off about that man."

"Pigs," Fiona said automatically. She glanced up at Christophe and hissed in a breath. "Your eyes. Tone them down. They're glowing."

He scowled but closed his eyes for a moment. When he reopened them, they were normal again. He leaned down and spoke into her ear, so as not to be heard, although it probably wasn't necessary in the din of the crowd's noise. "He's not human."

"Don't be ridiculous. I've known his family for years." But her gaze returned to Fairsby, now striding toward the exit. He had always seemed a little off to her, too. Aloof. Arrogant. Even more so than the usual English upper crust.

Not that she was a biased Scottish lass or anything.

She shook her head, though. "No, I don't think that's possible."

"Does your magic tell you when you're around other magic?" he asked, putting his arm around her shoulders and steering her toward the exit, following the crowd of media still shouting questions at Fairsby.

"No, but —"

"Mine does. That's how I knew you were there, outside the door of the jewels room before the guard opened the door. Trust me, that man is not strictly human."

She pulled free of his arm and headed for the gate. That was the problem, of course. Trusting him. Blackmail and wild sex did not make a terrific foundation for trust.

Ahead of them, Fairsby reached the street and slid into the backseat of his car, which immediately pulled away from the curb. The reporters took several final photographs and then turned around, almost as one, to face the Tower gate.

The Tower gate she was walking through.

Damn.

The first one recognized her and it was all over.

"Lady Fiona! Lady Fiona Campbell! Over here, Lady F," the lead photographer shouted, aiming his enormous camera at her.

At *them*, she realized, panic sweeping through her. She was about to be captured on film with Christophe. For all she knew, he could be a wanted fugitive.

"What are you doing here? Were you here for the press conference? What do you think? Are you going to write a book about the Scarlet Ninja?"

As they barraged her with questions, she tried to edge away from Christophe, but he was having none of it. He put his arm around her shoulders and grinned at the journalists. She gritted her teeth around a smile.

"I was just here showing my friend the sights, when we happened to see the crowd gathering," she said, as politely as she could manage. "Was that a press conference?"

The whirring of cameras sounded like a horde of locusts attacking, and she fought to remain calm. Publicity was the very last thing in the world she wanted at this moment.

"Who's the guy? Is this a new man in your life?"

"No," she said.

"Yes, definitely," Christophe said, flashing that sexy smile of his.

Two female journalists and one male in the front row nearly swooned.

"I'm going to kill you," Fiona murmured, smiling for the press.

"I get that a lot."

Of course, their different answers sent the reporters into a feeding frenzy.

"Who are you, anyway?"

"Are you Scottish, too?"

"Are you an author?"

"How long have you been together?"

"You can call me Christophe," her *partner* drawled. "Not Scottish, not an author. Just Fiona's bodyguard. Those kids at book signings can get kind of frisky, can't they, darlin'?"

He winked, as if sharing a great joke with the crowd, and they ate it up. Stupid charming man. Fiona shuddered to think of what the morning papers would be like.

More questions flew at them, this time mostly directed to Christophe. Fiona tried moving him along, but the fool was enjoying it.

"We haven't known each other long, but it was love at first sight, wasn't it, sweetheart?"

Her face went hot, and from the intensifying sound of the cameras clicking, the photographers caught it all.

"Christophe is just having a bit of a laugh. We're only just friends. Thank you all, but we've got to be moving along."

When the crowd showed no sign of dispersing, she came up with an inspired idea. "Of course, I'd be glad to talk about my new book, *The Forest Fairies*. I first thought of the idea for the book when—"

As if she'd sprinkled a little fairy dust herself, the reporters magically found other things they'd rather be doing. Amazing how interviewing an author about her book wasn't nearly as interesting as murder and mayhem.

"We're leaving. Now." She marched toward the street, texting Sean to meet them.

"Whatever you say, Princess."

"If you call me that again, I'll let Hopkins shoot you."

He laughed all the way to the car.

Campbell Manor

Fiona had never been so glad to return to her home. After the painfully long drive in the Saturday afternoon traffic, during which she'd done her best to ignore Declan's chattering and Christophe's responses, she practically flew out of the car.

As usual, Hopkins was standing in the doorway. "Anything you wish to tell me? Shall I offer my congratulations, perhaps?" His usual dry tone dripped frost.

"Funny. Did you see the press conference?"

He moved to let her pass by him into the house, then shut the door behind them, right in Christophe's face. "Yes. I also saw the bit where your new partner claimed the two of you were in love. Shall I serve lunch or retrieve the Glock first?"

She sighed. "I don't know what we can do, so long as he has blackmail material on me. We—"

The door opened, and Christophe sauntered in. "I guess you didn't see me," he said to Hopkins. "I'll give you a free pass this time, but don't let it happen again."

Hopkins looked at her. "Definitely the Glock."

"How about lunch? I'm starving," Declan said, following Christophe inside. "Hey, why are we standing in the hallway? Let's get some food. I'm off to get cleaned up, back in a jif." He bounded up the stairs, and Fiona spared a moment to wish she had some of his energy. She felt as if she'd been up for days.

"Indeed." Hopkins led the way to the dining room and then vanished, presumably to find something for a late lunch. At the thought, Fiona's stomach rumbled a little. She hadn't been hungry for the pastries and fruit they'd had that morning, due to pre–book signing nerves, and was surprised to be hungry now.

Someone claiming to be her had murdered those guards. "Brutally murdered," Lord Fairsby had said. The room suddenly spun around her and she stumbled, only to find a firm arm around her back.

"Are you okay? You need to eat and have something to drink," Christophe said quietly. "You may be dehydrated."

"No. No, I'm not okay. I'm not dehydrated. I'm thinking

about those men. How can you joke about love and lunch and whatever, when somebody killed them? Brutally murdered, he said. Somebody claiming to be me." Her chest was so tight. Too tight. Why was it so hard to breathe?

"Not somebody claiming to be Lady Fiona. Someone claiming to be the Scarlet Ninja," he said. "Nobody else knows that's you."

"Except you, and you've already proven you're capable of using it against me," she said, yanking her arm away from his hand. "Do you think that makes me feel safe?"

His lips tightened and his eyes turned to green ice. "My apologies for that bit of foolishness. I give you my word—no. I give you my oath, as a Warrior of Poseidon, that I will not betray your secret."

"Your oath?" She shook her head. "I don't even know you. Why should I trust your oath? What's a Warrior of Poseidon anyway?"

"I have been the victim of betrayal, Princess," he said, so softly she had to strain to hear. "I would never turn that anguish on another."

Hopkins chose that moment to pop his head out from the door to the kitchen. "Tea will be served in a few minutes. I shall serve, since I gave the staff the entire weekend off, due to our new circumstances. Do you have any preferences?"

The pain on Christophe's face vanished as if she'd imagined it, and he grinned at Hopkins. "How about some of those little cakes?"

Declan burst into the room. "Oh, yes, definitely cakes. Roast beef sandwiches, too, please. Thick ones—I feel as if I could eat an entire cow. Those book signings always wear me out."

Hopkins nodded and left the room again, and Christophe roamed around, pacing the floor, picking up objects and putting them back down.

"Casing the room, are you?" Hopkins said, returning through a different doorway.

Christophe shrugged. "You still won't tell me where the good silver is."

Fiona remembered the last time the silver had come up in

conversation, and her face heated up approximately a thousand degrees. Christophe must have had the same thought, because he flashed her a wicked grin.

Hopkins, unfortunately, must also have remembered, judging by the way he glared at them both.

"So, love at first sight," Declan said, breaking the heavy silence. "I always wanted a brother."

Chapter 15

Christophe patted his full belly and finally put down his fork. "I'll say one thing for you. You put out a great spread for tea. I expected something haggis-like, Your Scottishness."

He grinned as she put her head in her hands and quietly moaned. He was having a great time with this fake cowboy act—he'd encountered enough of them in America's Old West to know how to play it— and it was accomplishing exactly what he'd hoped. He'd kept her distracted and aggravated at him enough during the meal to help keep her from brooding about those murdered guards. She'd even managed to eat a little. Still, it was time to make plans.

"I'm going to hit the night side tonight. London's underbelly doesn't start rocking until after midnight. I'm heading out then to check it out and see who might know what about the theft."

Hopkins, who'd finally consented to sit with them, after Fiona had practically issued a royal command, nodded. "That's where you're going to find news, if there is any. I'm going with you. Declan can stay here with Lady Fiona."

Fiona put her teacup down with a distinct clatter. "If you

don't stop talking about me like I'm not in the room, I'm going to throw you both out of my house."

Declan chimed in: "You tell 'em, sis. Also, I'm going, too."

Everyone started arguing at once. Christophe watched Fiona, entranced with the way her cheeks flushed a dusky rose-pink when she was angry. The same color they turned when she was aroused. His pants started to feel uncomfortably tight, as he remembered the way she'd arched her back against the window, her pale skin glowing in the moonlight like a fever dream. He shifted in his chair, which was surprisingly comfortable, given the elegance of the room, and cleared his throat for attention.

All three of them ignored him.

"Hey. *Hey.*"

They finally stopped talking and he seized his chance.

"We can't all go," he pointed out. "Hopkins, I know I'd trust you to back me up in a fight, but you come off a little too much like a butler to go to the places I have in mind. The folks who hang in this kind of pub have never seen the inside of a drawing room."

Hopkins bared his teeth. "I *am* a butler. Also, appearances can be deceiving."

He stood up, hunched his shoulders, tilted his head to the right, twisted his mouth up a little, and suddenly, impossibly, the perfect, impeccable butler looked like a homeless drunk from the seediest part of the city. "Spare a euro, guv'nor?"

Fiona gasped. "How did you do that? That's rather terrifying."

Declan started applauding. "That's brilliant. You should be on the stage, Hopkins."

"Definitely brilliant," Christophe admitted. "But you're still not going. You're not a shifter, a vampire, or a sorcerer. You won't be welcome, and nobody will talk to you."

"There's no way anybody without magic pulled off that heist," Fiona said slowly. He could tell she was agreeing with him only reluctantly, but it was still agreement. He'd take what he could get.

"Unless it was an inside job, which, though doubtful, is still possible," he countered. "On a different but related topic, I don't believe in coincidences. Why is this sword suddenly so popular?"

"Let's adjourn to my office," Fiona said, glancing around. "We may be interrupted here."

Christophe followed the rest of them up the stairs, taking the opportunity to enjoy the sight of Fiona's lush, curvy ass. There was something about her. Something different. It wasn't just her body that was spectacular.

When the realization hit, it knocked him back a step. He didn't just lust after her. He *liked* her. He admired her courage. Sure, she was a thief, but she was a thief with integrity, if that even made sense.

A thief with integrity. Oh, boy. He was in trouble.

Fiona turned, waving Hopkins and her brother past her at the top of the stairs, and cast an impatient glance back at him. "Any day, now," she said, tapping her foot.

She was absolutely gorgeous and unbelievably desirable. He should run. He should run *fast*. Instead, he followed her up the stairs, wondering if this was how Prince Conlan had felt when he'd met Princess Riley.

Terrified.

Back again in her comfortable suite of office space, he commandeered the chair behind her desk, just to irritate her, and grinned when it was obvious he'd succeeded.

"So," he said, drumming his fingers on her desk. "Why Vanquish? There were plenty of jewels there that would have been easier to steal and more profitable to unload, right?"

She narrowed her eyes. "You first."

"What do you mean?"

Declan piped up. "She means, why were you after Vanquish?" The boy was nothing if not helpful.

"Shouldn't you be off chasing girls?" Christophe asked him.

"It's a fair question, *partner*," Hopkins told him. "Answer it."

Christophe swiveled in the chair to face him. "Why do you

always sound as though you'd rather shoot me than talk to me?"

"Perhaps because you have some measure of perceptiveness?"

Fiona held up her hands. "Enough, boys. Instead of shooting each other, let's find out what happened, who has Vanquish, and how they framed the Scarlet Ninja for the crime."

"If you hadn't left your calling card," Hopkins began, before he stopped and shook his head. "Forgive me, Lady Fiona. This is not your fault."

She raised her head, and Christophe had never seen despair written so painfully on a face in his centuries of existence. "Yes. It is my fault. I played this game, and now the penalty is mine. Those guards' families rightfully must be cursing my name. I owe it to them to discover the truth."

The sight of her face, ravaged by emotion, unlocked a door he'd forgotten was even buried deep inside his heart. He heard the click as the first barrier he'd erected all those years ago opened a slow and painful inch. It was enough to help him come to a decision.

"I need to tell you about me," he said. "Why I'm here for that sword. Although I don't really care about the sword, I just need the Siren."

"Need?" Hopkins said. "That's an interesting choice of words."

"A deliberate choice of words. I'm from Atlantis, and unless I retrieve that gem, the Seven Isles cannot rise from beneath the sea."

He didn't know what he'd expected, but it certainly wasn't what he got. Declan burst out laughing. Hopkins snorted in apparent disgust. Fiona did neither. She just looked at him, shock and then anger written on her face.

"If you don't plan to tell us the truth, that's one thing, but don't insult me by making up fairy tales," she said. "Did you think that since I write those stories in my books that I'd be charmed by another one?"

"Atlantis. Of course," Hopkins said. "Know many mermaids, do you?"

"Mermaids don't exist. I'd hoped that I could get a little trust on faith, but evidently I haven't earned it yet," Christophe said. "So here goes."

He called to power, reveling in the burning sensation as it flowed eagerly to his command. Towering sweeps of power, its intensity increasing every time he called to it these days. So much power that he almost feared that one day it would consume him.

Maybe one day it would. But not this day.

He formed twin spheres of blue-green energy in his palms and held them up in the air before sending them flying around the room, dipping and floating around and over Fiona, her brother, and Hopkins.

"My tie with Poseidon, as a warrior sworn to his oath, is one source of my magic. Water is our element to call."

"Sure it is," Declan said, grinning. "Cool magic trick. Do you—" His laughter muffled the next words, but he finally managed to get them out. "Do you ride whales down to Atlantis?"

Christophe glared at the youngling and contemplated how angry Fiona would be if he hoisted her little brother out the window and left him dangling by a ribbon of water. He decided against it based on the way she was already clenching her fists at her side.

A simpler demonstration, then.

A flick of his fingers sent the energy spheres whirling to two corners of the room. Then he called to water, the purest form of his magic, and it, too, responded willingly. He channeled the silvery streams of water to form a vortex around his body starting at the carpet and working its way up to the elaborately painted ceiling. He threw his head back and concentrated, though it was a simple enough working. He wanted this to be perfect—she was watching.

Why it mattered so much, he wasn't sure. He just knew that it did. He formed twin streams of water into perfectly symmetrical spears and hurled them directly at Declan. Hopkins jumped up, no doubt going for his gun, and Fiona cried out. Declan had no time to do anything but gasp before the streams spiraled into starfish shapes directly in front of him and, one after the other, splashed into the boy, thoroughly drenching him.

"No," Christophe said over Declan's sputtering. "We do not ride whales, either."

~~~~~

Fiona fell back into her chair, torn between warring impulses to laugh or yell at Christophe. Those spears had been terrifyingly real, but how many times had she wished for a bucket of water to drench her joker of a brother? The smile threatening to break free of the tight clamp she had on her lips faded, though, when she realized all that water was soaking her sofa, table, and the surrounding area. Even Hopkins hadn't escaped entirely, and he looked about to murder Christophe at any moment.

"Fabulous. You've got a store of parlor tricks, and you've drenched my furnishings. Does any of your magic show include picking up the bill for the cleaning?" She folded her arms across her chest and glared at him, which made not the slightest dent in that cocky grin of his.

"As a matter of fact," he said, raising his hands in the air again. She tried not to notice the sculpted muscles in his forearms beneath his rolled-up sleeves, but she was only human, after all.

Which, as he seemed to be trying to tell them, he might not be. Which was brilliant. She'd only just been hoping for more complications in her life.

Christophe gestured and a warm breeze swept through the room, flowing softly over Fiona before moving on. As she watched, the water soaking Declan and his surroundings simply disappeared. It didn't dry, leaving her brother rumpled and wrinkled. No, it was just gone as if had never been there.

Which, perhaps, it hadn't been.

"Sweet!" Declan yelled, patting himself and the pillows thoroughly. "Dry as a bone. That was awesome. Can you teach me that?"

Fiona ignored him. "Illusion?" She'd no sooner said the word than Hopkins was shaking his head.

"Definitely not. That water was real. A fine trick, and quite powerful," he said, frowning at Christophe. "But still no proof of this fantastic tale of the lost continent."

"It was never lost. We just hid it," Christophe told him.

"Of course," Fiona said, throwing her own hands up in the air. Sadly, that didn't cause any wild magical incident or she would have made them all disappear. She needed a nap and a headache tablet, not necessarily in that order. "You hid it. So how did you get here? Submersible? Dolphins? Magic bubbles?"

He lifted an eyebrow, and those wickedly gorgeous green eyes of his began to glow. "Magic bubbles is actually pretty close. We have a magic portal."

Hopkins rolled his eyes. "A magic portal. Of course you do. And probably a yellow submarine, too. I've had enough of this, Lady Fiona. I still suggest we throw the man out and take our chances. After all, if he discloses your identity, we can happily tell the authorities about his little expedition to the Jewel House, can't we?"

"Hopkins! You rolled your eyes," Declan said, grinning. "The nation will surely fail at any moment."

"I can call the portal and we'll all take a step through to Atlantis," Christophe gritted out. "Bunch of cynics."

"I believe you," Declan said.

"You believe in forest fairies, too," Fiona pointed out.

"And Saint Nicholas, until you were at least thirteen," Hopkins added.

"Hey, a sense of wonder is not a bad thing," Declan said, blushing.

Christophe closed his eyes, clenched his jaw, and raised his hands in the air again. Fiona caught her breath, in equal parts worry and anticipation. What would he conjure up this time?

They all leaned forward, waiting . . . waiting.

And, finally, after two long minutes—nothing happened.

Christophe opened his eyes and blew out a breath, then

muttered a long string of words in a language Fiona had never heard, though it had a bit of the fluidity and musicality of Italian. Maybe Italian crossed with Greek, on second thought.

From the tone of his voice and the way he glared viciously at the empty space in front of him, she had the feeling she didn't want to know the translation.

"Magic portal out of service?" she suggested sweetly. "Down for repairs?"

"Water damage, maybe," Declan said, breaking into a fresh peal of laughter, in spite of what had happened to him the last time.

"The portal can be capricious," Christophe snapped. "Sometimes it doesn't feel like opening."

"The door has feelings," Hopkins said slowly before turning to Fiona. "Lady Fiona, I fear we should call the home for madmen. Unfortunate that Bedlam closed. He'd have fit in quite well there."

She ignored Hopkins's jibes and studied Christophe's face. The frustration there was too real to be feigned. Either that or he was the best actor she'd ever seen. It was up to her to make the decision and stand by it.

"Look, let's leave it for now," she finally said. "You're either from Atlantis or you're up to something so secret you can't tell us about it. For whatever reason, I've decided to trust you, at least until you prove me wrong. Tonight you and I go pub-hopping in the low places to find out what we can, and Declan will use his computer magic to find out what the word is on the Internet."

She shot a warning glare at her brother when he looked like he might argue. "I need you on this, Dec. Nobody else has the skills you do."

"I'll put out word in my own network. Discreetly, of course," Hopkins said.

"You still haven't told me why you were after that particular sword," Christophe said.

Fiona shrugged. "I generally select an object that has no right to be where it is. An objet d'art with shaky provenance, where the owner either stole it personally or bought stolen merchandise, for example. Those owners are usually reluctant to get the police involved, and of course there are no insurance investigators involved, since the companies won't insure stolen art."

"Makes it easier to fence, too," Declan added.

She groaned. "I'm winning big sister of the year, aren't I? Introducing my baby brother to the world of stolen art before he's had his first real girlfriend."

"Hey, there was Nora," he protested, blushing fiercely.

"You were twelve. Anyway, to continue, this time was different. Word was put out through one of my usual fences that a buyer was interested in Vanquish. This buyer is supposed to be some oil hotshot, too, because my five favorite words were spoken."

Christophe tilted his head. "Free pints at the pub?"

"Money is not an object."

He laughed. "Women. Who can understand them?"

Hopkins nodded until he caught her glaring at him, and then he pretended to brush a speck off his spotless coat.

"This doesn't make any sense, and I hate coincidences," Fiona said, all but smacking herself in the head for her own stupidity. "Suddenly some rich oil guy wants Vanquish? At the exact same time you show up wanting it and someone else wants it enough to kill for? What don't we know about this stupid sword? I think we should make a point to find out what my contacts know about this mysterious buyer. I didn't ask enough questions this time, since so many programs need money so urgently. Maybe the buyer is counting on that?"

"I agree, we need to find out exactly who this buyer is and why he or she wants the sword so much. But I need the Siren. Just the Siren. You can have Vanquish," Christophe said, suddenly serious.

"What good does that do me? The value of the sword will drop considerably without it. I've got several new . . . ah, new dresses to buy," she finished lamely; suddenly unwilling to admit the truth and have him think she was playing the philanthropy card.

"New dresses. Right. I wasn't born yesterday, Princess," he said, stalking across the room toward her until he had her backed into the wall. "I know all about your Robin Hood tendencies. Which charities were supposed to benefit from this heist?"

"Ironically enough, we are saving the whales, though that's with my own money," she whispered, her heart pounding from his nearness. His masculine scent teased her senses, and she suddenly wanted to lean in and press her lips to his neck.

A black-sleeved arm inserted itself between them, rather ungently pushing Christophe away from her. "AIDS, children with autism, shelters for battered women, the homeless, a literacy group, and single mothers are on the list this time, to be precise," Hopkins said. "In point of fact, you have a charity engagement tonight. For the whales, I believe."

"Maybe Christophe should go. Some of his relatives might be there," Declan said, his voice strangled to hold in the laughter.

Christophe took a step back, the heat in his eyes and his sexy smile reminding her of all the things he'd done to her the night before. Definitely not thoughts she wanted to have right then.

"Try to remember I can kill you with both hands tied behind my back, kid," he told Declan. "If your sister is going, I'm definitely going. And I didn't say I was taking the Siren out from under you, Princess. I'll buy it from you."

"Oh, no," she protested. "You cannot attend this function with me, not after this afternoon. I'll never hear the end of this. Also, buy it with what? Have a spare few million euros lying around?"

"I'm going," he said, implacable.

"Did you happen to bring your tuxedo with you from Atlantis? That's the only way you'll get into that ball. Very snooty," Declan said.

Christophe's eyes widened and his mouth fell open in an expression of sheer horror. "A tuxedo? That might be a deal breaker."

She put the image of how fabulous he'd look in a tuxedo firmly out of her mind and shrugged. "Guess you're not going, then."

"A tuxedo it is," he said, lips curling away from his teeth. "I have things to do now, which apparently include finding a tuxedo. When should I be back?"

Hopkins checked his watch. "Ten past never?"

"Keep it up, funny man."

Fiona sighed. She really, desperately needed that headache medicine now. "Half past seven should do it," she said.

"Fine. Leave the tuxedo to me," Hopkins said. "If you're really going to allow this outlaw to accompany you, I'll be sure he looks at least somewhat presentable."

Christophe just laughed. "Three hours? That's enough." He nodded and turned to leave but stopped at the door, whirled around, and strode back across the floor to where she still stood near the wall. He put his hands on her shoulders and stared intently down at her, his eyes glowing again.

"Don't worry, Princess. We'll figure this out." Before she could respond, or stop him, he bent and pressed a brief, hard kiss against her mouth and left the room. He was gone before she could form a coherent response.

Hopkins cleared his throat. Loudly. "Shall we plan on an Atlantean wedding, then?"

Chapter 16

Three hours later, Christophe stared in disbelief at himself in the mirror of a lavish guest room decorated in dark greens and golds and paintings of fox hunts. Very traditional, proper British. He felt like a warrior trapped in a teapot.

"I look like a buffoon."

Hopkins sighed. "You *look* impeccable. You *are* a buffoon. There's a difference." He held out a scrap of black cloth. "I presume you don't know how to tie this, either?"

Christophe glared at him. "Been a little busy. Slaying vampires. Fighting rogue shifters. Saving your puny asses over and over again."

"Please refrain from commenting on the state of my buttocks," Hopkins said, making short work of the tie. "Also, you have never once saved me or mine from anything."

"Not yours, specifically. Human asses, generally." Christophe checked out his reflection again. He looked worse.

"I think this tie might be choking me," he said, tugging at it with a finger.

"Yes, I'm sure Lady Fiona will enjoy listening to you complain all evening. Do let me know how that goes." Hopkins left the room, closing the door with a polite but firm click.

"May as well get this over with," Christophe told his reflection. "Nice monkey suit."

He left the room and headed down the hall and then down the winding staircase to the front foyer, figuring Fiona wouldn't go straight to the garage. He spent a few minutes on the way down checking out the paintings of people who were probably Fiona's ancestors and wondered if the blank, empty space on the wall had been for the dastardly grandfather she kept talking about.

A ping at the edge of his consciousness signaled Denal trying to contact him. He reluctantly opened the mental doorway.

I haven't found out much. Humans don't know anything, and the shifters aren't talking. Alaric specifically forbade me to go to any vampire hangouts without you, something about safety in numbers, and they're not up for the day anyway. Spring sunshine. Where do you want me to meet you?

Christophe laughed out loud at the "safety in numbers" comment. Alaric, like most of the rest of them, still treated Denal like a youngling, and undoubtedly didn't want him anywhere near any vampires. It wasn't fair—the warrior was sworn to Poseidon like the rest of them and had slain more than his share of vampires.

Not his worry.

Change of plans. I want you here at Fiona's house. Hells, more like a mansion, really. Anyway, I want you to come keep her little brother company while we go out to some charity event.

Denal's amusement came through loud and clear.

Charity event? Really? Did you have to dress up?

Just get here, already. Christophe projected his location on the connection and then leaned against a wall, arms folded, waiting. Women were never on time, anyway; he probably had time to take a nap if he could find a comfortable sofa nearby.

The faint sound of an indrawn breath interrupted his mental musings, and he looked up to see Fiona posed on the landing of the staircase, looking like the princess he'd named her. Or a goddess.

Aphrodite had nothing on her.

The bodice of the shimmering green gown hugged her curves like a lover, and the bottom floated around her legs like the whisper of a dream. A single, square-cut emerald hung suspended on a silver chain between her perfect breasts, and smaller gems hung from her delicate ears. Her silken hair was pulled up and back into a style that had been popular in Atlantis thousands of years ago according to the mosaics in the palace garden pools. Popular with goddesses, too, if one believed the paintings and sculptures that graced the palace.

That made sense. The goddess thing. There was no way he was good enough for this woman. The thought stabbed him in the belly like a dagger, and he realized he was standing there staring.

"Princess." He swept his best court bow. "You are beautiful beyond any graceless words my poor warrior brain might conjure."

She lifted her chin. "You don't need to mock me."

"Trust me, Fiona. I am not mocking you." He put every bit of the heat he felt into his admiring gaze, and was rewarded when she gasped again.

"You—you don't look so bad yourself," she said, holding her skirt and descending the stairs.

He had no idea how she could walk in those high-heeled shoes and almost hoped she might stumble so he'd have the opportunity to catch her. Hold her in his arms. Strip that dress from her lovely body. They'd never make it to the charity event.

Another plus.

He met her at the bottom step, blocking her way. "A kiss for good luck, Princess?"

"You don't need luck," she whispered. "You seem to make your own."

"Only since I met you."

He wondered what would happen if he fell into the bottomless blue of her eyes and never, ever climbed out. He wondered if, finally, he might want to achieve the soul-meld when he'd dreaded it for so long. He wondered if he were going insane.

He kissed her. He could no more help it than he could silence his own heartbeat. He bent forward, barely touching her arms with his hands, and pressed his lips to hers. Just a feather-light touch at first, but then her breath warmed him and he caught her tiny sigh in his mouth. Desire turned molten, passion slowed the passage of time, and he was caught up in a tempest of emotion.

Surely no kiss had ever been so powerful. He wanted to protect her; possess her; consume her. He wanted all. He wanted everything she could offer and everything she was. Her scent tantalized him, something feminine and light and unmistakably her, and the silken softness of her skin was a marvel to his touch.

He lifted her off the ground, into his arms, and deepened the kiss, forgetting his vow to never get attached, forgetting his callous and careless image, forgetting his name.

She was everything, and he needed her more than he needed breath or life or hope.

Fiona's hands tightened on Christophe's shoulders as he lifted her, but she was helpless to draw away. His kiss was devouring her, consuming her, lighting her up with flames that she willingly embraced. The memory of their passion from the night before was there, but this was more, too. This was a new beginning; an innocence. This was discovery and exploration; it was comfort in a time of heartache. Somehow, he was almost part of her, and she had never wanted anything so fiercely as she wanted him to keep kissing her.

The sound of bells brought her dazedly back to her senses. She pushed against Christophe's shoulders and pulled away from his kiss. "That's the clock. It's eight o'clock. You have to put me down before someone walks in."

Christophe, breathing hard, rested his forehead on hers for a moment and then lowered her back to her feet. "I won't apologize for kissing you," he said, his voice rough. "I plan to kiss you again, as soon as I get you alone, so let me know now if you don't want me to do so."

Her cheeks felt like they were on fire. Damn the man for

making her blush so often. "I—I'll take that under advisement," she said, stepping back and casting a quick glance down at her gown to make sure nothing was out of order as she heard Declan and Hopkins in the hallway.

He grinned. "You look beautiful, Princess. Nothing out of place."

He, on the other hand, had a bit of a problem. She glanced down again. Make that a big problem. He caught her looking and laughed out loud, which didn't help the blushing at all. Still with his back to the hallway entrance, he whipped his tuxedo jacket off and held it in front of the large erection currently tenting the front of his pants. However, that left exposed the sheaths for the multiple daggers that crossed his chest front and center.

"Nice accessories," she said.

"Never leave home without them."

Declan burst into the foyer, holding something tiny and metallic in front of him. "Right, sis, I've got you covered. I'm going to wire you so we'll be able to hear everything you hear. We can record, too, so you and Christophe can go over the conversations later and catch anything you might have missed."

"Bad idea," Christophe said. "First, what do you expect to hear at the charity deal? Criminal pomposity? Second, electricity and Atlantean magic don't like each other. I was counting on it to short out the security system in the Jewel House, as a matter of fact."

Fiona looked at him in disbelief. "That was your plan? Stand around and hope for electrical failure?"

He tugged at his tie and looked anywhere but at her. "There was a little more to it than that."

"Like what?"

He grinned, and for just an instant, she could see the boy he must have been. "I hadn't actually gotten that far yet. You see, I ran into this gorgeous ninja—"

"I think we can all figure out the rest," Hopkins said dryly. "Will your electrical malfunction issue interfere with Fiona's microphone, as well? If we were to give you the equipment for her to wear later in the evening?"

Christophe shrugged. "I don't know. If I stay away from her, which I won't; if I refrain from using magic all night, which I won't; if all the fates are in our favor, which they never are—"

Declan groaned. "What happens? Will it short out and electrocute her? This is such a tiny mike, you'd more than likely only be shocked, Fee, not actually electrocuted."

"That's reassuring," she said, glad she'd taken the extra-strength headache powder. "Just give it to me. If it shorts out and somebody notices me jump, I'll claim I've been goosed."

Christophe gave her the oddest look. "Goosed?"

"Pinched."

He shook his head. "Just when I think I've gotten a handle on current colloquialisms. Also, if anyone gooses you, I'll cut his arm off for him, since Hopkins was kind enough to find me a tuxedo with room for my daggers."

Declan made quick work of showing Fiona how to attach the tiny mike so she could do it later. "Do you want the receiver, too, so you can hear us?"

Christophe answered for her. "No, she does not. We'll be able to handle it without instructions from here, but thanks."

She started to reply, but he held up a hand and then pointed at the door. "We've got company."

The door chimes rang, and all three of them stared at the door and then back at Christophe.

He shrugged. "It's a friend. He's going to hang out with Declan tonight and keep an eye out for any trouble that might have followed us home."

Hopkins opened the door and Denal, standing just outside, bowed deeply. "Denal of Atlantis at your service, sir."

"Brilliant. Another one," Hopkins said, standing aside and gesturing him in. "Is there any reason we should trust this young man with Declan?"

Denal's eyes widened. "I would give my own life to protect this human, my lord."

"I'm no lord, I'm the butler," Hopkins retorted, but Fiona could see him sizing up this new person in their lives.

For some reason, Denal reminded her of Declan—all fresh-faced youth with a bit of eager puppy in him. Their names even sounded similar. Except, this one was different. Older than he looked. There was a weariness in his eyes that matched the way Christophe's eyes looked when he didn't realize anyone was watching him.

She stepped forward. In for a penny, in for a pound. "I'm Fiona. Welcome to my home. This is Hopkins and my brother Declan. Thank you for your company, but I do hope that it won't come to giving anyone's life."

He bowed again, but as he straightened, his dark blue eyes widened until they seemed to take up half his face. "You're the princess? You're beautiful," he blurted out.

Yes. Just like Declan. She managed not to smile. "No, I'm not a princess. Christophe likes to tease me, that's all. Thank you for the lovely compliment, though."

She turned to Christophe, who was scowling at Denal. "We should be going."

"Ready when you are."

"Sean is pulling the car around to the front so you don't have to go through the garage in your gown," Hopkins said.

"Thank you."

"I'll have her home early," Christophe told Hopkins.

"No. You won't," she said.

"Discuss it in the car, Lady Fiona," Hopkins said, herding them toward the door. "Fashionably late is one thing with these charity functions, horrifically late is another."

"Christophe is nothing if not fashionable," Denal called, stifling laughter.

Declan grinned and punched Denal in the shoulder. "So, do you like pizza?"

"I have a feeling those two are going to get along famously," Fiona murmured to Christophe.

"Yep. You'd never know from the look of him that Denal has hundreds of vamp kills to his name, would you?"

Her smile faltered, and she swung around. "Hopkins, you're in charge."

Hopkins nodded. "Of course. I'll just clean the shotguns, shall I?"

Message received, in other words. There was trust, and

then there was "trust with her baby brother." Two very different things, especially from men who could so easily talk about killing vampires. The knot in her chest loosened and she put her hand on Christophe's arm. "Let's do this, then. Try not to offend anyone, that's all I ask. I have to associate with these people."

Christophe grinned down at her. "When have I ever been offensive? Oh, by the way, this is for you." He put a hand in his pocket and pulled out an object the size of a golf ball, which he tossed her way.

She caught it and then opened her hand and stared at a large rock. "Lovely. I've always wanted a—oh, for the love of Saint George, that's an uncut diamond."

Her knees wobbled and she had to lean against him for support. "That—that—it must be—"

"One hundred carats, give or take," Christophe said. "It should be ample to pay for your share of the Siren, don't you think?"

Hopkins crossed the room in three paces and lifted the stone from her hand. "That's ridiculous. It must be a fake." He examined it, holding it up to the light, turning it this way and that. "But it doesn't look— This can't be."

Fiona nodded, still staring at Christophe and then back at the jewel. "Trust me. I know jewels. Examine it, but I'm fairly certain that's an actual diamond."

"Should be excellent quality, too, but feel free to check it out for yourself," Christophe said. "Should we go?"

Fiona slowly turned to look at Denal. "Does he always do this? Give away fantastically valuable gems?"

Denal was watching Christophe, too. He slowly shook his head. "Never, as far as I know. Never took anybody to a ball, either, though, so what do I know? Next thing I know, we'll all wake up down Alice's rabbit hole."

"You're worried about rabbit holes, when you're from Atlantis?" Declan started laughing. "I think we're all in Wonderland. I also think we need a great huge pizza or two."

"At least two," Denal said, following Declan out of the foyer, headed to the games and media room, no doubt.

The bizarre juxtaposition of pizza and hundred-carat uncut diamond boggled Fiona's mind, and she stood, frozen, staring at the jewel in Hopkins's hand.

"If you have diamonds like this just lying around to give away, why do you need the Siren?"

"That, my beautiful one, is a very long story, and one I think we should save for later, before Hopkins yells at us again for being late."

Hopkins looked up, more off-balance than she'd ever seen him. "Late. Right. Go. We'll talk later." He closed his hand around the diamond. "Fiona, we can fund so many programs with this, if it really is what it looks like."

"You called me Fiona. This really is a banner day. Diamonds, book signings, and crime solving." She turned to Christophe. "Life is certainly interesting with you around," she told him.

"I was thinking the exact same thing about you."

Chapter 17

The British Museum

"Are you noticing a theme, here?" Christophe scanned the Great Court as they entered. "Our relationship is built on museums."

"We have a relationship?"

He was quick with a wolfish grin. "Oh, sweetheart. Are we ever having a relationship."

"We need to talk about that diamond."

"That was business. It has nothing to do with us."

"There's an us?"

He didn't answer, at least not in words, and she decided to ignore the implications of his wicked smile and take refuge in lecturing him about their surroundings. "The Great Court is the largest covered public square in Europe, with approximately two acres of space. It was designed by Lord Foster—well, redesigned, really—just in the late nineties and opened by the Queen just after the turn of the century."

"Turn of the millennium," he pointed out.

"Well, yes, that, too. You'll notice the ceiling—"

"Oh, yes. I couldn't miss that ceiling." He whistled, staring up at the glass-and-steel canopy.

"They constructed it out of more than three thousand panes of glass and, like snowflakes, no two are alike." She smiled. "I absolutely love it. I feel a sort of peace in this light, airy space."

He surprised her by putting an arm around her shoulders and pulling her close. "That's great news. If you like this, you're going to *love* the Great Dome of Atlantis."

Fiona started to snap out a retort, but the pleasure on his face as he looked up and around at the wonderful space stopped her. Maybe there really was an Atlantis. Maybe he really was from there. After all, it wasn't that long ago that they were all scoffing at the idea of vampires, and now there were certain to be some in attendance here tonight. Nothing, it seemed, was impossible anymore.

Not even Plato's mythical lost continent.

"Is it just a city? Or a whole continent?" she whispered, and he jerked his gaze down to stare at her in surprise.

"You believe me?"

"Maybe. Maybe a little." She laughed. "I don't know what to believe anymore."

"If you—" He paused and his eyes narrowed. "Who's the dandy on his way over here? He's staring at you like you're on the dessert menu."

"As did you, earlier," she pointed out.

"That doesn't mean any other man can do it," he growled.

"Lord Nicklesby," she called out. "What a delight to see you here."

"Fiona, my dear," he said, taking her hands in an overly effusive handshake. Now that she thought about it, Christophe was right. Nicklesby was a bit of a dandy. He had more gel in his hair than she did. "I was rather unpleasantly surprised to see you on the telly this afternoon. Bit of a strange situation, hmm?"

"Are you calling me strange?" Christophe's smile was all the more deadly for its veneer of politeness.

Nicklesby blinked. She'd bet he hadn't had much experience with Christophe's form of directness. She bit the inside of her cheek to keep from laughing.

"Certainly not, certainly not," Nicklesby blustered. "Just—ah, well. Quite right. I see Foster's new partner—vampire, don't you know. I'll just go over and say hello. Lovely to see you."

Before she could say anything, he was gone, practically jogging in his haste to be away from them. She finally released the laugh she'd been holding in.

"How do you do that? Make me laugh when my world is turned upside down?"

"When better?"

He flagged down a passing server with a tray of champagne. "When does the ale come through?"

The man shook his head. "Sorry, sir. I'm fond of a pint myself, but this is strictly a champagne kind of event."

Christophe pulled out a crumpled handful of euros. "This purple one is for you if you find me a pint. Find one for yourself, too."

The waiter's eyes grew huge. "Sir, I can tell you're not familiar with our currency. That's five hundred euros. I can't accept that."

Christophe grinned. "I like an honest man. Take it, and see what you can do." He tossed the bill on the waiter's tray and turned to Fiona. "Would you like a glass of champagne?"

She took a flute off the tray. "No, but I think I'm going to *need* a glass of champagne. Let's just put it that way."

She drained the glass in three swallows, and the server traded her empty glass for another and then took off, presumably in search of ale.

"Who is this delicious hunk of man, where have you been hiding him, and does he have a brother?" The voice was instantly familiar, and Fiona whirled around, delighted.

"Maeve! I didn't know you'd be here."

Maeve, dressed in a scarlet gown that set off her dark-haired beauty to perfection, tossed her head. "Saving whales is my life, don't you know? Or is it dolphins? What marine life are we saving tonight? And, I repeat, who is this lovely man?"

Beside Fiona, Christophe stiffened and his eyes flared a hot green for a split second before he bowed to Maeve.

"This is Christophe," Fiona said, not sure what to do about the no-last-name thing.

"I am delighted you brought your new man, Fee. Now where have you been hiding him?"

"He's not my *new* man," she said. "He's more my—"

"Her partner," Christophe said.

"Yes. Yes, my partner," she said, grasping the suggestion.

"And her lover," he said, ruining everything.

Maeve made an O with her perfectly red, shiny lips. "Oh, he is a rogue, isn't he? Lucky, lucky Fee. Shall we go and have a girly chat? I'll bring her right back, I promise."

With that, she pulled Fiona off, tightly holding her arm, leaving Christophe staring after them.

"Maeve, slow down. What on earth are you dragging me across the floor for? For Saint George's sake, this had better be good."

Maeve glanced back at Christophe, now a good twenty feet behind them. "Your boy toy there isn't human. Did you know that?"

~~~~~~

Christophe carefully unclenched his hands, firmly suppressing his instinctive reaction to fight to protect his woman. They were in the middle of a very public place, surrounded by other humans. Fiona would be perfectly safe talking to her friend, at least for a few minutes, even though Maeve was not human.

Maeve was Unseelie Court Fae.

Powerful, too. Her magic had the feel of ice and darkness. It reminded him of someone he'd met before. Someone he hadn't liked much. It was right there, on the edge of his brain, if he could only think of it. He felt someone approaching him from behind and whirled, hand under his jacket on his dagger.

"Your pint, sir." The man was beaming. "And two more, besides, back in the kitchen. Plus one for me."

Christophe took the pint. "You are an exceptionally fine human being," he said with feeling.

The server, not realizing how literally Christophe had

meant the expression, grinned. "Thanks. I still want you to take some change, though."

Christophe drank a long draft of the fine ale and then shook his head. "Not a chance. You earned it."

"Never thought I'd enjoy one of these events," the man said. "I'll be around. Let me know when you're ready for another."

"If I can get away with it, I'll be out of here by the time I finish this one," Christophe muttered.

"Lucky bloke." With a deep sigh, the server was off to foist more of the champagne on other guests.

Christophe returned his gaze to where Fiona was talking to Maeve, and nearly choked on his ale. She was gone. They were both gone. If that damn Fae harmed a hair on her head, he was going to murder her, peace treaty or no. He slammed his half-empty mug down on a table and set off to find her, walking fast.

A man swung into his path, moving so quickly that Christophe nearly ran him down. Only Atlantean reflexes saved them both.

"My apologies," the man said smoothly, extending a hand. "Gideon Fairsby."

"Lord Fairsby?" Christophe said slowly, recognizing him from the press conference. He did not want to shake the man's hand, but it would have drawn notice not to do so, especially since they were obviously the center of attention for quite a few groups of partygoers.

He focused on masking his own magic, but the faint, tell-tale giveaway of Fae magic stripped away his attempt.

"As I thought," Fairsby said. "What are you?"

"A friend of the whales," Christophe said, waving a hand at the crowd. "Aren't we all?"

"Don't be obtuse," Fairsby replied in a measured tone. "I know you're not human, but you're not Fae, either. What are you? Not a shifter, to be sure."

"Obtuse. Isn't that a triangle? How can a person be a triangle?" Christophe smiled in mock sympathy. "Too many glasses of that champagne, I bet. Right, old chap?"

The Fae's eyes flared a hot, molten gold and the monster

inside him showed through Fairsby's affable mask. "I saw you at the press conference," he said, suddenly changing the subject. "Why? What is your interest in Vanquish?"

"In what? Aston Martin had a press conference? That Vanquish is a sweet car," Christophe said, beginning to enjoy tying the Fae's guts into knots.

"Not the car, the sword, as you well know. Let me give you a little warning, fool. Stay out of matters that are none of your concern, and leave Fae matters to Fae hands. Do you understand me?"

Christophe glanced around and, seeing that nobody was within hearing distance, leaned in toward Fairsby, smiling as if offering friendly advice. Which, in a way, he was. "If any Fae *hands* so much as touch Lady Fiona Campbell or anyone she cares about, I will come for you first. I will rip out your lungs and feed your kidneys to the hounds of the nine hells. Do you understand me?"

Fairsby's eyes iced over, but he laughed. "I have been threatened by far better than you."

"Yeah," Christophe said. "I get that a lot. But usually only once."

Maeve's tinkling bell of a voice broke in before Fairsby could reply. "Boys, boys, boys, what are you talking about?" She put her hand on Fairsby's arm. "Is my dear cousin giving you a boring lecture on British crime, Christophe?"

"Cousin?" He studied them both. He was fair to her dark, but yes, he could see a slight resemblance, and it was true their power felt similar. Of course, with the Fae, anyone born to the same Court could claim kin right. Cousin, aunt, uncle, whatever. The Fae couldn't lie, but they could stretch the truth out of all recognition.

"Where is Fiona? If you've harmed her—"

He sensed her before he heard her, coming from the opposite direction than that from which Maeve had approached. The quality of the light actually changed for him—became brighter.

He frowned. If he was having thoughts about Fiona making the world a brighter place, he'd better go see Alaric and get his brain checked out. Maybe it was a tumor.

He crossed the ten paces between them in three strides and caught her arm. "Please do not go off on your own again until we get this situation resolved. I do not wish to worry for your safety."

She smiled up at him, her eyes sparkling. "You were worried for me? That's—"

"Unbearably sweet." Fairsby's dry voice interrupted. He'd followed Christophe. Maeve was right behind him.

"I see you met Lord Fairsby," Fiona said.

"We chatted for a moment," Fairsby said. "On a matter of little importance."

"It seemed quite important from a distance," Maeve said, staring avidly at Christophe. "Everyone was watching, too. I've warned you about that, you bad thing." She playfully swatted at Fairsby's arm, but he only tightened his lips instead of crushing her, so Christophe figured the two Unseelie had some sort of friendship going.

As much as the Fae could have friends. Mostly they only had rivals for power, cutthroat enemies, or former enemies they'd graciously decided to ignore. The occasional ally. Not really known for friendship.

Maeve pouted her red, red lips. "Don't keep secrets. It's so boring."

"No secrets here. Everything is out in the open," Christophe said. "Fiona and I are planning to dance. If either of you come near her, I will remove your immortal heads from your immortal bodies, which will be an extremely unpleasant way to spend eternity. Say hi to Rhys na Garanwyn for me, won't you? If you ever happen to socialize with Seelie Court Fae. Tell him he still owes me from our last poker game."

He inclined his head to them and, betting they wouldn't kill him in the middle of the museum, put an arm around Fiona's shoulders and turned his back on them, grinning at the hissing sound of rage coming from Fairsby.

"Shall we dance?"

Chapter 18

Fiona felt like events were swirling around her that she hadn't a clue how to decipher, and she didn't like the feeling. At all.

"Are you insane? You can't threaten my friends. They're going to call the police any minute!"

"They won't. They're Fae. They want nothing to do with the human police," he said flatly. "Also, stay away from her. Don't accept any favors from her, ever. Don't even say thank you. In fact, don't even say hello."

"Look, partner, you can't dictate to me what I do or do not do with my friends," she said. "I—"

"Let me guess. She told you to stay away from me. That I'm not human, right?"

That stopped her dead. "She did, actually. Why would she say that?"

He shook his head. "She said it because it's true. The better question is how would she know that, if she were human herself? Did she explain that?"

"No she didn't," she said slowly, revisiting her conversation with Maeve. Her eyebrows drew together. "I never knew Fairsby was Maeve's cousin, either. There are an awful lot of

Fairsbys running around. Also, stop dragging me. I'm getting a little tired of being pulled all over the Great Court."

"Cousin. That's one way to put it," he said grimly, maneuvering them out onto the space cleared for a dance floor. A small orchestra was playing something light and with a down-tempo beat suitable mostly for ninety-year-old dancers. She and Christophe must be the youngest on the floor. Or maybe not. Several things he'd said and done suddenly presented themselves in a new light.

"Just how old are you?"

He threw back his head and laughed, causing several heads to turn their way. "I quit counting at three hundred."

"Three . . . hundred? You—wait. This is like Atlantis, right? I believe it or not? You don't have any actual proof?"

"I don't have a birth certificate, if that's what you mean." He twirled her gracefully around an elderly couple she thought she recognized. The Hadley-Radfords, perhaps.

"I believe a record of my birth exists in the scrolls in Atlantis."

She sighed. "Of course it does. Is that where you learned to dance like this? I expected you to be stepping on my toes long before this."

"I learned it from my dance tutor, in the palace. It was required training for all warriors. Not all battles are fought on battlefields, Princess. Some are played out in ballrooms."

He smiled down at her and—for just an instant—Fiona gave herself permission to believe she was on a date. A first date with a fierce, unflinching warrior who seemed to be willing to protect her from all danger. It didn't make sense.

She didn't care.

"What did he want with you? Lord Fairsby?"

"Lord Fairsby, as he's calling himself now, and his *cousin* are Unseelie Court Fae. Very powerful, very bad news. The Unseelie Court is the dark side of the Fae, not that the Seelie Court is all flowers and little woodland creatures playing flutes. He has something to do with Vanquish disappearing, I'd put coin on it."

His arms tightened around her. "He is very, very powerful, Princess. Magically powerful, and with his official Scotland

Yard position, he has the weight of human bureaucracy behind him. He could make things difficult for you."

"The British have been making things difficult, as you call it, for the Scots for a very long time." She lifted her chin. "I'm not the first in my family, and won't be the last, to kick their arses."

He grinned down at her. "It makes me hot when you talk tough, did I mention that?"

Her pulse sped up, but she managed a shrug. "Everything makes you hot."

"When you're wearing that dress, yep. There go Fairsby and Maeve, heading out. We'll give them a few minutes before we leave. I don't want to give them a chance to get near you again."

He twirled her in a quick loop and then bent her down into a dip. Several of the people standing nearby started clapping, and she could hear the murmurs.

"Isn't that Lady Fiona Campbell? The book author?"

"Making a spectacle of herself—"

"That's the man who was on TV with her this afternoon—"

She pulled away from Christophe and walked off the dance floor, her head held high, smiling distantly over the heads of the nosy gossipmongers. He caught up to her in two strides of his impossibly long, hard-muscled legs and pulled her hand into his.

"Thanks for the dance, Princess. It's been a while."

"Really? Last year? Last month? When was the last time you treated anyone to your dance prowess?" She heard the sarcasm in her voice, but it was one of her defense mechanisms when she was embarrassed.

"Not hardly. The last time I danced like that was in those dance classes I told you about. The palace housekeeper's daughter took pity on us and rounded up some girls so we didn't have to dance with each other. I can tell you that even as a kid, Bastien—one of my fellow warriors—was huge and the gods know that he had at least three left feet." His shudder at the memory was so heartfelt that she laughed in spite of herself.

"These stories are very entertaining, whether they're true or not."

"They're true. I'll prove it to you soon, but part of me is hoping you come to believe me without needing evidence," he said.

She glanced up at him and his face had hardened into an expressionless mask. He'd put up his defenses again, and she knew the time for dancing and joking, brief as it had been, was over.

"Let's go and talk to some vampires, then," she said, changing direction to make for the exit. "I've already written my check to the hosting organization."

He tightened his grip on her arm. "There is no *we*. You are going home and Denal is going to babysit while I do some investigating. That Fae, and if I'm not very badly mistaken he's a Fae lord, which is even worse news, just warned us off of Vanquish. The last thing you need is to be caught anywhere near this investigation."

She yanked her hand away from his, stuck on a single word. "Did you say *babysit*? Do you think of me as a baby?" She kept the smile pasted on her face for the benefit of anyone watching, but fury was burning a hole in her throat. "Babysit?"

He put his arm around her shoulders again and herded her over to the Reading Room, where a bored-looking museum employee was standing guard.

"Sorry, no guests tonight, renovation," he recited in a monotone.

Quicker than thought, Christophe grabbed the man's chin with one hand. "We're going in," he said gently.

"You're going in," the man repeated, staring wide-eyed up at Christophe.

"Nobody else comes in."

"Nobody else."

"You never saw us."

"Never saw you."

Christophe released the man, who continued to stare straight ahead as if dazed or in a trance. Christophe pulled

Fiona into the room and turned left until they were out of the line of sight of the doorway.

"What was that? You have mind control, too?"

He shrugged, but the faint glow still reflecting light from his eyes was all the confirmation she needed.

"Is that what you did to me? Put some kind of mind control on me to make me go along with your crazy schemes? To . . . to get me into bed?"

All amusement drained from his face. An expression that almost looked like hurt flashed in his eyes, and then was gone. "Is that what I did, Princess? Be honest with yourself and with me. Which one of us cast the spell on the other? Because I can't seem to get through five minutes without wanting to kiss you. To strip you naked and taste your skin. Right now I'd bend you over that table and drive my cock into your perfect body if I thought you would let me, so tell me, Fiona. Who is in control here?"

He stood apart from her, his hands clenched at his sides, and didn't make a move to touch her. "Just go if you want to go. Hells, I'm used to it. I still plan to find the Siren and I'll give you Vanquish when I retrieve it. But you never have to see me again."

He meant it, too. She knew this man, somehow. He stood, shoulders hunched as if in defeat, waiting for her to leave. People had let him down before. Betrayed him. She could see the signs of it—the same signs that she'd seen in her father before he died, betrayed by his own father.

She'd always regretted that she hadn't been old enough to help her father. This time, with this man, she could do something about it.

"I'm not going anywhere," she whispered. "Let's figure this out together."

He raised his head, his eyes widening with disbelief or wonder. "Are you sure? I won't offer you an out again. I'm finding I like having you around."

She tried out her best seductive smile. "You may like me even more when I tell you I've absolutely nothing on underneath this dress. How long will that mind control hold over the guard?"

Christophe almost fell over. She wasn't leaving. She wasn't abandoning him, although she wasn't sure how to believe him about Atlantis or even his age. No, instead, she was walking toward him, smiling a wicked little smile, all but asking him to take her.

Who was he to turn down a lady?

He pounced on her, lifting her off her feet and into a fierce embrace. He found her mouth and devoured it, kissing her with all the relief and hunger he felt. A stark, implacable knowledge had risen deep inside him and was consuming him with forbidden flames.

She was *his*.

He put her lovely ass down on the nearest table and pulled her legs around him as he stepped into the cradle of her thighs.

"Really? Isn't that terribly decadent behavior for a princess?" He kissed his way down the side of her neck, kissed her delicate collarbones, and then kissed the rounded tops of her breasts. "Do you know, I've wanted to pop you out of this all evening?"

He proceeded to do just that, encouraged by her indrawn breath and the flush rising on her pearly skin. He scooped first her left, then her right breast out of the fabric of the dress and sighed in utter satisfaction at the sight of her rosy nipples hardening and pointing at him. "Like tiny little Atlantean blushberries," he murmured. "Just begging me to suck on them."

He pulled gently, them more firmly, on her nipple with his tongue and lips, his cock hard as tempered steel and growing harder by the second as she whimpered and pulled his head toward her with her hands.

"Oh, that's so good—oh, wait. Someone could walk in any moment," she whispered urgently.

"And that's even more exciting for you, isn't it?" He stood and stared into her eyes, while he slid his hands up from her ankles to her knees, pulling her knees farther apart, and then from her knees to her inner thighs, which were trembling. "We could be caught by any one of those aristocratic ninnies."

Her breath caught. "What about Fairsby?"

"They're gone, remember? Oh, what's this?" His fingers found liquid heat. "Are you wet for me, Lady Fiona?"

She trembled in his arms. "All the time, it seems," she confessed in a whisper. "If not mind control, what have you done to me?"

"The same thing you've done to me, I hope. And I plan to do it again, right now. Right here." He kissed her again, then unfastened his pants and released his straining cock. "I'm going to fuck you right here in the middle of the British Museum, and you're going to love it."

She caught his face between her hands. "You're going to love it, too," she said fiercely.

He centered his cock and plunged into her, and was rewarded by her tiny cry. "Oh, yeah."

She stopped him. "Condom?"

"Fiona, I swear to you on my oath as a warrior that we are safe."

She looked deeply into his eyes for a long moment, an eternity of a moment, and he had all but resigned himself to calling up an icy cold shower when she nodded.

"Yes. I believe you."

"Thank you," he said fervently, but then he didn't talk for a while, because he was too busy kissing her. He kissed her while he drove his cock into her warm, wet center; plunging deeper and deeper into her, answering every lift of her hips with another thrust. He couldn't get enough of her—he wanted her over and over, in every way possible.

He wanted her for always. The thought made him thrust deeper.

Her sheath tightened around him and she dug her fingers into his shoulders. "I'm—oh, I'm coming, Christophe. Please, harder. Faster."

"Anything for a lady," he said, his breath coming in harsh, rapid pants. He grabbed her hips and lifted her up and off the table, so her full weight was supported in his arms, and thrust harder, deeper, and faster, until she tightened around him and started bucking in his arms. He captured her cry with his mouth and thrust again, releasing his own seed, spurting long and hard into her welcoming heat.

When they both finally quit coming, he rested her back on the table and carefully, regretfully, withdrew. They were both breathing too hard to talk, so he removed from his pocket the handkerchief Hopkins had so thoughtfully provided and offered it to her.

"Thanks. I think I saw some napkins over there," she whispered, her cheeks blushing again. She was such a fascinating contradiction of wanton and innocent, his woman.

His woman. He was beginning to like the sound of that.

Maybe he was bewitched—but if so, it was the normal enchantment between a man and a woman. One he'd thought he would never experience. Far more than mere sex.

He filed the thought away to consider later. They cleaned up and he kissed her again. A long, slow, gentle kiss.

She took a deep breath. "Are you ready to go pub hopping?"

"I can't talk you out of this?"

"No. We're partners, remember?"

He took her hand. "You can never, ever leave my side. And if I tell you to run, you do it. Understand?"

"Perfectly."

"Okay, let's do this. And, Fiona?"

"Yes?"

"This is my new favorite museum."

She blushed all the way to the car.

Chapter 19

The slightly pointed tips of Gideon's ears had been practically on fire by the time he'd stepped outside the museum. Whoever—or whatever—that upstart Christophe was, Gideon would enjoy every second of the torture he planned for the man. How dare he touch Fiona? She was to be Gideon's. She would belong to him and only him. For a very long time. Eternity, perhaps, if he deigned to share the elixir with her before tiring of her. For her to be in the arms of another man made Gideon want to crush the entire museum into rubble, with the aristocracy still inside it. It would certainly be no loss to the world.

Not a good idea, though, considering his current plans. Still, Gideon wanted to lash out at *someone* to take the edge off his rage, but Maeve, the little coward, had run off to her car without a word, and now he was fuming in the backseat of his own car, like the impotent English lord he was supposed to be.

Enough. His meeting with Telios wasn't scheduled for hours, but since when did Fae lords need to adhere to schedules?

"Stop the car," he ordered his driver. "I'll get out here."

The driver, at least, knew better than to argue. He pulled the car to an immediate stop, and Gideon stepped out. He would make better time via his own method of travel, and he knew exactly where he was going. The St. Mary's tube station, on Whitechapel Road.

One simple bend in light and space later, Gideon stood inside the permanently closed station of London's Underground, looking around in disgust. A few burning torches lit the darkness to a dim glow. Most vampires were not known for attention to cleanliness, and Telios was no exception. At least there were no drained bodies lying about, although the stench attested to their recent presence. The rank odor of decaying flesh was practically suffocating in the claustrophobic space.

"What's the matter, Fae? A little too dark for you?" Telios's voice grated, as always, but this time it held a little more of an annoying quality. A bit of smugness, perhaps.

Gideon would enjoy crushing that.

"Do you know the history of this place?" Telios gestured at the rubble piled against the bricked-up platform. "Opened in 1884. Perfect timing for me, since there was always a fine hiding place in that storage room just off the platform. Ate a few workers, I did. But the station closed down in the late 1930s. They used it again as a war shelter against air raids for a bit during World War II, but a bomb smashed the building to bits. Too bad, really. It was easy enough to snatch a few of the fools rushing down into the dark to escape danger. Escaping the bombs, don't you know? Not so effective, when certain death lies in wait." He cackled and did a complicated kind of mincing dance. "Now that nobody ever comes down here anymore, it's mine. All mine."

Gideon's lips curled back from his teeth. The vampire truly was insane. But Gideon didn't care about sanity, so long as Telios had acquired the sword.

"Did you get it?"

Telios quit dancing and gave Gideon a far too shrewd look. "I may have."

"What does that mean? Either you did or you did not. Beware my anger, nightwalker. You are not immortal, for all of your pretense." Gideon called to the earth for power, but he was bricked away from too much of it for the surge he needed. Not that vampires had real life force to drain, in any case, but it would be satisfying to destroy this particular vampire.

Not yet, though. He needed that sword.

"I got it," Telios admitted. "It's not here, though. I almost got caught, getting away. Had to stash it. I'll go back for it tonight. There are other vampires searching for it, or so I've heard. Shifters, too. What is it about that sword?"

"Now, you fool. Get it now. I need that sword," Gideon roared, his hands clenching at his side. Twice thwarted in one evening was twice too much for a Fae lord who had not been denied his will in centuries. There would not be a third time.

"Bring it to me tonight. Or you will pay the price in pain."

"Why do you want it so much?" Telios's eyes gleamed a deep red in the flickering torchlight. "What makes that sword so important to you?"

Gideon hesitated. Perhaps, in his anger and frustration, he'd overplayed his hand. "I simply want it. There is nothing more important about it than any of my other treasures."

Telios nodded, but Gideon was almost certain he saw a flash of the vampire's fangs, as if it dared smile at him.

"All right then. Whatever you say. I'll try to bring it to you tonight. The price has gone up, though. I want six."

Utter revulsion gripped Gideon at the thought of turning over six wood nymphs to Telios for his sadistic pleasure. Not, of course, that he'd ever intended to relinquish even the two the vampire had originally requested in the bargain. Telios's death would solve that issue.

"You will not *try*, you will succeed," Gideon commanded. "Do not fail. Bring me that sword or else you will be very sorry. We will discuss payment later." He opened the fabric of space again and stepped through, not noticing until after he'd reached his destination—Fairsby Manor—that Telios was dancing again, and the vampire seemed far too happy for one who had been threatened by an Unseelie Court prince.

Gideon considered and discarded the idea of returning to Telios's lair and teaching the vampire a lesson. Instead, he lashed out and smashed the lamp off the table in his study, but it was a pathetically feeble outlet for his fury. Once Telios delivered the sword, Gideon would kill him, anyway. Simply to give himself pleasure in a day that had held little. Once he had the Siren, the Unseelie Court queen would understand what the Fae must do in this conflict. It was their time again. Time for the Fae to rule over all of humanity and destroy any vampire or shifter who thought otherwise.

It was Fae destiny. It was *his* destiny. He would be a god. If she were very, very lucky, he might make Fiona his goddess.

Chapter 20

Fiona bumped her head on the roof of the car as she shim-
mied out of her gown.

"I must be blessed beyond all men," Christophe said. "This
is twice so far this evening I'm getting you naked, and the
night's not even half over."

"A gentleman would turn his head," she said, pulling her
shirt over her head.

He started laughing. "You've got the wrong guy, Princess.
I don't plan to ever miss a chance to see you without your
clothes on."

She called the shadows and, bending light and dark to her
will, disappeared from view.

"That's so unfair," he growled.

"Don't mess with a ninja."

"You know, you could have done that in the museum if
anybody walked in on us."

"And wouldn't you have looked foolish standing there
alone with your bits hanging out?"

He grumbled something in that melodic language. She
wanted to ask, but was afraid he'd say it was, indeed, Atlan-

tean and they'd be back to that. She pulled on her underwear and jeans, tricky but not impossible in the backseat of the moving automobile, and finally dressed, she released the shadows and lowered the privacy glass and pushed her dress through to the front passenger seat. It landed in a heap with the bodice sitting upright.

"Brilliant," Sean said. "It looks like I was driving along, and my date melted right out of her dress."

"Better work on your conversational skills, friend," Christophe advised. "You probably bored her to death."

Sean glared at Christophe then met Fiona's gaze in the mirror. "So, do you really like this guy? Do I have to be nice to him?"

"Play nice, boys. Please. Sean, do you have my bag?"

He handed the leather tote back to her, and she pulled out a handful of chunky costume jewelry, her makeup kit, and a short black wig. She quickly donned the bracelets, rings, and necklaces, and then examined herself in the rearview mirror, considering. She added a pair of giant hoop earrings she'd never normally be caught dead wearing. Then she brushed on a thick layer of dark makeup. Smoky eyes, dark red lipstick, and bronzer. The final touch was the wig. She fit it around her head, pinning her hair underneath it. When she was satisfied that not a single strand of blond showed, she leaned back in her seat and turned to Christophe.

"What do you think? Uma Thurman in *Pulp Fiction*, right?"

"Who?"

"No movie theaters where you come from?"

"Sadly, no, but the prince's brother Ven has TVs and DVD players in all of his safe houses, so we've watched a lot of films."

"Of course. The prince's brother. Anyway, watch that one. American classic."

"I like the look. It's kind of hot."

She narrowed her eyes, and he raised his hands.

"Not as hot as you usually look," he said, backtracking.

"Way to go, mate," Sean said. "Smooth. Really smooth."

"Yeah. It's a gift," Christophe muttered.

"This is not a nice part of town," Sean said, turning down a road that was no bigger than an alley. "Are you sure about this, Lady Fiona?"

"Yes, I'm sure. We're going to The Melting Moon, and we need—"

Sean's yelp cut her off. "What the hell is that?"

He swerved the car and then slammed on the brakes.

A black vehicle—big, some kind of SUV—seemed to fill the windshield as it hurtled toward them at a very high rate of speed. Fiona cried out a warning or prayer or call for help; she wasn't sure which.

Suddenly, the bright glow of blue-green energy filled the car. Christophe grabbed her and yanked her down to the seat, covering her with his body. But the expected crash never came; instead the loud screech of brakes sounded in front of the car and, seconds later, on each side of the car, too.

"We've got trouble," Christophe said, unnecessarily. "Stay in the car."

He kissed the top of her head, threw the door open, and leapt out of the car. She heard a loud hissing noise and immediately flashed back to a visceral, terrifying childhood memory, and her blood turned to ice in her veins.

Vampires.

Daddy.

"No. Not again. Sean, stay in the car and get down on the floor." Calling to the shadows, she slipped out of the car behind Christophe, hiding from sight in the darkness and scanning the area. The dark forms advancing on them from the vehicle on this side of the car weren't alone. More shadowy shapes climbed out of the vehicles in front and on the other side, and as she watched, a fourth pulled up behind them. They were barricaded in like sheep in a pen.

She had no intention of being a sheep.

Sean jumped out of the driver's seat, a very serious-looking gun in his right hand and a wooden stake in the left. Hopkins must have been training him to do more than drive her around. She wanted to throw herself in front of him and protect him, as she had when she first met him, but she realized she'd do more harm than good. She was definitely firing that boy later, for his own good. For now, she flanked Christophe and ignored his stream of Atlantean cursing.

"Fiona, I can smell you," he said softly. "If I can smell you, don't you think they can? Or hear your heartbeat? Run, damn it."

She'd forgotten. A childhood memory of fear had driven away common sense. She called to her Gift again and used wind and shadow to disperse any sound and scent. In seconds, no trace of her remained, and yet Christophe turned and stared right into her eyes.

"I will always be able to find you. Get out of here before you get hurt. Please."

She knew what it had cost him to add that "please." He was a man used to issuing commands and having them obeyed. She could tell that from the effortless way he'd taken over a leadership role in their quest for Vanquish. She wasn't much for obeying, and she had a trick of her own—literally up her sleeve.

A ninja never left home unarmed.

"Nice night for an ambush," Christophe called out to the vamps as he balanced energy spheres in each hand. "Didn't have anything else to do? Polish your fangs, for instance?"

"You were heard inquiring about the Siren, human," the lead vampire hissed. "We would suggest you drop your inquiry."

"You need four carloads of goons to tell me that?"

"Bit melodramatic, wasn't it?" Sean said, moving into place with his back to Christophe's back. "I thought vamps could fly."

"Some can. This lot are obviously the weaklings."

"We plan to kill you," the vampire said. "Unless you tell us, right now, who has Vanquish and where it is."

"Interesting form of suggestion," Christophe said. "Lots of vampires have planned to kill me before, bloodsucker."

He hurled the energy spheres, twin gleaming arcs of death that exploded the heads of the speaker and another vampire on contact.

"Usually only once," Christophe added.

The rest of the vampires, shrieking and hissing, leapt and

crawled toward Christophe and Sean in a dark swarm of evil, bending and twisting in such inhuman ways that the mere sight of them almost made Fiona's heart stutter in her chest again. But she mentally kicked her own arse to get moving.

She was the Scarlet Ninja, for Saint George's sake. She was not a helpless ninny. She threw herself into a low somersault between the legs of two vampires leaping around the back of her car, and escaped the closing perimeter of attackers.

When she looked back at them, Christophe had daggers in each hand and was—unbelievably—grinning. It was the fierce, exultant joy of a warrior in action, and she instantly knew in her heart that everything he'd told her about Atlantis was nothing but the truth. She ran back a few steps, carefully checking the vampire's vehicle to be sure no one was hiding in it, and pulled the slender vials out of the pouches inside her sleeves.

One of Hopkins's inventions, the thick plastic vials hid in the draped fabric of her loose sleeves. They fit in the palms of her hands and she could rapidly uncap them with a thumb, which she did. Then she headed back into the fray to surprise a few vampires.

She dashed out from behind the SUV then stopped, frozen in shock by the battle being waged with tooth and dagger in front of her. Never once in her time as a thief had she encountered violence on an up-close-and-personal level, and it was nothing like in the films. This blood didn't spray artistically through the air.

No, it stained the side of Sean's head and ran down Christophe's arm and the side of his chest. They were black stains, glistening wetness in the dark. The vampires didn't bleed, though. They exploded into a greenish-black wave of slime, which she knew would be acidic to the touch. Christophe and Sean had already killed at least four of them, maybe more, but there were seven left and they were attacking in waves, too close for one of Christophe's magic spears to be effective.

He sliced at one's head with his dagger and it yanked its head back, laughing and hissing at him.

"Fool. Do you think we are all so easy to kill? I have—"

It stopped talking and shrieked, looking down. Though Fiona couldn't see its chest, it was easy enough to see what had happened.

There was a silvery tip poking out of the left side of its back.

Sean cried out as a vamp sank its teeth into the side of his neck, and the sight broke Fiona out of her shock. She heard a scream, the sound like that of a banshee's death herald, but she was running before she realized that *she* was the one screaming. She hurtled full speed into the back of the vampire attacking Sean, and dashed the entire contents of the vial onto the side of its face.

The vampire shrieked so loudly something in her ear canals popped with the pain, but she held on desperately to its shoulders as it released Sean, flailing around and clawing at the smoking ruin of its face and eye. The holy water carved crevasses in its flesh, and she threw herself away from it as it fell to the ground, screeching and hissing.

She dropped the empty vial, still holding on to the shadows that concealed her from sight, smell, and sound, and ran to the left a few paces away from the dying vampire. The rest of them had to know someone—or something—had attacked from behind, and she didn't want to be caught in a blind sweep.

"Princess, I'm going to kill you when we get out of here," Christophe yelled, fury riding the planes and angles of his face.

He launched himself into the air, pure blue-green fire shimmering in glowing streams around his entire body, and tackled three of the vampires who'd decided to leap over her car toward him and Sean. It was like watching a martial arts film where the action star was a master sorcerer. He twirled in midair and leveled a flying kick at the first vamp's throat, then followed it up with a dagger in its heart as it fell backward. Before that vamp even hit the ground, Christophe grabbed the head of the second vamp and slammed its face down onto his knee so hard that the resulting crunch sounded like lightning snapping a dead tree trunk. Energy pulsed between his hands, brief but fierce, and the vamp's head imploded, then disappeared.

Fiona didn't have time to watch any more, though, because one of the vampires was sniffing the ground, crawling on hands and feet like a deranged hound from hell. Its body moved in ways that bodies were not meant to move, as though it were boneless or at least had a flexible spine.

"I know you're here, *Princess*," it hissed, the sibilants hanging in the air. "Playing with toys you shouldn't have? I'm going to crunch on your bones when I'm done draining you dry."

She waited, silent as the grave she had no intention of going to—at least not today—until it was in range. Then she hurled the contents of the second vial into its face and threw herself back and to the side as fast as she could, to escape the reach of its arms as it threw its body forward in a last, desperate leap even as it screamed and squealed its way to a horrific death.

Over the drops of water that had fallen to the pavement a faint golden glow hovered for an instant before winking out, and she had a heartbeat of crystallized time in which to wonder what God thought about blessed water being used to kill. But then Christophe pulled her up and into his arms, crushing her in a fierce embrace until she thought her lungs might burst.

"Don't ever, ever, ever, do that again," he commanded, somewhat ruining the severity of his command by compulsively kissing her again and again.

She pushed him away after a minute or so, shoving against the rock-hard wall of his chest. "Really? Don't join in the fight when people I care about are in danger?" She glared up at him. "Have you *met* me?"

Then she ran to Sean, who was leaning back against the car, bent over and breathing hard, and threw her arms around him. "Are you okay? How bad is it?"

She pulled his head up so she could examine his neck. The wound was ragged but only dripping, not spurting, blood.

"Thank God, thank God, thank God," she said, over and over. "If you died because of me—"

"I'm too tough to kill," he said, managing a grin. "Anyway, this wasn't because of you. Far as I can tell, it was due to those vamps. Six of which I killed, by the way."

He straightened, puffing out his chest, and she couldn't help it. She pulled him to her and planted a big kiss on his cheek. Even in the dim light, she could see him flush hot.

"That, youngling, is why men the world over will do anything for a beautiful woman," Christophe said dryly. He gently nudged Fiona aside to examine Sean's wound. "You're going to have a scar, but it's not bad. Unfortunately, better clean it out."

He turned to Fiona. "Do you happen to have any more of that holy water, Invisible Girl? Sooner is better."

"This is going to hurt really badly, isn't it?" Sean's throat worked but he tilted his head so they could get at his neck.

"Like all the fires of the nine hells are searing your flesh," Christophe admitted, far too cheerfully. "Every warrior worth his daggers goes through it at least once, although our remedy isn't quite the same as yours."

"What do you mean?"

"Trust me, you don't want to know." Christophe looked around them, his eyes narrowing. "Anybody notice something odd here?"

"You mean, we're still in London, one of the busiest cities in the world, and nobody else has come down this alley during this entire time?" Fiona nodded, pulling another vial of blessed water from her sleeve and holding it up to Christophe, who nodded. "Yes, I noticed. In fact, how are they—"

"Accomplices," Sean said. "It's how we used to do it. Bloke at each end when there was going to be trouble. We'd call out a warning."

"A warning is one thing," Christophe said. "An empty alley for the better part of half an hour is another. I'd guess sorcerers. If they're enthralled, we're either in big trouble, or they're dead. Interesting that they thought we knew where the Siren is. Must mean the vampires don't have it. Or at least this group of vamps."

"Let's do this," Fiona said. She took a deep breath as if she would feel her own flesh sear. She wished it could be. *She* deserved it, not Sean. Her games as the Scarlet Ninja were what had put him in jeopardy.

"Just do it, Princess. Quick and get it over with," Christophe said, not unsympathetically. "The anticipation is almost worse."

She held her breath and upended the vial over Sean's wound, which sizzled and hissed like butter on a hot griddle. Sean sucked in a sharp breath and then said a few words she hadn't known he even remembered from the old days.

"More," Christophe said.

"But—"

"More."

She opened her last vial and poured it directly on top of the bubbling mess on Sean's neck, feeling the hot tears escaping her eyes. By the time she'd finished the vial, it poured clear and all signs of steam or infection had disappeared.

"That should do it," Christophe said, nodding once. "When it doesn't react any more, it's cleaned out. Now we get out of here."

"Home. Sean needs to rest. And you're bleeding, too." Relieved of the worry over Sean, she was swamped by fear for Christophe. She tore open his shirt like a wild woman to look at the wound in his chest.

He caught her hands in his own and kissed her knuckles. "I'm fine, *mi amara*. A scratch. Atlanteans heal faster than humans, too. Now we need to get out of here. Sean?"

Sean nodded and headed for the vehicle blocking their way, while Christophe headed for the one parked in the middle of the street.

"Search for anything interesting," Christophe called, and Fiona ran around her car to the SUV on the other side, leaping over the piles of still-dissolving slime that was all that was left of their attackers. A great many people were warning them away from the search for Vanquish. The important questions were why and who had it.

She made quick work searching the SUV, and found nothing, which was what she'd expected. The percentage of vampires who bothered to register with authorities and get any kind of official papers was still frighteningly small. Why lease a car when you could enthrall a human into giving it to you?

She made sure not to leave her fingerprints anywhere, slammed the door shut, and returned to Sean and Christophe. "Nothing."

"In either of these two, either," Christophe reported.

Sean shook his head, strain showing clearly on his face. "Not this one, either."

"Now. We leave now," Christophe said.

"I'm driving," Fiona announced. "Sean, you rest in the back."

Sean tried to protest, but Christophe opened the door to the backseat and pointed, and Sean half climbed, half fell into the car, the reaction from the battle finally hitting him. Christophe closed the door and turned to Fiona.

"I still need to go to those pubs and find out what in the hells is going on," Christophe said.

"Not without me."

"It's not like I will allow you to drive home unaccompanied, either. Not after that attack." He tilted her chin up with his finger and kissed her.

"I'm not a fan of the word 'allow,' but I'll admit the more the merrier," she said.

"Please, then. Please get in your vehicle now and drive home as quickly as you can, in a straight line."

She opened the door and paused. "Wait. Where are you going to be?"

He pointed up, then leapt into the air and, right in front of her eyes, transformed into a sparkling cloud of mist that soared into the air over the car and hovered there.

Please drive now, she heard in her head, and she didn't have any energy left to debate the possibility or impossibility of telepathic conversation. She just slanted her body into the car, turned the key in the ignition, and drove.

Chapter 21

Campbell Manor

Christophe waited, watching her every minute, but the shaking didn't start for a while. First, she'd seen Sean safely into Hopkins's care. Declan was sleeping, but she'd gone to his room and checked on him even after Hopkins reassured her. Denal sat in a chair by Declan's window, daggers resting on his lap. He rose when they entered the room, but Christophe had already communicated with him so he knew there was no threat.

She leaned over and kissed her brother's forehead, smoothing a strand of hair away, and Christophe was struck by the realization that she must have done the same so many times as the boy grew up. Declan didn't wake, but he smiled in his sleep.

Fiona raised a hand to Declan but didn't speak; she just turned and left the room. Christophe followed her, desiring with every fiber of his being that he could protect her from what came next, but helpless to understand how. If only Conlan were here, or Bastien. They were so much better with women and emotion.

He had never so desperately wished he knew how to comfort another.

She made it to her room and then to the shower, peeling her clothes and wig off along the way and letting them fall to the floor in a trail of discarded disguise. Moving robotically, stumbling as she walked, Fiona turned the water on to full heat and then climbed into the billowing steam in her glass-enclosed shower.

That's when the shaking finally began.

Full-body shudders wracked her body as she leaned against the wall, and the glass trembled with the force of her pain. Christophe stripped out of his own clothes in an instant and entered the shower, pulling her into his arms.

"Shh, *mi amara*. Shh. It's over now. Let it out, let it all out, but it's over now. It's all over. Shh. I'm right here for you." He smoothed her hair away from her face, over and over, as she sobbed as if her heart were shattering in her chest.

"He could have died. He could have died. Did I rescue him from his murderous father only to kill him myself? He's only twenty-two years old, Christophe, and he could have *died*." A fresh wave of grief and reaction took her, and he could do nothing but hold her, rocking back and forth, until it subsided a little and she could listen to him.

Listen to reason.

"You can't take the blame for that attack. They said they wanted me to stop asking about Vanquish. They didn't even know who you were, in that wig and makeup. Me. Not you. It is I who bear the blame."

She lifted her face to him, her eyes reddened with pain and fury. "No. No. Let's put the blame where it belongs. On those bastards who stole the sword, and murdered the guards. On those vampires who attacked us."

"I'm wondering if they're the same."

"If they already have the sword, why would they care about us?"

"It might have been misdirection. But we don't need to worry about this now. Now you should rest."

"No," she said again. "Now I want you inside me. I want

to feel something other than horror and fear and rage." She lifted her arms and put them around his neck. "Make me feel, Christophe."

And so he did. He lifted her in his arms and joined his body to hers, taking her there in the steaming heat. He directed the channels of water to swirl around her and caress her even as he held her and murmured nonsense words into her ear and thrust steadily home. She cried a little as she held him and kissed him, and the shudders of reaction gently, gradually, turned to trembling of a different sort entirely.

Their joining was not about passion and possession but a declaration of need; the simple need to experience warmth and light. To face their own mortality without doing so alone. He'd wanted sex after battle before, on many occasions. It was a purely chemical reaction to the adrenaline charge of a fight.

This was utterly, completely, different. This was seeking comfort and the welcome of home. He was fiercely proud to be the one she needed, and as if in reaction to the thought, the barrier between her soul and his began to open, surrounding them with heat and light. Her soul danced around her, a shifting dream of blues. But the lovely colors were darkened; tinged with black shadows and the somber gray of grief. It caught him off guard and he ceased to move within her.

She lifted her head from his shoulder, her eyes dazed and unfocused, and he decided to delay the choice. The time wasn't right—he'd once thought the time would never be right—for the soul-meld. He used every ounce of focus and discipline he'd ever learned to shut the doorway to his soul. To keep her own at bay.

The icy chill of loss swept through him, and he wondered if the miraculous gift of the soul-meld, once offered and rejected, would ever be offered again. But Fiona lifted her lips to his and he sought refuge in her warmth and her passion, and he achieved his release as she cried out her own climax. When he finally released her, they quickly finished their shower, dried in huge towels, and he carried her to bed, pulling her into his arms and tucking the coverlets around them.

He closed his eyes and concentrated, setting magical wards

around the room so none could enter it without his admittance, and then he kissed her.

"Rest now, beautiful one. Tomorrow we will figure this all out." He kissed her again, and then, wrapped around her warm, still-trembling body, he watched her for a very long time, until she fell into a troubled sleep. When her steady breathing finally told him she'd succumbed to her exhaustion, he lay there, content simply to hold her, until dawn brushed its golden fingers against her windows. Then, at last, he, too, fell asleep.

⁓⃯

Fiona woke up enveloped in warmth and the sensation of perfect safety for the first time since she'd taken up the role of the Scarlet Ninja. She blinked, disoriented by the large, muscular arm resting across her naked breasts, and then memory flooded back and her face and other, more intimate, parts of her warmed. Christophe. The shower. The way she'd practically begged him to make love to her.

Well. They were beyond petty embarrassments now. She was not a girl on a blind date. She was a grown woman. He was most definitely all man. Together, they'd battled vampires and survived. Anyway, he'd been more than willing.

"The thoughts running through your mind must be fascinating, if the expressions crossing your face in such rapid succession are anything to judge by," he said. His voice was a rumble in his chest against her side and made her want to rub her face against him like a kitten.

"I was thinking about last night. The vampires. And the shower, and the museum, to be honest," she confessed, her cheeks flaming again. Evidently whatever caused her to blush had not yet caught on that she was a grown woman.

"Ah, yes, the museum. One of my favorite memories of all time," he said, chuckling. "And yet waking up here with you counts as its equal."

She turned to look into his eyes. "Why? You must have woken up with many women before." She didn't want to think about it, but she had to face facts, especially if he really had seen more than three hundred birthdays. Even one or two encounters a year and that added up to . . . insanity.

She couldn't think about that now or her brain would catch fire.

"Never, in fact." He pulled her even closer and kissed her nose. "I don't sleep with women."

"Right. So you're a monk?"

"I have had sexual encounters, but I have never slept with a woman before this night. I've never met a woman I trusted enough to let down my guard that much." Sincerity and something else was in his gaze. A little embarrassment of his own, maybe?

She stared at him, fascinated. "Never? In all those years?"

"Never."

"I—I don't know what to say," she admitted. "I feel honored."

"You're the one who honors me, Princess," he said solemnly, but then a wickedly evil grin lit up his face. "If you want to honor me again, right now, you can climb on top of me and—"

"I get it, I get it." She leaned in to kiss him and took her time about it. When she pulled back, she took a deep, shaky breath. "You do amazing things to me, Mr. Atlantean warrior."

"Wait. Sean!" She pushed away from him and sat up, clutching the sheets to her chest. "I can't believe I haven't checked in on Sean."

"He is doing well," Christophe said. "I have already communicated with Denal. Sean's wound has begun to heal, perhaps due to the liberal application of blessed water so quickly applied."

She leaned back against the pillows. "That's good. I guess I can wait a bit to check on him in person."

"He, Denal, and Declan were planning a marathon battle of some video game after lunch," Christophe informed her, leaning over to kiss the top of her breast. "I think we can safely skip that."

"But Hopkins—"

"Let Hopkins get his own date." He pulled her over and on

top of him and proceeded to make love to her thoroughly for the next couple of hours, until they were lying in a tangle of rumpled sheets and bliss.

She traced a finger around the curves and lines of the tattoo on the upper left side of his back. "What does this mean?"

"That's the mark signifying my oath as a warrior. Poseidon brands us with it when we've completed our training to be a Warrior of Poseidon. A sort of graduation gift."

She caught the bitterness underneath the sarcasm. "You don't like it?"

"Would you want to be branded?" He sat up, pushing his dark hair away from his face. "It implies ownership. I have never wanted to be owned."

"What does it mean? The circle and the triangle and this symbol?"

"It's a symbol representing our duty. Poseidon's Trident bisects the circle representing all the peoples of the world. The triangle is for the pyramid of knowledge. All of Poseidon's warriors wear this mark as a sort of proof of service. It means we've sworn an oath to serve Poseidon and accepted the responsibility of protecting humanity."

"But you don't? Want the responsibility of protecting us from our own stupidity, I'm guessing?"

He glanced at her, clearly surprised. "You are very perceptive for a ninja, Princess. Let's just say I never did, before I met you. Now I'm starting to enjoy the job."

She punched him lightly in the shoulder. "I'm not a job."

"No, you, my beauty, are a privilege and a fantasy. I fear I might wake up from this dream and be bereft of your presence."

"Bereft. Nice. Poetic, even," she said. "Did you know an

eft is a kind of salamander, like a newt? Witches in the old days—or the poor women who were accused of being witches, at least—used to boil their tails in potions."

He started laughing. "Wonderful. I try to be romantic for the first time in my life, and you start talking about lizards. My poor ego may die a hideous death."

"But you're not," she said, serious now. "You're not a romantic. You're a warrior."

"Does that bother you?" His eyes cooled to green ice, but she recognized it for one of his many self-protective techniques.

"No. I'm still dealing with the fact that I killed those two vampires. I used blessed water to deliberately harm them and it caused their death. That was me. I am now a murderer." Her hands started to shake and she clenched them together.

"They were vampires."

"Vampires have rights as citizens now."

"They were trying to murder you. All of us. Self-defense and defense of others is still permitted, even in the screwed up new world you landwalkers are creating," he said, rolling over to sit up and stare down at her. "Don't ever think that you are bad or wrong for preventing them from killing Sean or yourself."

"You scared me a little," she admitted. "I'd heard you say the word—warrior. But I didn't have context. I didn't know how to believe it. Out there you were deadly beyond anything I've ever seen. So many of them and you were everywhere with your blades and your magic."

"Are you still afraid of me?" His eyes were shuttered again, and his jaw clenched as if against her response.

"Did I just act like I was afraid of you? When I had my lips around your penis, for example?" He stretched blissfully in reaction to her question, and she laughed but then grew serious again. "No, oddly enough, you make me feel safe. You have so much danger inside you, but you put your own life on the line for me and Sean. There's no way he killed six vampires, either, is there?"

"Let him think it, Fiona. He needs to be a white knight, especially after you threw yourself into the fray to save him."

Christophe lifted her hand to his lips and pressed a lingering kiss into her palm. "He's not the one who swore an oath, after all, which makes his courage all the more impressive."

"Do you want to tell me the words? The oath. I'd like to hear it, if it's not too private."

"The language is archaic. If you didn't like me being romantic, you probably won't like this, either."

"Please? But only if you want to." She couldn't explain, even to herself, why she wanted to hear it. She only knew that she did. Knew that if this man were capable of swearing an oath of one sort and following through on it, he was also capable of another kind of commitment. The *personal* kind.

The kind that suddenly mattered to her a very great deal.

He shrugged. "If you like. It goes like this: We will wait. And watch. And protect. And serve as first warning on the eve of humanity's destruction. Then, and only then, Atlantis will rise. For we are the Warriors of Poseidon, and the mark of the Trident we bear serves as witness to our sacred duty to safeguard mankind."

A thrumming sense of power rang through the room, resonating in the air and in her bones, under her skin and blood and individual nerve endings.

"That's beautiful," she whispered. Even she, with so little magic, felt the magic in the words. "But you don't like it?"

"It's not the words I don't care for, it's their meaning. Why should I care anything about safeguarding mankind?" His face twisted with a rage so intense she flinched away from him. "*Humanity* murdered my parents."

Chapter 22

Christophe leapt out of the bed and called to magic to clothe himself in pants and a shirt as he paced the room, suddenly feeling like a caged animal.

Like that little boy in the box, so many years ago.

"What happened?" Fiona sat curled up in the bed, her knees to her chest, classic protective body posture. She was probably afraid of him now.

He deserved it. He may as well tell her all of it now. Let her see how pathetic he'd been. How humans had destroyed his childhood.

"We used to walk the land, did I tell you that? Not just the warriors among us but the normal citizens. Scholars who wanted to learn about humanity, for example. People like my mother and father. They could travel through the portal and, maintaining anonymity, travel among humans and even live in one place for a little while. Studying and learning, gathering anthropologic data about different cultures, much like your own anthropologists who travel to different lands."

She nodded. "Of course. If you have all this magic, we must seem fairly uncivilized to you."

He laughed. "It's not just the magic. The magic is maybe the least of it. We had technology and books and treasures beyond all imagining. That's why humans tried to conquer the Seven Isles in the first place, more than eleven thousand years ago. That's when we knew we had to escape. Well, that and the cataclysm."

"Cataclysm?"

"The *Ragnarok*. The Doom of the Gods," he recounted. "The gods decided to take their petty squabbles to a world-ending level, and it happened to coincide with an attack upon Atlantis. The king and elders at that time decided we needed to remove ourselves from the battlefield before we were destroyed. So we went for a little swim, shall we say."

"Okay. Okay. Let me catch up here," she said, climbing out of bed and pulling on a cerulean silk robe. "You realize that *Ragnarok* is Norse mythology. Atlantis is Greek mythology. Your stories are becoming a little confused."

He whirled around to face her. "Do you think the gods care about how humans have classified them? Norse, Greek, Roman, whatever? Gods fight each other, fuck each other—and who or whatever they can catch, actually—and play games with human lives like you're all chess pieces on a giant board. No, not even as important as chess pieces to them. More like bugs underfoot. My ancestors didn't want Atlantis to suffer the same fate."

"But—" She shook her head, more to herself than at him. "No. That's not important now. Tell me how your parents died."

She walked toward him, hands outstretched, but he didn't want to touch her. Couldn't bear for her to touch him; not now. Not while he told this story that he'd never told anyone before. She was too pure, too perfect. Too good to hear his story of betrayal, torture, and death.

Oh, they'd known. The warriors who'd rescued him had certainly known some of it, suspected more. But he had never spoken a word of it in more than three hundred years.

She touched his arm and looked up at him with those blue, blue eyes. "Please."

And he was undone.

"My parents were among the lucky ones, in their minds. They were societal anthropologists, content to study farming villages in rural Ireland. Of course I didn't know that then, I learned about their study later. We lived on the outskirts of a tiny place, I don't even remember the name, if I ever knew it. We had a view of the sea. I spent most of the first four years of my life there."

Memories he'd buried for far too long surfaced: of playing in a field with his father, a man who always made time for a boisterous son. His mother telling him stories by the fire. He couldn't remember their faces. It had been too long. It was more of an impression of warmth and safety.

A feeling of *home*.

His eyes burned, and he turned away from Fiona, ashamed to let her see his weakness. "They only returned to Atlantis maybe once every few weeks or couple of months. I don't know. Time moves differently to a child, of course. We'd wait until the village was asleep and then my father or mother would call to the portal."

He laughed bitterly and ran a hand through his hair. "It always came for *them*. Maybe even the portal finds me tainted."

She put her arms around him and rested her cheek on his back. "No. Never. Not the man I've grown to know so well in such a short time. You're amazing. I can't believe you've done your job, protecting us for so long, even with so much anguish in your heart."

He caressed the back of her hand, but only for an instant; he still couldn't take her touch. Not now. Not during this story. He walked away from her.

"It was bound to happen. One morning one of the village women stopped by to talk to my mother about something. Some sewing circle, probably. I remember that she always loved the sewing circles." He smiled a little at the faded and out-of-focus memory of falling asleep at his mother's feet, tugging on her skirt, as she worked on some garment for him or for his father. She'd liked to sing as she sewed. He remembered that.

Perhaps it was why he never, ever sang.

"This stupid woman walked in as we were coming back to

the cottage through the portal. She ran, screaming as if the devil himself were after her. My parents knew it was over, so they hurriedly gathered their few possessions, but—" He doubled over, the pain of it fresh after so very many years.

"Christophe? What is it?"

"It was my fault. I killed them."

～～～

Fiona put her arms around him, tightening them when he tried to get away. "No. Shh. It's my turn. Let me comfort you."

He shook his head violently, his big body shaking in her embrace. "I can't—"

"Let me be the strong one this time? Yes. You can. I owe you." She stroked his back and murmured soothing words of comfort, much as he'd done for her in the shower. When his breathing slowed to normal, she let him escape her hug, but she kissed his cheek before he managed to pace away from her again.

"I ran away. Off to the fields to play or something. They called me and I thought it was a game, so I stayed hidden around the side of the barn. I remember the warmth of the sun on my head, and then nothing until a great shouting woke me up."

"Your parents?" She wasn't sure she wanted to hear the answer anymore; in fact, she was desperately sure she did not. But she knew he needed to tell his story, so the least she could do was muster the courage to hear it.

"They brought the sheriff. Or magistrate. Or what the hells ever he was called back then. But he was none of those things. He was Fae. Unseelie Court Fae. The murdering bastard killed my parents." He smashed his fist into his palm and the dark drive to seek vengeance was in every line of his face and clenched muscle in his body. He suddenly seemed taller and wider, and he was glowing again. Not the gentle blue-green of the energy spheres but the scarlet of fire and retribution.

She knew a little bit about retribution herself.

"He and his deputies dragged my parents out of the house. Then they sent the villagers away. I remember watching them go. It was so strange, how they'd come shouting and yelling down the lane to our house, but they ran away in total silence. They knew, you see. I figured that out later. They knew."

She didn't want to ask; more than she wanted to draw her next breath she so didn't want to ask, but she knew she must. "They knew what?"

"They knew the murderers were Fae and that they'd kill my parents. They didn't want to know, so they ran, but they knew."

He fell heavily onto her bed and the crimson flame vanished. "I could see, you know. I never told anybody, but I saw it all. They told me—the warriors who came for me, later, more than a year later when they finally found me—they told me that my parents had gone away to the Summer Lands. Silverglen, where Fae danced and animals talked and all manner of beings lived in peace and harmony forevermore."

"They lied? How could they do that? Who was it? I want to have a stern talking to with those men," she said, fisting her hands on her hips.

He smiled up at her, just a hint of a smile, but it was encouraging in the midst of this horrible story. "So fierce, *mi amara*. So fierce on my behalf. I truly am blessed among men."

"They told you, in effect, that your parents had abandoned you," she said gently. "That's a horrible thing to do to a child. Trust me, I know."

"No, it didn't matter," he said, shaking his head. "I knew what had happened. The Fae sucked the life force out of them until my mother and father were nothing but dust on the dirt floor of our barn. Dust mingling with dust. Of course, the symbolism was lost on a four-year-old child."

"What did you do?" She came to kneel at his feet and covered his clenched fists with her hands.

"What could I do? I was a terrified little boy. I lost control of my bladder—still to this day I remember how ashamed I was that my father would know I'd wet my trousers. Then I curled up in a ball and closed my eyes, wishing as hard as I could that it was all a nightmare and we were still in Atlantis with my grandparents."

Hot tears traced lines down her face and he followed their

path with one finger. "Don't cry for me, Princess. It was long, long ago, before even your grandfather's grandfather's day, more than likely."

"If not me, then who?" She leaned forward and put her arms around his waist, resting her head in his lap. "I think I've earned the right to cry for that little boy."

"I'm sorry. I didn't mean to add sorrow to your heart," he said, and he found that he meant it. He cared more for what pain he was causing her than for what relief the telling might bring him.

Possibly his first selfless thought in centuries.

The gods were definitely laughing at him now.

"What happened to you next?"

He sucked in a long breath. "I must have fallen asleep. When I woke up, the woman who'd discovered us that morning was staring down at me, and her face was twisted up like a monster. When I opened my eyes, she screamed."

"At a tiny child? What did she do?"

"She spent the next year of my life trying to beat, starve, and torture Satan out of me. She came close to killing me, but even then, even so young, I knew I wouldn't give her the satisfaction. She would never break me."

Fiona made a sound, and he realized he'd clenched his hands around hers so tightly he must be hurting her. He released her hands, pulsing a bit of magic into them to soothe any small pain.

"You were incredibly brave," she said, rising to sit next to him on the bed.

"I was a fool," he said, even now shuddering at the memory. "She broke me the first time she put me in the box."

Chapter 23

A discreet knock sounded at the door.

"Not now, please," Fiona called out, her arms wrapped around Christophe. He wasn't making a sound, but his body was shuddering so hard the bed was shaking underneath them.

"I'm afraid the lady insists," Hopkins said. "Lady Maeve Fairsby is here to see you and claims it is quite urgent."

Christophe's head snapped up, and all sign of the pain he'd been reliving had vanished, replaced by cold, deadly contemplation. "She may have news of why we were attacked. We need to see her. If nothing else, we can hold her hostage against her cousin."

He jumped up and began attaching daggers to his sheaths.

"We can't take my friend as a hostage, even if she is Fae." Fiona stood up, wondering which of him was the real Christophe—the terrified boy who'd seen his parents murdered or the lethal warrior who so calmly spoke of abducting her friend.

Both, of course, the answer sounded in her heart. What he'd endured as a boy had forced him to develop the cold shell over his emotions. His warrior training had completed the job. She felt a moment's despair that she would ever be able to break through to the man inside those barriers.

"Lady Fiona?" Hopkins never sounded impatient, but this was edging close. "Your response?"

"Please tell her we'll be down soon and offer some refreshments or something, Hopkins."

"I have already provided tea and cakes, of course," Hopkins said, and she could have sworn he sounded offended.

The world might be in jeopardy, but nobody insulted Hopkins's hospitality or service. She smiled a little at the few constants she'd known in her life: the sun, the moon, and Hopkins.

"Thank you, Hopkins," she called out, but all she heard was a hmph sort of sound.

She and Christophe showered and dressed quickly, and in fewer than twenty minutes they were heading down the hallway to the stairs. The door to one of the guest rooms opened, and Denal stepped out.

"Good night's sleep?" Christophe asked, his eyes glowing a hot green.

Denal's eyes narrowed. He clearly took the comment as a rebuke. "I patrolled the house and grounds until five this morning, when Hopkins took over for me. Then I had a nap and then lunch and stuff with Declan and Sean. This was just a brief after-lunch catnap." His scowl transformed into a grin. "Speaking of Hopkins, that man can fight, for a human. He showed me a few moves that would disarm any intruder in seconds flat."

"Hopkins has special talents," Christophe said, relenting. "We're going to meet a friend of Fiona's who just happens to be Unseelie Court Fae."

Denal whistled long and low. "That's not good. Aren't we forming an alliance with the Seelie Court through Rhys na Garanwyn and his scary brother Kal'andel? They won't like it if we get tangled up with the Unseelie Court."

"We don't have any intention of getting tied up with them. We might tie *her* up, if she doesn't cooperate."

"Sounds fun," Denal said, grinning wickedly.

Suddenly, the hallway felt full of far too much testosterone, and Fiona made a break for the stairs. "No one," she said emphatically, "is tying Maeve up."

∼⌒⌒∼

Maeve sat on the white sofa, her elegant form arranged as if the furniture served only as a pristine backdrop to her emerald-green dress and her overall impeccable perfection. Fiona searched her features closely, looking for any hint of Fae, and suddenly a realization hit her.

"You've never aged," she blurted out. "We've been friends for ten years, and you look exactly the same now as you did when we met."

"As I will for the next thousand years, undoubtedly," Maeve replied, carefully placing her cup on its saucer on the tea table. "Of course your lover has told you what I am."

"Why didn't you ever tell me?" Fiona felt inexplicably hurt. "All of these years of friendship?"

"To what purpose? So that you could think of me as strange or different, or someone to fear? I have plenty of subjects and sycophants to do that. What I don't have—what I never had, until you—was a friend." She stood and took a step toward Fiona. "Our friendship has meant more to me than you can ever imagine."

"Stop right there, Fae," Christophe commanded from the doorway. "Don't touch her."

"Don't be ridiculous," Fiona snapped. She took the next step and hugged Maeve, as she'd done so many times in the past decade. "She's my friend."

Christophe growled, actually growled, and she didn't have to guess to know he was frustrated. Today was a great day, however, for him to realize he couldn't order her around. Never put off a difficult task, Hopkins always said.

Maeve hugged her back, hard, and then stepped away. Her dark eyes began to change, swirling with power, and she held her arms out to the side. An icy breeze carrying the scent of winter's deepest night flowed through the room and centered on Maeve. She seemed to grow taller where she stood, and the sensation of a deep, terrifying power swept through Fiona, raising the hair on her arms.

"Call me by my name, mortal," Maeve said, her hair lifting in the breeze her power had created. Her voice was thunder and darkness given sound, the compulsion contained within it so powerful that Fiona had to grit her teeth and lean into the breeze in order to be able to stand her ground against the urge to run or hide or kneel before her friend's unearthly beauty.

"I am Maeve na Feransel, Princess of the Unseelie Court, and you will bow to me or pay for your insolence," she thundered. Her voice shook the very walls and carried to Fiona the desperate urge to do just that, to bow and worship Maeve's beauty for eternity, but also the knowledge that it was no ordinary beauty. No, Maeve's power was a dark and biting thing; knives wrapped in velvet—swift cuts tempered by sweetness. Her chosen would bow to her and live in pain and ecstasy. Begging for more. Begging to escape. Not knowing which they wanted more.

The few seconds it took for Fiona to realize all of that were enough for her to break free of the compulsion, but another sound helped even more. Christophe. He was clapping.

"Bravo, *Fae*. Maybe for your next act, you can pull a rabbit out of your ass?"

Fiona winced at the crude words, and fury crossed Maeve's face, but it was followed quickly by amusement. Her glamour, if that's what it had been, vanished, and she was suddenly just Maeve, Fiona's friend, albeit with silver chips like ice floating in her eyes.

"Never out of my ass, mortal," she said. She laughed, and her laugh held as much compulsion as her glamour had. Fiona wanted to curl up in Maeve's laughter and bathe in it; revel in the joy of the Fae princess's happiness for the next fifty years or so.

"Wow. That's pretty powerful," she managed to say, breaking free of the compulsion again. "Is that how you always got out of tests at university?"

Maeve laughed again, but this time it was an ordinary

laugh, just like thousands they'd shared before. "You have no idea, Fee."

"What do you want?" Christophe's voice was pure menace. She glanced back to find his eyes glowing a hot green and both of his hands holding daggers.

"Well, I'd love to find out what exactly you are, Warrior," Maeve said. "But I'll settle for my original purpose in coming here. Fiona, darling, you need to get out of town for a while. Forget this plan of stealing the Siren. Far more powerful beings than I are in battle for that gem, and you have no chance against them."

Fiona suddenly had a hard time breathing. "I—what are you talking about? What's a Siren? Why would I—"

Maeve cut off her babbling. "Too little, too late. I know you're the Scarlet Ninja. Others know, too."

"What are you talking about, Maeve? Really, I think you drank too much champagne—"

Maeve waved a hand in the air, and an image of Fiona, dressed as the Scarlet Ninja, climbing out of the trellised upper window of the Trehorne estate, appeared for a few second before vanishing.

"Trehorne is Fae. You're lucky he found you amusing, or you'd be licking his boots in the Summer Lands for a few centuries, Fee."

Fiona abruptly sat down, not trusting her legs to hold her upright any longer. She'd thought she was so clever. So discreet. And who knows how many Fae not only knew her deepest, darkest secret, but found her *amusing*.

"Listen to me," Maeve said, suddenly urgent. Her features hardened into an expression of imperious command, and it wasn't difficult for Fiona to believe that she truly was a princess of her race. "The Siren has become known to us as a weapon of great power. It is said to have the ability to enthrall large numbers of shape-shifters simultaneously. This would be extremely valuable in the war for control of this world. The Seelie and Unseelie Courts have decided to join in to prevent the vampires from gaining complete domination. We wanted to stay neutral; the Moon Goddess herself knows we have enough discord on our own without becoming involved in this fight. But if the vampires succeed, they will turn all mortals into sheep on which to be fed, and we cannot allow total desecration of your race." She laughed and was again the friend Fiona had known for so long. "Plus, we need your kind. I simply cannot survive without Chanel lipstick."

"Who has it now?" Christophe stalked over to her. "Who has the Siren now?"

"Do you ask a boon of information, mortal?" Maeve licked her lips, suddenly almost feral. "I will gladly grant it."

"I ask nothing. I know how your kind works, and I have no desire to be indentured, or worse, to you," Christophe snarled.

"Oh, I could find something very pleasant for you to do," Maeve purred.

Fiona wanted to rip her eyes out.

Denal burst into the room. "Can you believe they're still playing that game? I think Sean is ahead, a zillion to one, but perhaps Declan is letting him win, since . . . oh. My apologies, Lady Fiona," he said, all but skidding to a halt. "I did not realize you were still entertaining your guest."

Maeve's eyes widened. "Oh, Fiona, you bad girl. Not one, but two of them? You must share, you know."

She crossed the room to Denal, and her walk was pure sex; a gentle sway making the most of her curves. Christophe watched her, and Fiona now wanted to scratch *his* eyes out.

If this was jealousy, it was exhausting.

"Why don't you come play with me for a while, handsome man?" Maeve's voice was honey and cream, whispering a tale of seduction older than time.

Denal was clearly entranced. He bowed deeply. "I am Denal of Atlantis, my lady, and you are?"

Christophe slammed his daggers back into their sheaths. "She is the Unseelie Court Fae I was just warning you about, and you are supposed to be undercover. Certainly not telling Unseelie Court princesses about Atlantis."

"Atlantis?" Maeve whirled around. "Oh, so that explains the smell and feel of your power. It has the resonance of the ocean crashing into the moonlit beach, sorcerer."

"I am no sorcerer, I am simply a humble warrior," Christophe said.

"Anything but humble, I think," she answered, a dark light in her eyes. "But enough of this. I will give you a gift, none beholden, none owed. I do not know who has the sword, but fear the vampires have acquired it. The sometimes-leader of this region is an ancient vampire named Telios. Find him and you may find what you seek, although it is true there are factions who oppose him."

"Why would you help us?" Christophe asked.

"Who says I'm helping you? Perhaps there is simply another I wish to oppose." She laughed, a sound like silvery chimes mixed with a child's laughter, and turned to Denal. "Come and play with me for a while, fair one."

"Yes," Denal said, taking her hand. "I will."

"No!" Christophe leapt toward him, but it was too late. Maeve cast a magical barrier between them that shimmered like a net of the finest gauze, if gauze were made from diamond dust.

"Willingly spoken, Atlantean," Maeve said. "Take care of Fiona or I will have more than words for you when next we meet."

With that, she and Denal vanished.

Fiona gasped and then fell back into her chair, her lungs suddenly unable to fill with air. She began relaxation breathing of long, slow inhales and exhales. "You know, I think that this was perhaps an inch or two beyond what my rational mind can take right now. Atlantis, magical gems, Fae royalty, and vampire attacks. Oh, and let's not forget sex in museums. Now my best friend is a Fae princess who just stole your best friend. I've had it. I'm done. I'd like my straitjacket now, please."

"He's not my best friend," Christophe said.

She let her head fall back on the chair and started laughing. "Right. Because *that's* the important part of what I just said."

"Is one of your new books in here?"

"You want to read? Now?"

He just stared at her, clenching his jaw, and not in a good way, so she sighed and pointed to the bookshelves. "Bottom shelf on the left. It would be bad form to display my books like some sort of trophy, of course."

"Hopkins?"

"Are you kidding? Hopkins would hang framed posters of all my covers in the foyer if I'd let him. That was a classic grandfather-ism, always going on and on about bad form. He's probably rolling over in his grave to think I'm anything as common as a children's book author."

He came up with a copy of *The Forest Fairies* and flipped through the pages as he walked over to her. Then he dropped the open book into her lap.

"There. On the right."

She glanced down at the painting she knew so well, then back at him, puzzled. "Yes? What about it?"

"What does he say? To the human child?"

She looked again, but she knew. She *knew*. She recited it from memory, not needing to see the words on the page. "Oh, no. Oh, no. He says, 'Come and play with me for a while, fair one.'"

"Yes, he does. And an assent, willingly spoken, means that your friend the Fae princess can do whatever she wants with Denal, for as long as she wants to do it." His face was grim, promising retribution and death.

Fiona shivered. "But she's my friend," she protested. "We can surely get him back."

"Yes, maybe. But who knows how many years will have passed for him? Time does not pass the same in Silverglen as it does here or in Atlantis. We Atlanteans do live a very long time, but it is nothing to the Fae. He could be a very, very old man by the time we see him again, even if she returns him to us tomorrow."

"What can we do?" She was the type to take charge, but she didn't know how to combat Fae tricks. Especially since only yesterday she hadn't even known that the Fae really existed.

"We go to Atlantis. I need to report in, and we need a way to fight on more than one front." He bent his head for several seconds and then looked up at her, his eyes burning pools of green. "If only the damn portal would respond to me. I don't understand why it won't."

Before she could reply, a shimmering oval of light appeared in the middle of the room, immediately in front of Christophe. He jumped back, giving it room to expand and lengthen.

Fiona slowly stood up and circled the apparition, not coming within five feet of it until she was close enough to take Christophe's hand. "Is that what I think it is?"

"Welcome to Atlantis," he said, tightening his grip on her hand. He pulled her forward, and together they stepped into the portal and fell through into a shimmering, cascading tunnel of light.

Chapter 24

Atlantis

Fiona called on every single ounce of manners, decorum, and British stiff upper lip she possessed to keep from allowing her jaw to hang open like some sort of unfortunate fish. Like, for example, the thirty-foot-long fish swimming by just outside the dome.

The dome that was quite clearly *underneath the ocean*.

The dome of Atlantis.

Christophe grinned and put his arm around her, which was actually quite welcome since her knees were a bit wobbly from the journey through the magic portal.

"So, Alice and the rabbit hole had nothing on this. Did you ever bring Lewis Carroll down here?"

"Not that I know of, but it would explain a lot, wouldn't it?" He laughed. "Which one of the guards would be Tweedle Dum?"

One of the guards, standing by the glowing portal, which was absolutely enormous on this side, put a hand on his sword. He looked to be in his mid-thirties, so he was probably five hundred. "Watch it, my friend. I still owe you for that fur-brained lummox comment."

Christophe shrugged. "I call it like I see it. Plus there were a few pints of ale involved. I'm not sure I can be held responsible for what I said."

The second guard, an older man with graying hair and a beard, threw back his head and laughed. "As I recall it, Christophe, you challenged every man in the place to darts and beat them all soundly."

"Except for me," the first guard said, grinning.

"Really?" Fiona said dryly. "There's something you're not good at?"

"Oh, please, my lady, don't inflate his ego any more than it already is," the older man said, groaning. "It won't fit under the dome before much longer."

Christophe tossed an energy sphere in his left hand. "You know, I can crush you like a bug, Marcus."

"Not till you take Alaric up on his offer and join the priesthood," Marcus replied, unruffled. "Until then I can whip your youngling behind with a trick or two."

"The priesthood?" Fiona stared at Christophe. "When were you going to tell me that?"

"Um, look at the fish!" Christophe pointed to the fish she'd seen earlier, or one of its mates. He suddenly looked a bit like Declan had when she'd caught him filching the biscuits before his tea. She put on her best stern big sister expression and he twitched a little.

"No time to discuss this now," he said, taking her arm. "Must get to the palace and report in."

He started walking, pulling her along, and then cast a dark glance back over his shoulder. "Marcus, I won't forget this."

The elaborate sound of a fake yawn floated through the air and Fiona had to stifle a laugh. "Marcus doesn't sound very afraid of you."

He kicked a white glossy stone on the path and then grinned. "Yeah. It's so hard to get good help these days."

"We're in Atlantis."

"I know."

"No, I mean, we're *in Atlantis*." She finally remembered to look up and leaned her head back as far as she could to stare into a cloudless, sunny sky.

"It's sunny."

"Usually is."

"No, you don't seem to understand what I'm saying." She clutched his arm and stopped walking. "We're in Atlantis and we're underneath a dome *underneath* the ocean, and it's *sunny*."

He bent down and kissed her so thoroughly that her fingers were somehow twined in his hair by the time he stopped.

"That was lovely, but it doesn't speak to the question," she whispered, trying to catch her breath.

"What question? Was there a question in there?"

She gestured around them with a sweep of her arm. "Every bit of this is a question. I'm going to be asking questions for hours. No, days. Years, maybe. This is amazing."

"Is this where I say 'I told you so' and you agree I'm the most wonderful man you've ever known?" He kissed her again.

"No, definitely not. There should be no 'I told you so' between us, ever," she decided. "However, you are quite wonderful. Now, where is that palace?"

She started walking again, only noticing after about ten steps that he wasn't with her. She turned and he still stood in place as if frozen, staring at her with the oddest expression on his face.

"Are you coming?"

"Yes." He caught up to her, and they walked down the path into a fantasy.

Everything, everywhere she looked, was impossible. Far too fantastical to be real. Even the trees and flowers in the garden were unlike anything she'd ever seen before, as if she'd stepped into the most secret imaginings of a master horticulturalist or possibly a Dr. Seuss book. Sweeps of vivid purples from an insane version of the color chart complemented shades of green from all ranges of the spectrum. Every color she'd ever seen and many she couldn't conceive of existing in nature—they were all represented in a fabulous palette that somehow, in some crazy way, was absolutely beautiful together.

And the scents . . . oh, the scents. Human perfume makers would go mad trying to take it all in. Each section of the garden carried its own distinctive bouquet of fragrance, shading from light to intense. By the time they reached the palace itself, she was nearly drunk just on the pure sensation of it all. Sight, scent, touch—for of course she'd had to touch and feel the petals on the blossoms, the rough or smooth bark on various trees—it all overwhelmed her until she believed she'd be completely unsurprised to see a white rabbit consulting its pocket watch at any corner.

"How can you ever bear to leave it? I would never spend a minute indoors if I lived here," she whispered, not wanting even the sound of her own voice to disturb the moment. "I have to set a book here. My fingers are itching for my paints. Oh, the children are going to love it. If there were only a way to bring these fragrances to the pages of a book."

He looked around as if seeing it for the first time. "It's pretty."

"Pretty? Are you kidding? This is the most glorious garden I've ever seen, and I've seen a lot of gardens. Even the queen's gardens at Buckingham Palace."

He laughed. "Well, if you think about it, this is a queen's garden, too. Or at least a high princess, soon to be queen. Atlantis is a lot older than England, too."

"I don't want to meet her, Christophe. I'm dressed like—like—"

"A lot like me, actually," a friendly female voice said from behind them.

Fiona turned to find a smiling woman with vivid reddish-gold hair walking toward them. She, like Fiona, was dressed simply in trousers and top. The woman held out her hand and Fiona shook it.

"Hey, Christophe, I thought you were in London. Oh, which I guess would explain the British accent of your friend."

Christophe bowed. "Princess Riley, this is Lady Fiona Campbell of Scotland by way of London."

Fiona wanted to crawl in a hole and pull the dirt in over top of her. "Oh, Your Highness, I'm sorry. I'm so pleased to meet you." She bowed her head a little, since curtseying would look ridiculous.

The princess laughed. "No bowing, no Your Highness–

ing, please. Just Riley. It is a true pleasure to meet you." Her dark blue eyes were glowing, not with magic but with simple joy.

"Truly a pleasure. You are most welcome," Riley said, her voice slowing. She turned to Christophe. "Really? Finally? Oh, I'm so happy for you!"

Fiona watched in utter shock as the high princess of Atlantis jumped across the space separating her from Christophe and threw her arms around him. "I knew it. I knew it, I knew it. Underneath that surly exterior, I knew there was a heart beating."

"Yes," Christophe said, raising one eyebrow and tentatively patting the princess on her back. "My heart grew three sizes today."

Riley pulled away and punched his arm lightly. "Funny guy. I have to quit letting Ven raid my Christmas video collection. You are all taking over my best lines."

She put her hand on Fiona's arm. "Let's go find something to eat and have a long chat, shall we?"

Fiona stared back at Christophe, but he just grinned and held out his hands, helpless against Hurricane Riley. So Fiona did the last thing she ever, in her lifetime, could have imagined doing. She went to have lunch with the princess of Atlantis.

❧～～❧

Christophe watched as Riley herded Fiona off toward the terrace, probably to stuff her with food and pump her for information. Riley was *aknasha*, and with her Gift of emotional empathy she had clearly picked up on his feelings for Fiona. Maybe now she could explain them to him. He felt like his insides were tangled up into knots of razor wire mixed with flowering vine. Every moment he spent with Fiona made him want to be with her more, but danger haunted his footsteps. Danger and violence. She'd already seen too much of it. He'd thought his heart would explode out of his chest when he saw what had happened to that vamp and realized that she must be the one holding the blessed water.

"Can't stay with her. Can't leave her. Where does that leave me?"

He felt Alaric's presence before the priest appeared, and he weighed the odds of getting away. Slim to not a chance in the nine hells, he figured.

"You do not have the Siren," the priest said even before he'd fully transformed into his corporeal shape. "And yet you have returned. With another human. Perhaps we can open a nature preserve for humans?"

"You are dangerously close to sedition, my friend," Prince Conlan growled, appearing next to Alaric.

The two of them were getting far too good at popping in and out. Made a man feel spied on. Christophe stood his ground, but bowed to his prince.

"Really? You're bowing to me when there's nobody here to see it? Are you feeling okay?" Conlan reached up a hand as if to brush Christophe's forehead.

"Bad habits must be wearing off on me," Christophe muttered, ducking.

"Bad habits? More bad habits? You're already a walking cornucopia of bad habits. One more might send you into the abyss, screaming," Alaric said.

"I'm the horn of the goat who suckled Zeus?" Christophe tilted his head. "I've been called worse, I guess."

"Nice. Greek mythology for ten points, ding, ding, ding," Conlan called out. "Next up, hot human women for twenty."

"Your wife might not appreciate you calling another woman hot, Your Highness," Christophe pointed out.

"Your Highness me again and I'll kick your ass. Also, last week she told me not to release Liam on unsuspecting women because he is, and I quote, 'hot enough to blister paint.' Don't worry about me and Riley, Christophe. We're doing just fine." The prince's wicked grin left Christophe in little doubt of that, but it was all far, far beside the point.

"Not that talking about women isn't fun, guys, but I have news and it's all bad."

"The Siren?" Alaric's eyes glowed a hot metallic green. "Tell me the Siren isn't in the hands of the vampires."

"I'd love to tell you that, but I can't. I don't know where it is, yet. And I can go one worse. Denal willingly went to the Summer Lands with a Fae princess."

"What?" Conlan smacked his hand against the trunk of a tree. "Our alliance with Rhys na Garanwyn is supposed to prevent this. I'm going to have his arrogant ass on a platter for this one."

"Leaving aside the truly nasty visual that creates, you can leave na Garanwyn out of this. Maeve na Feransel is Unseelie Court."

Dead silence. Alaric looked at Conlan. Conlan looked at Alaric. They both looked at him. Just when Christophe started to sweat, Conlan finally spoke.

"I think we'd better go inside and call Ven. We're going to need to do some planning."

"Fiona deserves to be in on it," Christophe said. "She has a stake in this, too."

"What are you talking about? What *stake* could a human female possibly have in one of the missing gems of Poseidon's Trident?" Alaric made no secret of his belief that only the Atlantean priesthood had a claim on the sea god's most precious object of power.

"It's kind of complicated," Christophe said. "But she's secretly a ninja, both vamps and Fae may want to hurt her, and the Unseelie princess who invited Denal to play? She's Fiona's best friend."

The priest and the prince both froze and stared at him for several long seconds.

"Yes," Conlan said finally. "We most definitely want to talk to your Fiona."

Alaric raised an eyebrow, as if waiting for Christophe to deny that she was *his* Fiona. When he didn't, the priest sighed. "And so another one, as Princess Riley would say, bites the dust."

Chapter 25

**Atlantis, the palace war room,
half an hour later**

Fiona swallowed past the lump of awe that seemed to have permanently settled in her throat. First she'd had fruit and juice with the princess of Atlantis, who offered her the use of the palace gardens for her next book any time she wanted, so long as she promised to autograph a book for Prince Aidan.

Then Christophe had come to find her, told her she was needed at a war council, and she'd walked through the palace—a classic concept of mythology turned historical fact. Now she was sitting at a scarred wooden table that was probably older than Scotland. Surrounded by unbelievably gorgeous men who were all cut from the same genetic cloth as Christophe. Tall, dark-haired, and muscular. High cheekbones and sensual mouths. Men to make women sit up and notice.

They were almost as devastatingly attractive as Christophe. She only hoped *devastating* wasn't the operative word.

"Shall I make the introductions?" Riley briefly rested a hand on Fiona's shoulder before taking a seat on the other side of the table. Without waiting for a response, she began, pointing to the various people as she named them. "Everyone, this is Lady Fiona Campbell, currently of Campbell Manor, Coggeshall. She also has a secret identity, but I think I'll let her tell you about that."

Fiona flushed, wondering why in the world she'd revealed her secrets so easily to Riley. There was something about the princess, though, that invited confidence.

"This is my husband, Conlan." A tall man with a distinct air of command bowed to Fiona.

"Your Highness." She tried to rise from her chair, which wasn't that easy with Christophe holding her hand, but Conlan shook his head.

"Please don't. We're pretty informal here, as you'll soon notice. Please call me Conlan, Lady Fiona."

"Just Fiona, please."

"This is Ven," Riley continued. "My partner in crime in the love of B movies. He's also Conlan's brother."

"Pleasure to meet you," Ven said, his eyes lit up with definite amusement. "Especially with Christophe."

Christophe narrowed his eyes but didn't release her hand.

"We spend way too much time in here, by the way," Ven grumbled. "I'm leaving after this to join Erin in Seattle at her witch's coven meeting."

Fiona's eyes widened until she was afraid they'd pop out of her head as Ven described what Erin was doing with her coven. Very powerful magic designed to aid the human rebels, from what she could glean from his brief description.

"His wife is a very powerful witch. Human," Christophe said quietly.

"Is it some kind of rule? That you marry humans?"

Christophe laughed. "No. Until Conlan met Riley, it was a rule that we couldn't."

Ven wound down his report and Riley pointed to a man, dressed all in black, who sat at the far end of the table. "That's Alaric, Poseidon's high priest and head of the Temple of Poseidon."

Fiona gasped. "But—that seat was empty. Are you Fae, too?"

"I certainly am not," Alaric said, his lips curled back from his teeth. "You may want to learn that to accuse an Atlantean of being Fae is a serious insult."

"You may want to learn that Scottish women don't appreciate being threatened," she snapped right back at him.

Alaric put his elbows on the table, rested his head in his hands, and groaned. "Here we go again. I just know it. Poseidon's balls, here we go again."

"I hate to point this out, but isn't that blasphemy?" Fiona said. "Perhaps you aren't the best person to lecture me about insults."

Ven grinned. "I think I'm going to like you."

It came to her that she was sitting with the crown princes and princess of Atlantis and she was insulting their god's highest priest. She felt about two inches high.

"I beg your pardon, Your—ah, Conlan. And yours as well, Alaric. I am feeling a bit overwhelmed right now, but it shouldn't make me forget the courtesies due to my hosts," she said.

Alaric flashed a smile that probably made sharks cry. "I liked you better when you were putting me in my place."

She laughed. "Noted."

"Perhaps we can get on to the point of this?" Ven said. "I'm thrilled Christophe finally became a real boy and found a girlfriend—hopefully you can keep his ass in line, Lady Fiona—but why are we in war council over it?" He aimed a mock glare at Fiona. "Is Scotland planning to declare war on Atlantis?"

She didn't know what to answer first, but her cheeks were burning over that "found a girlfriend" comment.

Christophe beat her to it. "My love life is none of your business, King's Vengeance or no. But if you'd like to meet me in the arena to discuss it—"

"Oh, pipe down," Fiona said. "Don't we have enough problems without you fighting amongst yourselves?"

He snapped his head around to glare at her, but then his gaze softened and he raised her hand to his lips and kissed her knuckles.

When she turned back to the table, every face but Riley's reflected varying degrees of shock. They were all staring at Christophe like he'd grown another head.

"Moving on," she said pointedly. "We've had a busy few days since we met in the Tower of London the night we both tried to steal the same jewel."

It took a few minutes for the questions and comments to quiet down, and then Christophe and Fiona took turns telling the rest of them everything that had happened since they'd met, leaving out nothing except their . . . personal interactions. At some point during their recounting, people brought food in, and they all fell to, but they kept at it, one talking while the other ate, and then trading off.

"There is, unfortunately, nothing at all we can do about Denal. He went willingly with this Fae, and is gone for as long as she chooses to keep him. Nothing short of a full-scale assault on Silverglen would gain us the slightest hope of even finding him, and that would put us at war with the Unseelie Fae. Possibly the Seelie Court, as well, since we'd be invading the Summer Lands," Alaric said.

Christophe slammed the table. "No. He was under my care. I should be the one to retrieve him."

Conlan shook his head. "Christophe, the truth is that Denal is a grown man and a warrior, much as we all still treat him as the youngling we met all those years ago. The Fae cannot tell a direct lie. If she said he spoke willingly, then she hadn't enchanted him. He wanted to go, and he went. Perhaps he simply needed a respite. The gods know he's been through enough lately."

Fiona noticed that Riley's cheeks turned pink, but the princess's eyes were sad.

"I wish—well, I wish I could have done something. I wish I'd known Maeve was Fae, or even known Fae existed, or . . . I don't even know what I wish," Fiona said. "I'm sorry my friend took yours. I hope she'll bring him back soon. She really is a kind person. I've known her for more than ten years. You can't fool somebody for that long."

"The Fae can keep up a simple deception for one hundred times ten years, or even more if they so desire," Alaric said.

"It's true, though, that the Fae was different with Fiona," Christophe said. "Talked about how much it meant to have a friend who liked her for herself and not for her position, that sort of thing. If Maeve na Feransel actually cares about any human, it is Fiona."

"Time will be the only answer to this dilemma," Conlan said. "We must move on to the matter of the Siren. We can assume it is in dangerous hands—but whose?"

"I'm betting the vampires," Christophe said. "The plan to enthrall shifters is in full swing in Europe, the same as everywhere else on the planet. What we know of the Siren is that it gives its wielder vast power over shifters and can even force them to shift back and forth between their animal and human shapes."

"Perhaps the shifters stole it," Riley said. "You've already mentioned the possibility that the Tower robbery could have been an inside job and that some of the Tower guard are wolf shifters. What if they took it, to keep it out of vampire hands?"

Alaric drummed his fingers on the table and then made a flicking motion with his right hand and sent a trail of tiny, perfect triangles of blue-green flame tumbling down the center of the table. They rolled over the fruit bowl and then vanished when they fell off the other end. Nobody else but Fiona paid any attention to them, so she guessed the little magic was the high priest equivalent of when she tapped her pencil while thinking.

"We must find it," Conlan said. "Christophe, you're obviously stirring things up, so you continue to do what you're doing and even step it up. How much help do you want?"

"Let me do the reconnaissance on my own, and then I'll call in the troops," Christophe said.

Fiona cleared her throat. "Excuse me, but why do you want this gem so badly? Are you planning to use it against the shifters, yourselves? I'm sorry, but I can't go along with that."

"Remember when I said that without the Siren, Atlantis couldn't rise to the surface again? I wasn't joking," Christophe said. "More than eleven thousand years ago, the elders of Atlantis took the Seven Isles to the bottom of the ocean. Before they did, they removed the seven gems of Poseidon's Trident and scattered them to the corners of the world. We've recently learned that unless and until we restore them, we're trapped here. If we attempt the magic to cause Atlantis to rise to the surface, we'll be destroyed."

Fiona looked from face to face. They were dead serious. "The actual Trident belonging to the sea god Poseidon? Brother of Zeus, *that* Poseidon?"

"Yes. He takes an active interest in Atlantean affairs, you might say," Christophe said wryly, tapping his shoulder. She remembered the tattoo.

"The question, I believe, is why *you* want the gem, Lady Fiona," Alaric said. "We know you're a thief, by your own account. Nevertheless, Christophe appears to hold you in high esteem. So please grant us the favor of explaining your own interest."

"Watch your mouth, priest," Christophe growled. "We never have gone head-to-head, but if you insult Fiona again, you're going to find out just how strong I've become."

She put a hand on his arm. "It's fine. He has a point. I mean, you need it for the safety of your whole continent, and I only wanted it for the money."

"The money you use to provide support for so many charities I can't even count them all," he said.

"Yes, I have heard that reported," Alaric said. Fiona wondered if there was anything the priest didn't hear about or know. The man was scary.

"I have also heard that the Scarlet Ninja only donates a sum equal to precisely half the value of any stolen item. So what do you do with the rest of the money? I imagine you have a very nice home." Alaric opened his hand and an image of Campbell Manor appeared in the air.

Christophe shot up out of his chair, but Fiona grabbed his hand before he could go after Alaric. "Stop. Please."

He slowly sat back down. "You don't have to answer any of this, if you don't want to. You're a guest here—my guest—not a prisoner to be interrogated."

She leaned up and kissed him. "No, it's okay. I'd wonder, too, if I were them." She turned to address Alaric and the rest of the group. "Fifty percent of the value is correct. Of course, from any fence, even my most trusted ones, I'm lucky to get sixty percent of an object's recorded value. In theft, as in the corporate world, there are unfortunately a great many middlemen."

"And the rest?" Conlan asked gently. "To support yourself and your family?"

She shook her head. "No. I have never once kept a single penny of any proceeds from one of the Scarlet Ninja's heists. There are many charities we support that are desperately in need of funding but they can't accept money if they know it comes from the proceeds of crime. Those, we funnel through my offshore accounts that my computer genius of a brother and my very talented butler assure me are virtually untraceable. Of course, a few others are happy to receive anything the Scarlet Ninja has to offer, and they appreciate the intrigue of it all. They count our donations, given through intermediaries, as anonymous and laugh all the way to the bank."

"I knew I liked you," Riley said, smiling across the table at her. The princess glanced over at Alaric. "She's telling the truth. Her emotions reflect nothing but absolute sincerity."

Fiona blinked, startled. "But I thought you were human?"

"You, too, are human, but have a secret Gift, don't you? Mine is emotional empathy, or what the Atlanteans call being *aknasha*. I can read emotions. My sister can, too." Riley's smile held a hint of sadness. "I miss her. She'd like you."

"My brother would like you, too," Fiona assured her. "Actually, he'd go stark raving mad with excitement over all this. I'd love to be able to bring him someday. Hopkins, too."

"Your butler?"

"He has been like a father to me since my own died," Fiona said. "He's an amazing man."

"Keeps threatening to shoot me, though," Christophe said.

"I like him already," Alaric said.

"Why the Scarlet Ninja?" Riley asked.

"I don't exactly know how to explain it. I guess I've never said any of this out loud before." Fiona thought for a little while, took another drink of water, and continued. "I want— no, I need—to help restore to the people of Great Britain a sense of hope. The prosperity we enjoyed before the vampires declared themselves."

"That's a lot to take on all by yourself," Conlan said quietly.

"One person can make a difference," she said. "Especially if each one of us determines to be that person."

"Amen," Riley said. "That's what I had to believe when I was a social worker, or I would have given up in utter despair."

"Turns out that the majority of the aristocracy have some vampire branches of the family tree. In retrospect, it makes a lot of sense. As far as I know, we didn't, but not for my grandfather's lack of trying. He was still trying to bribe his contacts to turn him when he was murdered. I have the feeling they didn't want him around for all eternity." She shuddered. "He was a horrible man."

"So when the vampires revealed themselves, you were suddenly back to the bad old days where lords and ladies ate off gold plates and drank from jeweled goblets while the peasants starved and died in the streets?" Alaric's eyes were shadowed.

She wondered briefly if he'd seen any of those bad old days in person, but she wasn't about to ask him.

"Yes. That's exactly it," she said, holding up the sturdy but plain glass that held her water. The same type of glass that the princes, Riley, and the high priest had at their place settings. The plates were simple stoneware, although she recognized neither the stone nor the glaze.

Riley caught the direction of her gaze. "Our housekeeper does try to insist we use the special dishes sometimes, but we're not very fancy," the princess admitted.

"Social worker? So you weren't always a princess."

Riley laughed. "Oh, heavens no. Getting used to the palace and servants has been a trial for me and them. You should have heard how the cook scolded me when she caught me doing my own dishes after we had a midnight snack."

Fiona was fascinated. She'd never had the opportunity to wash a dish in her life. "Did you stop doing the dishes?"

"Yes, but I worked a deal that I can cook our own dinner at least once a week, and I get to throw a big bash once a month and everybody has to come. House staff, guards, everyone." She grinned at Fiona. "I usually make the warriors clean up."

"That sounds so lovely," Fiona said wistfully. "Our staff

won't eat with us. Not from any class issue, I think their lives are just too busy. Sometimes it gets lonely."

"But not now," Christophe said, squeezing her hand.

"No. Not recently," she said, smiling at him.

"Your grandfather worked with vampires? Was he a thief?"

"Yes, although he called it business. His corrupt dealings with vampires in Scotland, long before they ever outed themselves to the rest of the world, got my father killed. A revenge plot, Hopkins finally told me, years later. Grandfather stole money from vampires, can you imagine?"

Christophe raised his eyebrows.

"Right, yes, I see where you're going, but I have anonymity and some measure of recourse," Fiona answered his unspoken question. "Now that vampires have proclaimed themselves citizens of the European Union, they have to follow our laws. Back then, they killed with impunity, and they used my father to prove a point to my grandfather."

She realized her voice was trembling, and she took another sip of water. "They were fools. He didn't care that my father was dead. He only cared that he lost everything else. They took it all away, and then they killed him, too. They probably would have killed me and Declan, too, but Hopkins took us away and hid us. After they killed Grandfather and had stolen all of his lands and money, they didn't care about a couple of kids all that much, I guess."

"Where was your mother?" Christophe's voice was unbearably gentle.

"She died when Declan was born." She saw a reflection of her own grief in his eyes and realized that his empathy and sympathy ran far deeper than the surface, since his own past had been visited by the same horrible tragedy. "She left the house in trust for us through Hopkins. She knew enough before she died to realize that Grandfather would find a way to steal it out from underneath us if she didn't."

"So you became the Scarlet Ninja, and you've spent your lifetime stealing back everything they took from you," Christophe said, touching her cheek. "But you give it all away. How can you possibly be real?"

She looked deep into his eyes, and everyone else in the room vanished from her awareness. Only he and she remained, captured in a crystalline moment of perfectly shared understanding. "I feel that way about you," she whispered. "It's like you stepped out of my dream of a hero and came to life just for me."

Someone cleared his throat and the moment was broken. She raised her chin and looked, in turn, into every pair of eyes at the table. "I have made a name for the Scarlet Ninja. A thief, true, but one who preys on the evil and the vile. Well, to be honest, occasionally, I borrow things just for fun and to keep the authorities guessing."

"The Raphael?" Christophe grinned at her.

"Yes." She sighed. "It's on the schedule to be returned next month. I'm really going to miss that painting. Saint George is a kind of hero to me."

"We have a painting of his dragon around here somewhere," Alaric said casually. "I think the dragon lived a very long life."

Fiona opened her mouth, but then closed it again. No. Later. She was *not* asking about dragons now.

"But the sword, Vanquish? You planned to return that?"

"No, actually. I have some guilt about that, but I did plan to provide a perfect copy, or at least the best I could devise, for the display. It might not even have been noticed for a very long time. But so many people are starving right now, thanks to the worst unemployment rate we've ever had. So many are homeless, thanks to the vampires claiming ancient homesteads and tangling property up in the courts. People need help, and the sale of that sword was going to fund a huge number of programs."

"Including the whales," Christophe reminded her.

She blushed. "No, that was my personal money, remember? I only use the Scarlet Ninja's money for humanitarian causes. I have several animal charities that Fiona's Friends, my personal charity, supports."

"Fiona is a very successful children's book author," Christophe told the rest of them.

Riley smiled. "I know. She's going to autograph a book for His Royal Drooliness. I'm so excited to have her paint in the gardens here."

Alaric groaned for some reason, but said nothing.

"Thank you. I'm very honored and hope to have the chance to do that someday. But right now, I need to focus on getting my name cleared. The Scarlet Ninja stands for something. I've been a symbol of hope to a lot of hopeless people. I'm not going to let these thieves destroy that by portraying me as a murderer."

"We'll help ," Christophe said.

"If it doesn't interfere with our retrieval of the Siren. That is our clear priority," Alaric said.

Christophe slowly shook his head. "My priorities seem to have shifted. I will retrieve the Siren, but I will also help Fiona clear her name. I hope you'll all help me, but I'm doing this no matter what your decision."

"We cannot let you have the Siren, Fiona," Conlan said. "Your English queen only had the gem on loan, whether or not she knew it. The gem has waited more than eleven thousand years to return to us, and so it shall."

"I understand," she said hastily. "I wouldn't do anything that might harm you or Atlantis. Anyway, the diamond Christophe gave me will certainly fund my programs for more than a year."

"The diamond?" Conlan's face was twitching, as if he was trying not to laugh. "You gave her a diamond?"

"It was mine to give," Christophe muttered.

"Oh, my friend. It's going to be an interesting journey for you." Conlan lost the battle with himself and started laughing.

"It won't be easy," Christophe warned her, ignoring his prince.

"I hate to sound like a walking cliché, but nothing worthwhile ever is," she replied.

"Then we're done here," Conlan said, rising. "Riley and I have a baby to feed. Christophe, why don't you show our guest some of Atlantis before you have to return?"

"Just what I was thinking," Christophe said.

"Thank you. All of you," Fiona told them. "It's good to feel like I finally have allies."

"Oh, the more the merrier, certainly," Alaric said darkly. "Will there be more diapers? I love diapers."

Riley burst out laughing. "Ignore him. He gets a little moody sometimes."

As they all filed out of the room, Christophe pulled Fiona to him for a hug. "It's all going to work out."

She looked into his lovely green eyes and smiled. "I know. After all, what could defeat a team made up of an Atlantean warrior and a Scottish ninja?"

Chapter 26

Christophe watched Fiona as she wandered through the palace and the grounds, exclaiming over and over in wonder like a child. His facial muscles felt strained from the unfamiliar smiles. Everything held for her the joy of discovery, from the tapestries on the walls to the throne room to the kitchens. Even the taste of her first Atlantean blushberries, which she savored so sensuously that it made his cock harden in his pants.

He could tell by the way her eyes flew open and her cheeks turned pink that she remembered exactly where she'd heard the fruit's name before.

"Oh! You said—"

"Yes, I said," he agreed, stalking her around one of the smaller garden fountains. "I'd like to say it again. Would you like to make love in Atlantis?"

"Here?" She looked around, almost as if she were considering it, but then she shook her head. "No, of course not. What if someone came along and saw us?"

"They'd be jealous?"

Her lips curved. "Funny, but no."

"I was thinking my rooms, Princess."

"Don't call me that. There are too many princesses in our lives. Riley and now Maeve. It's just odd."

"Neither of them are *my* princess." He pulled her in for a long, deep kiss and only released her when they were both breathless. "My rooms?"

"Your rooms."

They didn't run, as much as he would have liked to, but walked at a barely more than normal rate of speed up the staircase and through the hallways of the palace, until they came to the warriors' wing and threw open the door to Christophe's suite of rooms.

"What do you think?" He figured it wouldn't be very impressive to her. After all, she lived in a mansion, and he only had a few rooms. But they were pretty nice rooms, after all. He did live in a palace. The view from the balcony was stupendous.

She ran across the room and opened the glass-and-crystal-paned doors. "Oh, Christophe. This is absolutely magnificent."

He followed more slowly, enjoying the view of her lovely round bottom as she bent over the waist-high barrier and looked down. "The gardens are lovely from here, too. What a wonderful place to live. You are so lucky."

He fitted his body against hers from behind and put his arms around her. "You live in a mansion, my ninja. You're pretty lucky yourself."

"We survived a vampire attack, too," she reminded him. "We're both pretty lucky."

"That's skill. Not my first vampire attack." He kissed his way down the side of her neck, enjoying her shivers, and then he slowly reached around in front of her and unfastened her silk trousers.

"Christophe," she gasped, capturing his hand. "What are you doing? Someone could see."

"Not unless they can see through walls, and there's not a single recorded incidence of that in the history of Atlantis." He pointed to the walls dividing his balcony from its neighbors and then to the solid barrier in front, which covered her completely from toes to just under her waist.

"Nobody can see me do this, for example," he whispered

in her ear as he slid his hand down her silken belly to find the nest of curls between her thighs. "Or this," as his hand moved even lower, and he traced her clitoris ever so lightly with the tip of his finger.

Her sharply indrawn breath was her only reply, so he nibbled the edge of her ear and whispered a few suggestions as to what he'd like to do to her. She stood perfectly still, except for pushing her hips back until his cock was nestled against the sweetly firm cheeks of her still-covered ass.

"I want to hold your breasts in my hands."

"No, someone might see," she said breathlessly. "We should go inside."

"We will. But first I want to watch you come in the bright magic of Atlantean sunlight." With that he slid his fingers farther down, until they touched her liquid heat. He coated his finger in the slick wetness and then rubbed up and along her clit again, causing her to buck against him.

"Christophe, I can't—we can't—"

"Oh, yes, we can," he said, tilting his head to take her mouth. He kissed her long and hard while his fingers continued their play, until she started shaking in his arms.

"Now, please, I want you inside me," she whispered against his mouth.

"Your wish is my command." He unfastened his own pants and then pulled hers down as he leaned forward slightly, bending her just the tiniest bit over the rail.

"Now, you said," he reminded her. He plunged the thick head of his cock into her silken sheath and she bit her lip against crying out. Then, slowly, ever so slowly, inch by blissful inch, he entered her, his body barely moving, until his cock was so deep inside her that he felt like part of her. He stood perfectly still, unmoving, as she clenched around him, and then his fingers resumed their rhythmic stroking on her swollen clit.

"You have to move," she whispered. "You're driving me crazy."

"That's the idea," he said, alternating pressure with his fingers. Firm, then gentle. Rapidly, then slowly.

"Oh, no. There's someone coming." There was real panic

in her voice, so Christophe reminded her that nobody could see her from the waist down, especially from the ground below.

"Hail, Christophe," the man called up. It was one of the palace gardeners. "You owe me another chance at darts."

"Soon," he promised, waving to the man in hopes he'd get the hint and move on. Which he did, thank Poseidon.

Fiona collapsed forward onto her folded arms, which rested on the balcony ledge. "I can't believe that I—that we—oh."

"Well, we didn't yet, but we're going to, now." He withdrew a little and then, grasping her hip with the hand not busy driving her to an exquisite madness, he thrust into her, hard. "I told you nobody can see you."

"Of course. Nobody can see me. Why didn't I think of that?"

A split second later, she disappeared, for all intents and purposes. He stood holding her ass, his cock buried in her warm, sweet heat, but all he could see of her was a swirl of light and shadow.

It was simultaneously the oddest and most erotic experience of his life.

"I won't come without being able to see your beautiful face, but that doesn't mean I can't make an invisible woman have an orgasm right here on my balcony," he said, teasing her, his fingers stroking harder now.

She bucked against him, frantic now, trying to get him to move, but he laughed and held her still against him, barely pulsing his cock in tiny movements inside her. The rhythm of his motion matched that of his fingers, and it took only seconds more for her to reach her climax, spasming around his cock like a velvet glove. He nearly came then himself, but instead he lifted her by the bottoms of her thighs so that he was carrying her in almost a seated position in front of him. He made it to the bed in seconds and gently lowered her to her hands and knees and then took a firm grip on her hips and released the power he'd been holding back.

He drove into her, over and over, and she let go of her shadows so he could see every gorgeous inch of her. Her luscious ass rocked with his motion and she'd thrown her head back so her hair trailed along the curve of her pale, perfect back.

"More?" He sped up, thrusting harder and faster. "Do you want more of me?"

"All of you," she said breathlessly. "I want all of you."

He bent down and pressed a kiss to her spine. "I want all of you, too, Lady Fiona Campbell."

She cried out, coming again, and he thrust into her, over and over, riding the wave of her orgasm to his own. They collapsed in the bed, exhausted and safe, and she almost immediately fell asleep. He, however, lay awake for a long time, again contemplating the irony of humanity, his most hated foe, giving him such a gift.

Chapter 27

Atlantis, the royal suite

Conlan smiled to see his son mash banana slices into his own hair. "He's clearly a brilliant child."

"Hey, buddy," his princess and bride said, pulling him down for a kiss. "You did the same thing at your age, bet on it."

"I'd do the same thing now, if I thought it would relieve some of this worry."

Riley nodded. "Denal?"

"All of it. Denal, the vampires, the impending war, the jewels for the Trident." He ran a hand through his hair, wondering when he'd pull enough of it out to go bald. "Hells, what *isn't* going wrong? Will I ever be able to live up to the demands of being king? Alaric keeps pushing for the coronation but I don't feel like I'm even handling the high prince job well yet."

"Do you have to become king?"

"You mean could I abdicate?" He smiled at her. "I tried that once, for you, remember? Poseidon wouldn't let me go so easily."

"What about Christophe and Fiona? Does that worry you,

too, my handsome prince?" She cleaned up their sleepy son as they talked, so she could put him down for his afternoon nap.

"Should it? I don't know. What right do I have to meddle in the warriors' private lives? But he has been so close to the edge; so dangerous and out of control with his power. Is he even safe for her to be around?"

"Maybe only for her, but yes, she's safe with him. It's anyone who tries to hurt her I worry about," she said.

"They must find the Siren. All hope of Atlantis rising is lost without it."

"They'll find it. Now, come take a nap with us. Even high princes are allowed to rest with their family once in a while."

Conlan held his wife and son close while they slept, but his own eyes couldn't close, nor could his mind shut down. They were so close to retrieving all the jewels. Maybe he should send someone else. Christophe had always been . . . unpredictable.

And now this new element, this Scarlet Ninja—and the Unseelie Court Fae.

"I'll put the word out to na Garanwyn," he told his sleeping wife. "If the Fae are facing a civil war, the Seelie Court needs to know about it."

His tiny son belched, a huge noise for such a small boy. Conlan sighed and nodded. "I feel exactly the same way, Aidan. Exactly the same way."

Chapter 28

Campbell Manor, later that evening

Hopkins was standing in the middle of the floor when Fiona and Christophe stepped through the portal into her drawing room.

"Welcome home, Lady Fiona," he said. "Would you care for tea?"

She started laughing. "Only you, Hopkins. Only you would offer me tea when I'm stepping through a magic doorway."

"If it were my place, I would be asking where you've been for the past several hours. I might ask where Denal is. I might ask how you stepped through a ball of light to appear in the middle of the drawing room. But I won't ask any of it. So I repeat, would you care for tea?"

Only a slight reddening of his face and his exceedingly clipped tone gave away how worried he must have been, and she felt like an utter heel. She hugged him. He stepped away, but not before she saw the relief on his face.

"I do adore you, Hopkins. And I owe you an explanation. Why don't we have tea, and I'll tell you all about Atlantis. How is Sean, and where is Declan?"

"Sean is fine, healing rapidly. Sunday is his day off, of

course, so he's off with his friends somewhere. Declan is doing the same. I made up a story about you showing Christophe the sights of London when he asked where you were."

"Thanks. I wouldn't want him to worry, and I'm sorry I made you do so."

They followed Hopkins into the kitchen, and he set about making sandwiches while Fiona filled the kettle and put it on to boil. While they ate, she told him about Atlantis, and after the first thirty minutes or so, he finally quit treating her as if she were mad. Christophe sat silently, eating several sandwiches, and let her tell the story. A couple of times she caught him examining her as if she were a new species of butterfly and he a scientist. It was oddly disconcerting.

"I can hardly believe you were really in Atlantis," Hopkins said. "Maeve a Fae princess. Now, *that* I can believe. I always thought there was something off about her."

Christophe's expression darkened. "If she harms him, she will answer to me. I have little love for the Unseelie Court."

"I truly believe she won't," Fiona said.

"I hope you're right."

He didn't sound convinced, but to be honest with herself, neither was she. The Maeve who could hold such secrets so closely for so long wasn't the woman Fiona knew.

"I'd love to see it someday," Hopkins said. "I've long been a student of mythology—although, we'll have to reclassify, won't we? You've just changed everything. Fiction has become fact."

"The world should be used to that, after vampires and shape-shifters revealed themselves," Christophe said. "But we're not openly announcing anything until we can raise Atlantis to the surface to take its place in the world once more."

"It seems like a lot of people know," Fiona said doubtfully.

"Yes, but what can they say? Atlantis exists? It would show up as a tabloid story." Christophe shrugged and, standing, took the plates to the sink and turned on the faucet. "We still have to retrieve the Siren and two other gems before Atlantis can rise."

"I can understand your urgency," Hopkins said, jumping

up to help clear their few dishes. "Even after you gave us your proof, we didn't believe you. I'd so very much like to see it."

"That can be arranged," Christophe said, grinning. "Be nice to me and you'll get your chance."

"Then again, I've heard Morocco is an interesting place to visit," Hopkins replied, not missing a beat.

Fiona laughed at the two of them and crossed over to the sink where Christophe was washing their dishes. She picked up a hand towel and began to dry them.

"Lady Fiona," Hopkins said, sounding shocked. "A lady does not do dishes."

"You know, that's silly," she said. "I have to eat. Why should I be exempt from cleaning up after myself? If you really want to help, will you please figure out another disguise as good as the Uma Thurman look? We're heading out to a werewolf pub, and this time we're taking the Ducatis."

Chapter 29

The Melting Moon

Christophe parked the motorcycle next to Fiona's and removed his helmet. There was something very sexy about her on a bike. Raw power controlled by a delicate, graceful woman.

Come to think of it, that came uncomfortably close to describing their relationship. He was certainly acting completely out of character lately. Wanting to actually *sleep* with a woman; his reluctance to leave her; even defying Conlan and Alaric—

Nah. That last was pretty normal.

Her eyes sparkled, framed by long, lush lashes and sparkly makeup. She looked like a celestial fairy from a bedtime tale. A wicked one. She carefully shook out her hair.

"I like you as a redhead. Hot and spicy," he said, his voice pitched low.

She flashed a sexy "come hither" smile. "Really? Tell me more, big boy."

"Smile at me like that again, and you'll see how big I can get," he growled. "Everything about you makes me hard. I'm worse than a youngling with his first woman."

She tucked her helmet under her arm and put a hand on his chest. "I like it." She kissed him, but he forced himself not to linger over the taste of her lips. Not in the parking lot of a shape-shifter pub.

"I've never been here before," she said, looking up at the pub's sign. A full moon, painted a stark white against the dark wood, dripped a single crimson drop onto the words "The Melting Moon." "Beautiful sign. I wonder how old it is. Pub signs have become a hot collectible, did you know that? Some of the old names are so evocative, like this one. I always like the ones with animal names and figures. The White Boar, the Blue Sow—"

"The Red Dragon," he said, smiling at a distant memory.

"Oh, you've been in a few pubs in your centuries, haven't you? It's hard to remember that you're so ancient." She dodged when he tried to grab her.

"I'll show you ancient later when I get you alone and naked."

"Now, there's a promise I like," she said, putting her arm through his. "Come on, let's go and meet some werewolves. Maybe we'll meet an American one, here in London. Get it?"

He didn't understand why she started laughing when he shook his head.

"I'm not sure there will be any American wolf shifters here, and they prefer that term, by the way. The word 'werewolf' is a grave insult. Most stay near their home packs."

She laughed harder, and then she started humming something about werewolves in London. He was beginning to realize he understood far less about women than he'd ever suspected.

The first thing he noticed when they walked into the pub was the spicy, almost pungent scent of wolves. Lots and lots of wolves. The crush of bodies in a fairly small space made him twitchy, but they needed information and he'd learned that this was the home base of the London pack alpha and her mate.

"Are you sure this is the right place?" Fiona had to speak almost directly into his ear to be heard over the din of conversation and the pounding beat of rock music. Her warm breath on his ear made his cock twitch, and he firmly told it to behave.

First he was talking to pigeons, now body parts. This was not good.

"I smell human." A shifter who looked about the size of an orca lurched over from the bar to stand in front of Fiona, swaying and drunkenly leering at her. "Want to give me a little taste, sweetkins?"

She took a step back and tilted her head to look all the way up into the drunk's face. "Right, then. Definitely the right place."

Christophe sighed. "I knew I'd wind up in a fight if we came here, but I didn't think it would happen this early."

"I knew this was too much cleavage," Fiona said, peering down at the creamy expanse that her very low-cut shirt exposed.

"Oh, Princess. I hear the words 'too much cleavage,' but my brain doesn't understand the meaning." He winked at her, so hopefully she got that he was kidding and not turning into a lecherous pig. Although lately, around her . . .

"I'm taking your woman, funny boy," the shifter mumbled. "Wanna play with the pretty human."

"I beg your pardon," Fiona said, all haughty lady of the manor. It was kind of hot, especially combined with her sex-kitten disguise. "Please address your comments to me. The human does not want to play with you. Be on your way."

She made shooing motions with her hands, and Christophe sighed again. Like waving a red flag in front of a Minotaur. The shifter, predictably, snarled, showing a tangle of yellowed and broken teeth.

"Dental care, my friend. The great blessing of the modern age," Christophe advised him.

The enraged shifter turned his attention away from Fiona, fisting his enormous hands. If he landed a punch, he might knock Christophe into next week. Best not to let him land a punch.

He stepped into the arc between the man's burly arms, and before the angry drunk could form his next thought, Christophe had one dagger digging its tip into his throat and a second into his balls. The shifter made a noise between a yelp and a squeak, higher-pitched than Christophe would have thought the hulking man could utter.

"You'll leave the pretty human alone now?"

The shifter nodded carefully, since his motion caused the dagger to slice a bit of the flesh from his neck. "Just funning," he muttered as his blood trickled down his skin.

Christophe moved back and out of arm's reach before returning his daggers to their sheaths, being sure to let everyone in the crowd gathering around them see the many weapons strapped to his body. Then, just for extra insurance, he channeled enough power to cause his eyes to glow a bright green.

The crowd around him jostled to get away.

"We don't want any trouble, sorcerer," one of them said. She was a tall female, curvy and muscular both, leaning against the bar. Her dark hair hung in a thick fall to her hips, and the promise of a wicked sensuality shimmered in her eyes. "Maybe you should go somewhere else to drink this night. Or at least let the human leave and you can stay and play with me."

Fiona captured his hand and stared defiance at the shifter. "I think not."

Amusement warred with anger on the woman's face, but she finally settled on the first. Smiling at them, she indicated they should follow her. She made a gesture to the bartender, who nodded, and then she strode across the floor in a way that probably made every male in the place thank the gods for the invention of pants. If Christophe hadn't met Fiona, he would have been one of them. Now, strangely enough, the shifter female's rolling hips didn't cause him even a twinge of desire.

She sat at a large table in the back of the pub, one that had been completely empty in spite of the large crowd. A slender man walked out of the shadows from a back room and silently joined her. She indicated the chairs across from her.

"Please. Sit."

Christophe moved one chair so its back was to the wall as much as possible and sat, pulling Fiona into the chair to the left of him so anybody in the crowd who tried to get to her would have to go through him first.

"Fee, this is the alpha and her mate," he said.

The alpha laughed; a deep, throaty sound of sex and pain and pleasure. "Correct. Most mistake me for my mate's tame lapdog."

"They're fools, then," Christophe replied honestly.

She laughed again and extended a hand. "Lucinda. This is my mate, Evan."

He shook her hand. "Christophe, of Atlantis. My m—uh—*partner*, Fiona."

Damn, but he'd come close to saying the words "my mate, Fiona."

Fiona glanced at him as if she'd noticed his slip, but she said nothing.

Evan wasn't as courteous. "Claim her before another does, my friend." He had a slight accent. Spanish, perhaps.

"I don't know you well enough to be your friend yet," Christophe replied evenly. "And we do things a little differently in Atlantis than you do in Pack hierarchy."

"Maybe I'm the one who should claim *him*," Fiona said, clasping her fingers around his on the table.

"You have bite, little human," Lucinda said. "I almost feel like I recognize you, but you've never been in my pub before."

"No, I haven't. But it's a lovely place," Fiona said, gracious as usual in spite of her circumstances. "I'll be sure to tell my friends about it."

"Be sure not to," Lucinda said dryly. "They might wind up as lunch. Now. Christophe of Atlantis, tell us why you are here, and what you want. I'd also like to hear if you have any American friends we may know."

He knew what that meant. Squeezing Fiona's arm so she didn't start singing that ridiculous song again, he smiled at the alpha and her mate. "Lucas of the Yellowstone Pack sends you his fond regards."

"Does he?" She tapped a very long, crimson-tipped nail on the table. "Just who is he?"

Christophe grinned. "Lucas said if you asked me that, I should remind you that he rescued one of your children who'd strayed too near a geyser on your vacation."

Lucinda smiled—a real smile—and the force of her power

washed over his own. "Stupid pups have no sense at that age. Now that all of them are teenagers or grown, I long for those innocent days."

She turned to Fiona. "Do you have children?"

"Not yet, but I hope to one day," Fiona said. He could tell she found the question to be overly personal and slightly offensive, but she presented a calm, smiling face to their hosts.

"Did you hear that, sorcerer?" Evan laughed and threw an arm around his mate's shoulders. "Are you ready to be a daddy?"

"Have I done anything to offend you?" Christophe was getting a little tired of the man's attitude. Sure, being mated to the alpha female must be exhausting, especially with Lucinda's obvious power, but there was no need to vent his anger all over Christophe.

"Not yet," Evan replied, a dull red light glowing in his pupils. "I'm sure you will before you leave. I don't like sorcerers."

"Neither do I, fur face. Not a sorcerer. Deal with it."

Fiona sighed. "Really? Is everything about proving who possesses the bigger man parts?"

Lucinda roared with laughter. "Man parts? Oh, that is priceless, human. Now tell me what you need while I'm still amused."

"We are trying to find out information about the theft of Vanquish," Fiona said. "Anything you might know could help us out, and we'd really appreciate it."

The alpha stared at Fiona in disbelief. "Anything we might know? You'd *appreciate* it? You dare ask us of Vanquish when it contains the Siren?"

Evan growled, deep in his throat, and Christophe got a sudden impression of predators stalking squealing prey. He smiled, a simple baring of his teeth, and Evan subsided. Wolves weren't the only predators who hunted in the night.

"Have you heard the rumors of what that gem can do?" Lucinda snarled the words. "Enthrall my kind, perhaps permanently. What kind of a death wish do you have to come in here and tell me you're looking for it?"

"That's one of the reasons we're after it," Christophe said.

"We in Atlantis don't want it to fall into vampire hands any more than you do. If you know Lucas, then you know about our mission."

"Protect humanity, noble sacrifices, whatever." Lucinda shrugged. "Nothing to do with me or mine. I have heard nothing of the ones who took it, but if I do, they will regret the day they first conceived the idea. This Scarlet Ninja is already a dead man, though he doesn't know it yet. If, to compound his transgression, he is working with the vampire Telios, we will make sure his death takes hours. Perhaps days."

Christophe very carefully did not so much as glance at Fiona.

Lucinda planted her hands on the table and leaned forward, all crouching, feral fury. "If you discover anything, you will tell me about it. Immediately. You can consider yourselves emissaries of the wolves from here on out."

Fiona shook her head. "With all due respect—"

"Anyone who uses that phrase is generally going to be quite disrespectful, I've found," Evan said.

"I don't intend to be. I simply want to say that we all want the same thing—the Siren off the market. It's an Atlantean gem and belongs to them. We're going to find it and restore it to its original place of honor. A strictly ceremonial thing, of course. Since there are no shifters in Atlantis to be enthralled, you have nothing to worry about." Fiona smiled and nodded as if everything were now solved.

"Princess, life isn't like one of your books. You can't tie everything up neatly with a bow all the time," Christophe said, casting a resigned look at Lucinda. "Now we're in trouble?"

"Now you're in trouble."

The first wave of shifters came at them hard, fast, and low. Christophe barely had time to pull his daggers again before they were on him, but they ignored him and went for Fiona first. There were far too many, and they were far too fast.

Christophe shot out of his chair so fast it flew through the air and smashed into the wall behind him, but Evan dove for his legs and knocked him flat against the table so hard Christophe's head bounced off the wood. The two shifters in the front wave of the mob coming after Fiona grabbed her and yanked her away before Christophe could reach for her. He roared out his fury and denial, and the sound took shape into a glowing ball of forbidden fire, the flames as scarlet as Fiona's costume.

Flames licked the edge of the table and Christophe took advantage of the distraction to slam his elbow back into Evan's face. The shifter howled as the force of the blow caught him in the nose and mouth and flung him back and off Christophe.

Lucinda jumped up, the predatory grin on her face fading into a scowl at her mate's pain.

"Release her, or I'll burn this whole damn place and everyone in it to the ground," Christophe snarled, standing his ground. The shifters who held Fiona could kill her before he could reach her, which neutralized any potential move.

"I don't think so, sorcerer," Lucinda said, pointing to Fiona. "If you so much as blink, they will rip her throat out. Now make your pretty fire go away."

Christophe analyzed every option available to him in the space of a single breath, but the damn alpha spoke the truth. She had the upper hand, for now. He extinguished the fireball.

"Now you're in a *great deal* of trouble," Lucinda said, and then she started laughing.

Chapter 30

Fiona had the craziest urge to give in to the giggles. The entire situation had a distinct evil villain vibe to it, and she half expected Bond, James Bond, to show up any minute and get Lucinda to launch into a monologue about her plans to take over the world. Didn't look like that was going to happen, though. Instead, Fiona drew a deep breath and analyzed the situation.

Chance of escape? None.

Chance of winning a battle, against these odds? None. Or at least none before she'd be dead and bleeding out on the floor. Christophe might be able to fight them or escape, or both.

Chance of negotiating? Better than average.

"Lucinda—"

Somebody smacked the back of her head, hard.

"Speak to our alpha with respect, human. You're not fit to say her name." The words came out in an animalistic growl, but she had no problem understanding either their meaning or their menace.

"I do apologize, but that is how she introduced herself to

me. Is there a form of address you'd prefer I use?" She smiled calmly, as if this were any cocktail conversation in any drawing room in the country.

"You've declined my very reasonable request," Lucinda said, stalking her way across the room. "I don't care what you call me, you're in trouble."

Christophe roared out a warning, and Evan, his nose crooked and bleeding, smashed a chair into the back of Christophe's head. Christophe went down hard but was back up in a few seconds.

"If you touch her, I will kill you all," Christophe said, his voice carrying throughout the room. His eyes burned like deep green pools of molten emerald and flashed a warning or a signal to Fiona. She had no idea what he was trying to convey, not that there was much she could do about it anyway. She was surrounded by drunken, angry, excited, and possibly hungry shifters. That last adjective alone accounted for the shiver of terror trailing its cold fingers down her spine.

"You should watch your mouth, warrior," Lucinda replied. "She will be dead before you can make your first move."

Fiona could tell by the way Christophe clenched his fists that he knew as well as she did that it was the truth.

"Please let them entertain us, my mistress," one of the shifters called out to his alpha. "If we are not amused, they can be food."

"I can be very entertaining," Fiona said quickly.

A few of the shifters laughed, and she smiled at them. Diplomacy never hurt, though she didn't think they'd go as far as disobeying their alpha. Lucinda was the key.

"You offer, then?" Lucinda smiled. Her mouth surely hadn't had so many teeth in it before.

"No," Christophe shouted. "She doesn't understand. Take me."

"Too late, Atlantean. Offered and accepted," the alpha replied, never taking her eyes off Fiona. "Well, little human, which will it be? Fight or fuck?"

Fiona gasped. "I beg your pardon?"

"Little too late for that. Now you entertain my people. If

they decide you've done a good enough job of it, we let you go. Do you choose to fight or fuck? Either will suffice. Pain or pleasure?"

"I don't—I—who would I have to fight?" Delay. Keep Lucinda talking. Fiona's heart was about to beat out of her chest, and she was sure the shifters surrounding her could hear it, since they were crowding closer and closer, some snuffling at her like . . . animals.

Brilliant, Fee. Of course, like animals.

Evan shouted out a laugh. His nose seemed to be healing already. "Guess you're not satisfying her, Atlantean, if she'd choose to fight a wolf shifter rather than fuck you for our viewing pleasure."

"I'll only be satisfied when I have a wolf-skin rug in front of my fire," Christophe said, scorn dripping from his voice. "Why don't you fight me, if your Pack wants some real entertainment? Or is the little puppy afraid to come out from behind Mommy?"

Evan launched himself at Christophe again, but Lucinda made a hand gesture and several of the shifters grabbed him and held him back.

"Evan," Lucinda said patiently. "He's trying to provoke you into fighting him so the debt is paid and we can no longer accept his mate's offer. Try to think with your brain instead of your . . . man parts."

She had the effrontery to wink at Fiona, as though they were just gals in on a lovely joke. Fiona suddenly, fiercely, wanted to smash the smile off the woman's face. Naturally, it would be her last act on the earth, since shifters were far stronger than humans, but perhaps the wave of personal satisfaction would be worth it.

"I have another idea," she said instead. "A counteroffer, if you will. I will entertain you in my own way, with a story. The tale of what happened when your own moon goddess came to Scotland and fell in love with a Highlander."

Lucinda tilted her head. "And if I accept and we are not entertained by your story?"

"Then I surrender gracefully and buy drinks for everyone

in the pub, which, you must admit, would also be entertaining." Fiona kept her head raised high but didn't stare directly into Lucinda's eyes. She'd read somewhere about displays of dominance in the shifter world, and she didn't want to appear to be challenging Lucinda's authority in her own pub. She and Christophe were in enough trouble already.

Lucinda appeared to be at least considering the idea. One of the younger females surrounding Christophe spoke up.

"Mother, if you please, I have not heard this tale and would like to collect it for my book. I would ask as a boon to me that you allow the human to tell her story."

Mother? Lucinda in no way looked old enough to have this grown woman as a daughter. Fiona knew the shifters lived longer lives than humans, but she hadn't realized they retained their youthful appearance for so long.

When Lucinda didn't immediately dismiss the idea, Fiona allowed herself to hope, but said nothing further. She'd played her hand. It was all Lucinda's decision now.

Finally, the alpha nodded. "Because my cub wishes it, I will allow you to tell your story. Be sure, though, that it is the finest tale you have ever told, or you will regret it. You will *also* buy drinks for everyone in my pub, so they may soothe their dry throats while they listen."

Fiona knew when to give in gracefully. She very carefully reached into her pocket for her credit card, since she hadn't brought nearly enough cash to buy pints for a room full of thirsty shifters. Lucinda nodded, and her daughter walked over and took the card from Fiona. She hadn't gone three steps toward her mother, however, when she gasped and whirled around.

"Fiona Campbell? *The* Fiona Campbell? *The Forest Fairies* and *The Selkies Return* Fiona Campbell?"

Fiona nodded, sighing. She hadn't really expected to be recognized in a shifter pub, but of course werewolves had children, too. She fought back another wave of giggles at the thought, realizing it was simply a crazy reaction to the relief that she wasn't going to be eaten.

At least, not for however long it took to tell her story.

"Mother, this is Fiona Campbell!"

Lucinda rolled her eyes. "Yes, I think even a deaf person would have gotten that by now. Who is Fiona Campbell?"

"Only the most famous children's book author and illustrator in the United Kingdom!" Lucinda's daughter was all but jumping up and down, a reaction Fiona usually only received from fans about fifteen years younger.

"Ginny, calm down," Lucinda ordered, and Ginny immediately dropped her head submissively. "Now, slow down and explain."

"Do you remember that book I showed you? The one with the painting of the forest in Scotland that you said was so vivid it reminded you of your childhood in the country? That's Fiona Campbell."

"Now that we're all friends, perhaps you can ask your associates to let me pass?" Christophe called out.

"Not a chance, sorcerer." Lucinda gestured to Ginny and the young shifter approached her mother and spent several minutes whispering urgently to her. Lucinda finally nodded and Ginny moved a few steps away.

"Famous author, maybe. It seems you have a fan in my daughter," Lucinda told Fiona. "But your companion poses too great a threat. However, we have our own magic here. If he will agree to be bound, we will consider allowing you both to leave unharmed. *After* your story, and if it pleases, of course."

Christophe's face drained of all color, and Fiona realized that nothing could be worse for him than being bound. Not unless they planned to lock him in a box, and they'd only do that over her dead body.

"No," Fiona said. "Let him go. You can bind me or whatever you need to do."

"No!" Christophe shouted. "Leave her alone. Let *her* go. I'll agree to anything you want."

Lucinda smiled. "Most do," she said. "You two are so touching. Ah, here is help."

The oldest woman Fiona had ever seen in her life chose that moment to make an entrance from the back room. Fiona supposed she must be a shifter, too, considering the company, but she looked like Mother Earth or the moon goddess herself. In spite of the dire situation, Fiona's fingers itched for her paints.

The old woman's pale, pale eyes widened, and then she laughed. Her laughter held so much power that even Fiona could feel it. All the wolves but the alpha bowed, and even Lucinda inclined her head.

"No, child, I am no moon goddess, though you flatter me with the comparison," the woman said, moving toward Christophe. "Now let's see about the magic in this man. It tastes of sea and salt and ancient days, but not at all of sorcery."

Christophe bowed his most elegant court bow. "As I have told your friends, Wise One."

The old woman smiled and patted his cheek. "Melisande will do, Atlantean. Simply Melisande."

He tilted his head, studying her. "How did you—"

"I know much beyond the purview of you youngsters," she chided him. "Do you swear by your sea god to harm none here?"

Christophe scanned the room, his gaze finally coming to rest on Lucinda. "I will harm none so long as my mate is not harmed, Lady Melisande. I do so swear it by my oath to Poseidon."

Fiona tried to mask her shock. His *mate*?

"Such pretty manners in this boy," Melisande said, chuckling. She turned toward Lucinda. "You may let him go now."

Lucinda made another gesture, and the shifters surrounding Christophe melted away, as did the ones around Fiona, although one of them took one long, last sniff of her hair before he moved off. Christophe leapt across the space separating them, so fast he was a blur, and pulled her into his arms.

"Never again," he whispered into her hair. "If something happened to you— Never again."

"We're not out of the woods yet," she murmured, as Lucinda approached.

"I loved that painting," Lucinda admitted. "The Scottish forest. That was you? You don't look—"

Fiona interrupted her with the simple action of pulling the red wig off her head and shaking out her own blond hair. "It's easier to go out, sometimes, when people don't know who I am. I'm in no way famous like an actor or TV presenter, but I do get recognized, and people—parents, especially—seem to be disturbed by the idea that the woman who writes their children's bedtime stories might be seen in a pub." She smiled ruefully. "I rather think they expect me to live in one of the forests from my paintings."

Lucinda nodded. "I once did. Perhaps someday I'll tell you about it."

Christophe leaned forward, and Fiona squeezed his hand in warning.

"I would enjoy hearing it," she said. "Perhaps in another venue?"

"I apologize for our lack of hospitality," Lucinda said, handing Fiona's credit card back to her. "Drinks on the house, while The Melting Moon's first guest author tells us her tale," she shouted, and a rousing cheer shook the walls of the pub.

Fiona finally, very carefully, allowed herself to breathe a sigh of relief.

✧～～✦

Christophe, with Melisande ensconced in a chair nearby, watched as a room full of wolf shifters, among the deadliest of all predators, sat entranced and listened to Fiona tell a tale. Although, to be sure, the story was one of the finest he'd ever heard. The wolves' own moon goddess, known for her incredible beauty and the vanity that was her greatest downfall, had apparently taken a little jaunt to Scotland one day and fallen hard for a Scottish warrior.

The warrior and the goddess. It named his own story, and he wasn't sure his was fated to have any more of a happy ending than Fiona's tale. A mere mortal wasn't meant to love a goddess, and Fiona shone brighter than any mere moon. She was brilliant and brave beyond anything he had ever seen in a human. She'd faced down Lucinda's threat with a smile and an offer of her own.

She was incredible.

He could never deserve her.

"Don't wait too long before claiming that one for your own," Evan said from behind him. "She is a treasure, is she not?"

Christophe turned to find the alpha's mate, his nose healed and his face cleaned of blood, leaning against the bar next to him. Evan raised his mug to Christophe in a wry toast.

"Truce?"

Christophe nodded and raised his own mug. "Truce. Although it would have been a far different story if you'd hurt her."

Evan shrugged. "No need for posturing now. The crisis is past. Our two alpha females worked out their own balance, I think."

Christophe nodded, his gaze returning to Fiona, who was gesturing animatedly with her hands as she told of the warrior's fearsome jealousy.

"It is not always easy to fall in love with the brightest star in the firmament. I know this." Evan nodded to Lucinda, who sat with her daughter, both of them clearly enraptured with the story. "I had to kill three challengers for her hand before I won her."

"Things are different outside the Pack," Christophe said.

"Yes, and no. You feel you are not worthy of her, I think," Evan said shrewdly. "Get over it, before she believes it, too."

"You always talk to strangers about their love lives?" Christophe drew another long pull on his ale before putting it down. "Bit presumptuous, don't you think?"

Evan smiled. "I am Spanish, my friend. Nothing in the world is as important as love."

He walked off to join his mate at the table, leaving Christophe staring after him in astonishment. First the man tries to kill him, then he gives him advice on his love life. Christophe didn't know whether to be amused or offended.

The roar of applause, accompanied by whistling, hooting, and stomping feet, snapped him out of his musings and he made his way through the noisy crowd to Fiona's side. She was flushed, clearly enjoying the shifters' reaction to her story.

She turned a shy smile up to him. "Did you like it?"

"It was a wonderful story, *mi amara*," he said, pulling her into his arms, simply because he needed to feel her close. "Perhaps now we leave?"

The crowd quieted down, and he watched Lucinda cross the floor to the two of them.

"Thank you," the alpha said, her eyes bright. "That was a lovely story. You are welcome here at The Melting Moon anytime, Lady Fiona Campbell. Your mate, too."

Fiona smiled and held out her hand. "Thank you. I am very honored."

The crowd cheered again, and Christophe marveled at Fiona's instinctive ability to do and say the exactly right thing at the exactly right time.

"I promise you if we find news of the Siren, we will send word to you," Christophe said quietly, for Lucinda's ears alone. "I would not want a gem that could cause harm to my people in vampire hands, either."

Lucinda nodded, and Evan, who'd walked up behind her, smiled.

"You would make a fine shifter, my friend," Evan told him. "Fearless and honorable. It is an unbeatable combination. Remember what I told you."

Christophe bowed to the two of them, one of his best court bows, and when he rose, Lucinda was grinning.

"Oh, he is too pretty, Fiona. You, too, are a lucky woman." She put her arm in her mate's.

"Yes, I am," Fiona agreed. "We must be off now. Please tell Ginny I'll call her soon to talk to her about writing."

"She'll be thrilled. Good luck, both of you, and be careful. If Telios is indeed behind this, he is a very, very dangerous enemy to make. He is deadly and completely insane. A terrible combination." Lethal-looking claws suddenly ripped out of the ends of her still-human hands. "I will gladly tear his throat out and eat his heart if I find out he threatens my kind. We have feelers out, too, but vampires do not talk to shifters about this, as you may imagine. Perhaps you will fare better."

Evan nodded solemnly. "If it comes to war, you of Atlantis will have to choose sides."

"We are on the side of humanity," Christophe said flatly. "Through oath and precedent of more than eleven thousands of years. But should it come to a battle between shifter and bloodsucker, we will never take the side of any who try to enthrall others, this I swear to you."

Fiona nodded. "It's wrong. We'll do whatever we can." She leaned in toward Lucinda and spoke in a quiet, confiding tone. "It might help with public relations if you stop threatening to eat humans, you know. Just a thought."

The alpha's laughter followed them all the way out of the bar.

Chapter 31

Once they hit the sidewalk, Christophe took a firm grip on Fiona's arm and headed straight for the bikes. He was taking her back to her nice, safe home, where he didn't have to worry about being ambushed while anybody threatened to eat her.

A ragged group of shifters was crowded around the Ducatis, admiring them. When Christophe approached, one of the bigger males put a hand on the seat.

"This bike used to be yours, human? Because I'm thinking it's mine now. I'll take your pretty little woman, too."

The rest of the thugs laughed and nudged one another, egging the stupid one on.

Stupider one?

"I'm guessing you weren't inside," Christophe said.

Before the shifter could move, Christophe's dagger shot through the air and buried itself in his throat. As the man gurgled, blood spurting out around the blade, he began to fall, and Christophe snatched his blade back, wiping it on the nearest shifter's shirt.

"He'll heal. Eventually. Anybody else?" He channeled power

until it seared his skin and lit up the night sky with an eerie blue-green glow.

The rest of them uttered hasty denials and dragged their friend away. Christophe turned to find Fiona staring at him, her eyes huge.

"I've had enough of people threatening you," he said flatly. "The next time it happens, I'm going to start killing them." It wasn't a threat, it was a simple fact. They'd threatened his woman. The next person to do it died. Anyone after that to do it, died.

Simple.

"You can't keep treating me like I'm some fragile princess you have to protect," Fiona said.

"It's not only my sworn duty this time. It's personal. Get used to it."

"No. I won't. Listen to me, Christophe, and listen closely. This can never work—our partnership, our relationship, whatever we have here—unless you treat me like an equal."

He didn't understand why *she* didn't understand. "You're not equal. Not as a warrior. You don't have offensive magic, only defensive, and you don't have centuries of battle training and experience. How can I possibly treat you like an equal?"

She sighed and took his hands in hers. "I'm not talking about that kind of equal. I don't claim to have any of that. But I have a brain. I'm the one who got us out of that mess in the pub, didn't I? You have to trust me, too."

"Not everyone is going to be a fan of your books, Fiona. Sometimes it's going to take fighting our way out, and I won't allow you to be in situations like that."

"When it does involve fighting, I'll let you lead the way. I'm not an idiot. But you have to let me make the choice of what I do and where I go, and you have to let me stand by your side when we can do more together than apart." She released her hands and took a deep breath. "Also, you need to forget the word *allow*. Or I'll go my own way now. Trust me or lose me, that's the choice. Now it's up to you."

With that, she swung one leg over her bike, put her helmet on, and took off. He stood watching her go for a few seconds before he climbed on his own bike and followed. Trust her or lose her. How could such a simple decision be so damn tough to make?

~~~~~~

Fiona concentrated on the road, the traffic, and not crying. In that order. She was looking for the nearest coffee shop that was at least ten kilometers away from that damn pub. Nothing like fear of being an evening snack for a bunch of wolves to shake a girl up.

The truth wasn't that simple, though. It wasn't about fear. It was about finally finding a man who excited and challenged her on every level— physically, emotionally, mentally—and then learning he couldn't put aside his need to protect her long enough to consider her a true partner.

A true equal.

She'd seen what happened to women who allowed men to dominate them. Her grandfather had bullied her grandmother into an early grave. Even in the name of protecting her, Christophe couldn't take over her life. If she let him begin now, he'd never stop. Slowly, gradually, he'd wrap her in a lovely, soft cocoon—with him in control. The Scarlet Ninja would be no more. Fiona herself would disappear, taken over by a useless version of herself who was very well-sated in bed but not in any other way.

No. He had to learn, or he had to go.

By the time she pulled the bike over to the side of the road underneath the welcoming coffee shop sign, she'd all but resigned herself to never seeing him again. So when the roar of the second Ducati sounded beside her, she half wondered if she were imagining it.

The bike shut off.

"I'm sorry. You were right," Christophe said.

She smiled and scrubbed the tears off her cheeks before she looked up at him. "My new five favorite words."

"I can't pretend this will be easy for me, but I'll do my best," he said. "I can't walk away from you. Not now, maybe not ever. I don't pretend that's easy for me, either. You've turned my world upside down, so the least I can do is trust you."

She wanted to throw herself into his arms. She settled for taking his hand.

"Coffee? While we plan our next move?"

"Our next move is clear," he said. "We're going to Daybreak, the vampire club. Did you happen to write any vampire stories?"

Chapter 32

The Daybreak Inn, East End

The soulful sound of jazz piano and a sultry female voice singing about heartbreak and the man who done her wrong met them when they walked in the doors of the Daybreak club. Fiona had never been in a vampire nightclub, so she looked around her with some interest.

It was nothing at all like she'd expected.

Soft lighting turned the space a mellow, smoky gold. Deep chocolate walls and dark brown leather booths accented the rich golden tones of the wooden tables and the spectacularly polished bar. It looked like an old world, old money gentleman's club from a novel.

The people who occupied the space were similarly golden. Too beautiful, too perfect to be real. Or at least too perfect to be human. These were all vampires, she'd bet, and every single one of them had turned to look at her.

"Nice the way you make instant friends wherever you go," Christophe said next to her ear.

"It's my natural magnetism," she murmured.

"Actually, it's the scent of *his* blood." The man speaking

stared at them with glowing red eyes across a dozen or so paces of open floor. "There's something different about it. Not human, not shifter, not Fae. So what does that leave us?"

He was movie-star gorgeous. No, not even that. Movie stars would give everything they owned to look as good as this man. He wore a black silk shirt and black trousers as if they had been made for him. They probably had. That kind of casual arrogance only came with title, money, and position.

She glanced at Christophe and amended the thought. Or Atlantean warrior training and a great deal of magic.

At the moment, Christophe was busy staring down the vampire. Finally he replied. "Alien. I'm a little green man from outer space."

"We're not fans of aliens here."

Fiona put on her best "lady of the manor" smile. Old money, indeed. She could carry her own on this. "We're just here for a drink."

"I don't think so, Lady Fiona. How is Lucinda doing, by the way? Evidently you made quite an impression."

"You're very well informed," she said.

"We simply want to live our lives in peace. The word is out about the two of you, and if I let you drink in my bar, I have trouble with Telios. Nobody wants trouble with Telios, especially me."

Christophe stepped right up in the vampire's face. "Does he have Vanquish?"

"Even if I knew, do you think I'd tell you? Whoever you are, whatever you want, get the hell out of my club and stay out. I'm not involved in any of that, and I plan to keep it that way."

Christophe started to respond, but Fiona grabbed his arm and shook her head. They were slowly, stealthily being surrounded, and this time she didn't think she could talk her way out of it.

"Let's go. He has the right to be left in peace," she said.

The vampire turned his dark gaze to her. "Yes. We do. We are content to live in a society without the fear of mobs with torches for the first time in our existence. Leave us be."

"If Telios has his way and starts a war against humanity, you'll be right there with those torches again," Christophe said. "You're going to have to choose sides soon."

"Perhaps. But not tonight. Now leave."

They left.

~~~~

Fairsby Manor

"What do you mean, you can't find him?" Gideon kicked the cringing vampire in the ribs again. "How difficult can it be to find a single insane vampire?"

"I don't know where he is," the vampire blubbered. "We lost several of our number when they attacked that human, except he's not human—no way is he human—and those of us who are left can't find Telios."

"No, Christophe is definitely not human," Gideon agreed. "But what?"

"I don't know that, either," the vamp whined.

Gideon kicked him again. "I wasn't asking you, you pathetic waste of space. Get out. Try again. Follow any rumor or possibility, no matter how far-fetched."

"Well, there was one thing, but it was ridiculous."

"What?"

"I heard he was seen entering a shifter hangout, but that's just stupid," the vamp said, all but falling over itself in the hope to prove useful.

"Go!" Gideon screamed. "Go now. To that shifter place and *find that vampire* or I will chain you in a box with silver and crosses for the rest of eternity, you miserable leech."

The vampire leapt out the window so fast it nearly flew. Or maybe it did fly. Gideon didn't know and didn't care. All he knew was that if Telios was suddenly going to shifter venues, then the vampire might very well have discovered the Siren's secrets. Which could be bad for Gideon.

Very bad, indeed.

At least until he figured a way to fix it. So Gideon did what he had always done best: he started drawing up a strategy to make others suffer and bleed. He would call in another of his minions, this one Fae. They'd put part two of his plan into motion.

And that was very good. Very, very good.

~~~

Campbell Manor

"That was a useless night," Christophe said as they walked up the stairs from the garage.

"No, it wasn't. We learned what is not true, so we can start to deduce what is true. The shifters don't have the sword, or they wouldn't have reacted like that. Telios terrifies even the vampires he might recruit to be on his side. There are even rumors, although I think it's ridiculous, that he might be the real Jack the Ripper."

"Aha!" Christophe shouted.

Fiona shushed him. "Aha, what? Also, be quieter, please."

"Nothing. Just a hunch I had. Anyway, Telios may have the sword. A powerful enough vampire could get past the security in the Jewel House easily enough," Christophe mused. "He doesn't seem to be the type who would share the news, either. So we can't rule him out."

"So tomorrow we go after Telios?"

Christophe shook his head. "Tomorrow I go after Telios. Alone. A very old, very powerful master vampire is my domain, not yours, won't you agree, partner?"

She narrowed her eyes, and he tensed for another battle, but then she sighed and smiled. "Yes, I do agree. There's not much I can do other than get in the way. But I'm going to be working on a plan for how to clear the Scarlet Ninja's name."

"Agreed."

A sound in the hallway alerted them to Hopkins's presence. "Glad to see you home safely, Lady Fiona. I'll say good night."

"You didn't need to wait up for me, Hopkins," she said, smiling at him.

"Of course not, my lady." He bowed and retired to his

quarters, leaving Fiona staring after him with a mixture of fondness and exasperation.

Christophe knew how she felt. "Annoying, isn't it, when nobody does what you say?"

She stuck her tongue out at him and ran down the hall to her room. He gave her exactly three seconds' head start, and then he gave chase.

He burst through her door and she was nowhere to be seen. Maybe she'd headed to the bathroom to freshen up. He slowed to a walk, trying not to look like a love-struck fool, and someone pushed him from behind, and then laughed.

Fiona's laughter. She was shadowing.

He removed his daggers and then grinned and ripped his shirt off over his head, not bothering with the buttons. "I'm happy to play, Princess."

She laughed again and smacked his ass. He jumped a little. Hadn't been expecting that.

"You know turnabout is fair play, right? Just warning you that now I get to spank that luscious ass of yours," he growled, unfastening his pants and sliding them down. He stepped out and, totally nude, turned around. He couldn't find her at first, though. That unique pattern of swirling light and shadow he'd learned was Fiona didn't appear.

"I'm learning to mask any trace of myself, even from you," she said, from the opposite corner of the room. "Did you know you have a lovely body?"

Seemingly from thin air, her shirt flew through the air and hit him in the chest, followed shortly thereafter by the wisp of lace that was her bra. His breathing sped up, and his cock, already hard, swelled even more.

"You want to put your hands on my lovely body?" he asked, stalking toward her. Or where he'd thought she was. He realized he was wrong when another scrap of lace hit him in the back. He whirled around and caught her underwear before it fell.

"A trophy?" He held it up and grinned. "A keepsake?"

"If you like spanking," she purred, this time from near the bathroom door, "that can be arranged."

He caught his breath. His prim, proper Fiona was turning a little kinky for him. He liked it. His entire body tightened, and he thought he might go insane if he didn't get her under him in the next few seconds.

"Go lie on the bed," she commanded. "On your back, arms out."

"If you—"

"Now," she said sternly. "Don't make me punish you."

"Oh, by all the gods, I'm going to make you pay for this," he warned. "I'm going to make you come so hard and so long that you're screaming for a week."

He heard her quick, indrawn breath, but she quickly masked it.

"Big talk, big man," she taunted from near the bed. "Are you afraid of little old me?"

A silk scarlet ribbon waved in the air and then floated to the bed. Another quickly followed it.

"Tie your left hand to the bedpost, then lie back and I'll tie your right hand," she ordered. "If you move, you lose points. If you touch me first, you lose points."

"And what do these points gain me?"

She laughed a sultry, sexy laugh that shivered its way from his head to his toes by way of his cock. "Silly man. They gain you me."

He flew to the bed and did what she'd asked, although it took every ounce of determination to lie still when he felt her delicate fingers tying his wrist with the ribbon and tightening it.

"Can you be good or do I need to tie your feet, too?" she teased.

"I'll be good," he gritted out the words through clenched teeth, hoping that he wouldn't spurt out of control and come all over himself at her first touch. He'd never been as aroused as he was with this woman. Never, in all the centuries of his existence.

"Have your wicked way with me," he invited. "Please."

Silence. For a moment, the thought crossed his mind that it had been an elaborate trick and now she'd gone off to shower and laugh at his foolishness. But then her mouth closed around the head of his cock and his entire body arched off the bed.

"How's that?" She gave him a long, slow lick.

He moaned and his hips bucked involuntarily. He still couldn't see her, though now he could once again distinguish the shadows that bent to hide her. It was like making love in a dream, almost unbearably erotic but still not enough.

"I need to see you. I need to know it's you touching me," he said roughly. "Nobody else but you, ever again. Let me see you."

Slowly she appeared before him, curled around his hips. First she released the shadows, so she seemed to be made of pure light. Then she released the light and she was back. Fiona. Just Fiona. A miracle made into a woman, created especially for him.

"I need you. Now. Please."

Fiona's teasing response faded on her lips, as the intensity in Christophe's face and voice captured her. She nodded.

"Yes. I need you, too." She rose above him and lowered herself on his erection, then slowly slid down its length until she rested against his body. "I need you now."

She leaned forward and released the silk ties so he could hold her. He pulled her down into a desperate kiss, devouring her mouth as if kissing her was the only thing keeping him sane. Her hands were trapped between them, resting on his powerful chest, and then he flipped her over and yanked her legs up.

"Need you now," he said roughly, thrusting into her over and over and over. "Now. Always."

She couldn't talk, speech was impossible, nothing was left to her but pure sensation. She was the flame to his candle, and together they were incandescent. She climbed so high she knew the fall might kill her, but she didn't care, she only knew she wanted him. Now and forever. Just like this, inside her body and inside her heart.

He cried out and she came apart around him, and together they fell off the side of the world and into each other's soul.

Christophe knew exactly what was happening to him, and

the terror he'd expected was nowhere to be found. It was the soul-meld, and he'd told himself he'd never, ever allow it to happen to him.

Now he welcomed it.

Her soul was warmth and light and color, it was a landscape painted by a true master. He saw her childhood and the dark grays and shades of black for the terror and sadness she'd experienced with her grandfather and father. He swam through the blues and greens as she grew older, began to move on, cared for and loved her brother, was cared for and loved in return by both Declan and Hopkins. He saw the scarlet of excitement and adventure as she took on the persona of the Scarlet Ninja. Watched her go on her first heist.

Cried with her when she was finally able to help people the vampires had harmed.

Her soul was as beautiful as she was and the same glorious contradiction; neat, orderly, and organized in certain parts, and wild, flowing, and free in others. She was a woman made up of so many different and contrasting colors that she absolutely took his breath away, and the realization smashed into him as he reveled in the fire of her stubborn and courageous heart: he was hopelessly, irrevocably in love with her.

Fiona clutched Christophe's shoulders, almost feeling as if she actually were falling off the edge of an impossibly high cliff into a terrifying abyss below. Somehow, she didn't understand how or why or if it were even real, but she was falling into Christophe's memories.

Darkness surrounded her, and fear and pain swallowed her up until she screamed. She was so young, no, *he* was, it was Christophe who was the child, this was his memory, and his poor, broken and battered body lay curled up in the corner of a rough wooden box. The darkness stank of urine and terror, and Fiona wanted to kill the woman who had done this to him. Even the rational realization that the woman was long dead, that all the townspeople who'd turned his parents over to the Fae were long dead, did nothing to reduce her need for vengeance.

They deserved to hurt and suffer for what they'd done to him. They deserved—but then she fell again. Fell into warmth and confusion. His grandparents had loved him, but he'd been closed off, terrified, angry.

Why hadn't anyone saved him? Why hadn't they saved his parents? Why were they lying to him? His young mind couldn't understand it, couldn't find a way to ask, so he reached the only decision he could. He quit trusting. Anyone, ever.

She fell again. Warrior training. Finally the belief that what he was doing was right. He could avenge his parents. Only to learn that his duty was to protect the very humanity who had caused his family's murder. Doing his duty, year after year, while the anger, pain, and futility ate at him.

Falling again and again. The magic in him. So powerful. Alaric's edict that he join the priesthood, learn to train and channel the power. Christophe's refusal. Again feeling like an outsider. As though he weren't good enough.

She fell again, this time into a pool of golden warmth. Felt bathed in hope and reassurance; a sense of belonging. A feeling of *home* after so many long centuries without. She looked into the light, the source of this wonderful, soul-renewing hope.

And she saw her own face smiling back at her.

Chapter 33

Christophe held Fiona as tightly as he dared, rocking her back and forth as she cried in his arms.

"How did you stand it?" she finally said, her sobs slowing. "So alone for so long. How could you bear it?"

He considered the question and realized he didn't know how to answer it. "I didn't know any different."

"What *was* that? What happened to me?" She wiped her wet face on her pillow and then sat up, taking deep breaths. "How did I see your memories?"

"What you saw was actually my soul." He sat up, too, pulling her close to him. He needed to be touching her. "That was an ancient Atlantean . . . ritual? Experience? I don't even know what to call it. A blessing, perhaps. It's called the soul-meld and what you experienced—no, what *we* experienced—was a journey through each other's soul."

"But how is that even possible?" She trembled against him. "You saw my childhood, too? Lived through my pain? I don't know what to say."

"I did, *mi amara*, and your soul is beautiful beyond the fantasies of the gods. You are courage and goodness made into light and formed especially for me. You must know that you are mine." He pulled her into a tight embrace, wishing he could hold her there forever, just like that, with no vampires or Fae or missions to ever come between them.

"What does that mean, that I am yours?" she asked, her voice muffled against his chest.

He loosened his arms, but she didn't pull away.

"Is that some kind of magic binding? Do you—what does it mean? Can it be broken?"

He fought against the terror biting into him with sharp metal teeth. He'd finally found her and she wanted to find a way to escape him. He wanted to shout and rage against the injustice, but that would frighten her, and he found that he cared more about her feelings than his own. He almost laughed.

Love, then, was a fool's game.

"Yes, it can be broken. Or at least, it can be ignored," he said. "The most precious tenet of Atlantean life is free will. The soul-meld, though it comes but rarely and offers a gift beyond price to a relationship, can be turned down. Refused."

He inhaled a shuddering breath and said the hardest words he'd ever had to speak. "Tell me to go, and I will."

She put her hand up to his cheek and stared up at him, her blue eyes drowning with some emotion he couldn't translate. "Christophe."

"Don't," he said, throwing himself away from her and out of the bed. "Don't try to be kind. Don't try to let me down easily. Just tell me to get out, and I'll go."

He stopped, realizing he still asked too much. "No. You don't even need to say the words. I'll leave now."

He reached for the sheaths with his daggers and knocked over a vase of flowers. Instead of righting it, he hurled it against the wall and howled out the anguish that bubbled out of his chest until he thought it would consume him in its scarlet flame.

"Christophe. Christophe, listen to me." Fiona knelt beside him, though he didn't know how or when she'd gotten there.

She shook his shoulders again. "Christophe! Don't make me smack your bottom again."

Tears ran down her face, silvery tracks not marring her incredible beauty but merely changing it, transforming it to something bittersweet. "I don't want you to go. I love you."

He raised his head and stared at her. He thought she'd said . . .

"What?"

"You can't go. Don't leave me. We can figure this out. I love you, you crazy Atlantean madman," she said, laughing and crying at the same time. "I'm not sure why you'd want a cat burglar, but you're mine, too, so let's make this work, okay? No more talk of leaving me. Not ever."

He couldn't make a sound. He took her in his arms, swept her up off the floor and back into the bed, and made his clothes vanish with a thought. Before he could speak, or think, or even offer up a prayer of thankfulness to all the gods who might be listening, he was inside of her again.

"Mine," he said. "I love you, too. This is where I belong. For always, my princess, my ninja, *mi amara.*"

She traced her fingertips down his spine and smiled. "What does that mean? *Mi amara?*"

"My beloved. It means my beloved, and you are."

Then he made love to her, gently and sweetly, for a very long time.

His. She was his. He would never let her go.

～～⁓

Fiona woke up gradually, swimming through sleep to consciousness in stages. First she realized her body was slightly sore, and she smiled at the memory of the lovemaking that had caused it. Then she remembered the rest of it, and her heart rate felt like it doubled as her eyes popped open.

Christophe came walking out of the bathroom, hair wet and a towel slung low on his hips, and strolled over to the window to look out. She took a few moments to enjoy the view before she let him know she was awake. His broad chest tapered down into sharply defined abdominal muscles, which

veed down between his hips. He was a purely perfect speci-
men of masculine form, and he was hers.

"Good morning," she said, and enjoyed seeing that she'd
surprised him.

"I thought you'd sleep for quite a while." He crossed to the
bed and leaned down to kiss her.

She enjoyed the kiss, but decided to table any further dis-
cussion of soul-melding and forever until her emotions were
on more solid ground, so she took refuge in practicality.
"What's on the agenda for today?"

"Change of plans. You've got a lot of friends who might
be Fae, whether you realize it or not, and I think we can kill
two barnacles with one shell."

She started to laugh. "It's kill two birds with one stone."

He grimaced. "Why would I want to kill birds with stones?
Anyway, the only ones slow enough for that trick would be
the palace peacocks, and even I think they're too pretty to
kill."

"I feel a little like I've fallen down the rabbit hole again,"
she moaned, still smiling at him so he knew she was teasing.

"Look, forget birds. We're going Fae hunting. I think the
Fae may be pulling a double-cross, here, urging both shifters
and vamps to believe it's the other who stole the sword and
the Siren. Also, we can ask about Denal. Are you with me,
partner?"

She jumped out of bed. "I know just the place to start. One
of my contacts, the first to give me the tip about the man who
wanted Vanquish, actually. He owns a pub, and he's Maeve's
cousin."

"Which means he's Fairsby's cousin, too," Christophe
said. "I knew that damned Unseelie Fae was involved in this
somehow."

She headed for the bathroom. "Give me twenty minutes
to shower."

His eyes flared hot, and he followed her and tossed his
towel on the rack. "We're not in that big of a hurry. I think
you need me to wash your back."

It took far longer than twenty minutes.

~~~~~~~~

The Prancing Pony pub

It had taken a while to get Hopkins and Declan caught up, and even Sean had eaten breakfast with them. Hopkins had already called Fiona's assistant, Madeleine, and given her the week off and done the same for the rest of the staff, so there would be no interruptions or distractions. By the time she and Christophe managed to escape, it was nearly lunchtime. Sean had dropped them off, darkly muttering something about errands, and promised to be back in two hours unless Fiona needed him sooner.

She had never spent so much time in pubs in her life. A lady didn't frequent pubs, of course. She defiantly took another sip of her ale, sending a mental *piss off* to her grandfather.

"I've never liked ale before, but it's really quite perfect with the fish and chips, isn't it?" She chose another chip and blissfully poured vinegar on it and doused it with more salt. "I could quite get used to this pub food."

Christophe grinned and shook his head. "I'm corrupting you. Today ale and pub food, tomorrow who knows? Reality TV?"

"You know about reality TV? In Atlantis?"

"Riley told us about it. Another sign of the decline of humanity, if you ask me." He nodded toward the bar. "There he is."

She turned. It was him. "How could you know which one is Maeve's cousin?"

He was right, though. "Yes, that's Paul."

"Not exactly a brilliant deduction. He's the only Fae who walked behind the bar like he owned it." He leaned forward. "You've got a little salt right there."

Instead of wiping the corner of her mouth, he kissed it, and then he kissed her some more, and soon she was necking in a pub like a proper ninny.

"Stop," she said, pulling away. "I have a reputation to uphold."

"I look at it more like I have a reputation to destroy. Namely, yours." A slow, wicked smile spread across his face. "Sex on a balcony in broad daylight, kissing in a pub—what's next? The fall of the British aristocracy, I bet."

"Shh!" She looked around, but nobody was paying them any attention, except for Paul, and he was too far away to have heard. "You're too bad."

"Nope. I'm just bad enough, and you love me."

She sighed. "Yes, and you're going to hold that against me, aren't you?"

"Every chance I get." He tilted his head toward the bar. "Why don't you go find out what Paul knows, soften him up before I come over? I'll stay here and rescue any of my chips you didn't manage to steal."

"I *am* a cat burglar," she whispered.

She stole another chip and waved it just out of his reach before she slid out of the booth and headed for the bar.

"Hello, Lady Fiona," Paul said, wiping down the already spotless bar. "Surprised to see you here."

"Yes, I'm sorry I haven't made it over more often. Deadlines and such. You know how it is." She smiled, inviting him to agree.

He didn't.

He didn't smile, either.

"I know you know about us now, Fiona," he said, his formerly warm voice gone cold and hard. "What do you want?"

She allowed a little of his wintry coldness to seep into her own voice. "I want to talk to Maeve, Paul. She took a friend of mine when she poofed out of my house, and I want to be sure he's all right."

He turned to aim his stare at Christophe. "Your friend from Atlantis is fine. You can tell *him* that, and get out of my pub. Both of you. I'm in danger just from your presence."

She glanced back at Christophe, and quicker than thought, he was standing next to her. She'd wanted him and he was there. Warmth spread through her veins, as though he superheated her blood simply with his presence. The soul-meld? Perhaps. A topic to be tabled until later, certainly.

"Where is she?"

"She's in the Summer Lands, fool. You know that and you have no recourse." Paul picked up a wickedly sharp knife and started slicing through limes like they were butter. "I like cutting things, Atlantean. How well can you bleed?"

"Are you threatening me?" Christophe's voice was calm. A little bored, even. She could actually *feel* that he didn't consider Paul to be the slightest small threat.

Christophe answered her unspoken question out loud. "Fae vary as dramatically in power as humans do in physical or mental ability. This one isn't much of a power. Barely even much of a Fae."

Paul's hand tightened on the knife until his knuckles turned white, but he didn't challenge Christophe. Instead, he sighed.

"Just leave. I can't force you to do it, but if you don't, I'm going to suffer for it. If you ever liked me at all, Fiona, please just leave."

She stared at him, looking for any hint that this was yet another deception, like the bit with the knife, but all she saw was weariness and a hint of fear.

"Who is frightening you like this, Paul? Tell us and we can help you."

He laughed, and it held genuine amusement and utter despair. "You can't help me, Fiona. You can't even help yourself. Get out of London while you can. Run. Run all the way to Atlantis. Swim, if you have to. He's after you next. He's going after the Siren and then he wants you, and I don't even know why."

Christophe reached over the bar and grabbed Paul by the collar and lifted him up and halfway over the polished wooden surface. "Who wants her? Tell me or die now, Fae."

Paul looked down at the fruit staining the front of his shirt and then raised his head, and a corpse's smile spread across his face. "Maeve's brother, of course. Fairsby is Gideon na Feransel, Prince of the Unseelie Court, and he has decided to take a human bride. He's after you, Fiona. You need to run."

Christophe released him, and Paul slid back down his side of the bar until he was standing there, grinning at them, his eyes twin holes blazing in his pale face. "He has old business with you, too, Atlantean, or so he claims. You should both run."

He started laughing, clutching his middle, insanity rising in the shrieking tones of his voice. "Run, run, run. Run, little human, but there's no place to hide. The Siren is back, the wolves will fall, Atlantis will be destroyed. Run, run, run."

Fiona grabbed Christophe's hand and pulled him toward the door. She managed, only just barely, to keep from covering her ears with her hands to block out the horrible laughter. The mad refrain of "run, run, run" followed them out the door and at least fifty feet down the street.

That's when the pub exploded behind them.

Chapter 34

The wave of heat and power almost preceded the noise, or at least smashed into them simultaneously, so that Fiona was flying through the air as if knocked aside by a giant's hand before she realized what had happened. Through some miracle of balance or Atlantean magic, Christophe performed an amazing twisting somersault in midair and caught her before she crashed down on the concrete, headfirst.

Together, they sat up and stared at what was left of the Prancing Pony. Fire, smoke, and death.

"They're going to think it was terrorism," she said. "We need to leave. Slowly and inconspicuously."

"I think it's too late for that," Christophe said, pointing.

A crowd was boiling up the street toward them. No, too big to be a crowd. More like a mob. But no ordinary mob. This one was utterly, completely, silent.

"They're all shifters," Christophe said, pulling Fiona back into the doorway of a shop. "Every single one. They're shifters, and they've been enthralled."

"So many? At once? That's not possible," she protested. Then realization dawned in spite of her brain still feeling dazed from the blast. "He's got the Siren. This is a demonstration or a taunt, or something. Fairsby has the Siren and he's already using it."

Christophe's face was grim. "Either that or Telios does. One of them must be behind the explosion in the pub, too. Whichever it is, he's making some kind of point, and he's making it here. We're caught in the middle of it."

Behind them, the shop owner locked the door. The old woman's worried face appeared in the glass for an instant, and then she ran away, into the back of her shop, or possibly out a rear exit.

"We have to get out of here," Fiona said. "You can't fight that many shifters."

"I won't have to," he said as the first ranks marched right past them. Every single shifter stared straight ahead, eyes blank and glazed over. "They're not here for us."

Fiona scanned the street. "Everybody is running and hiding, but they're ignoring the people for now. What is this about?"

A flash of bright blue caught her eye and she cried out. "Christophe, that's a child. He's caught right in their path. If they don't stop, they'll trample him."

She tried to run out there, but he yanked her back. "Let me."

Before she could argue, he transformed into a cloud of sparkling mist and swirled rapidly through the crowd of shifters, then circled the sobbing child and, still in mist form, lifted him off the ground and above the heads of the oncoming shifters, who kept marching as if they'd seen none of it.

They probably hadn't.

Christophe carried the child to his mother, who'd fallen down while chasing him but appeared unhurt. She took her child and hugged him close to her body, surreptitiously making the sign against the evil eye at the sparkling savior who'd delivered her baby safely to her arms.

Fiona wanted to smack her. Superstitious fool. Christophe had saved her child. She hoped he hadn't seen the hurtful gesture.

He returned to her and transformed back into his physical self. She launched herself into his arms, kissing him all over his face. He pressed her against the wall and returned her kisses so thoroughly she was trembling by the time he released her.

"You are my hero," she said, hoping every ounce of her love for him showed in her face.

His eyes widened, and his expression rapidly cycled through smugness, terror, and an almost tentative happiness. Her own eyes widened when she realized she wasn't reading all that from his face. She was actually feeling his emotions.

"The soul-meld. Can it, does it make me feel your emotions? Like, what did you call the princess? *Aknasha?*"

"Only for me, and I for you. But let's discuss the finer points of the soul-meld later. Now we need to see what they're up to, but it's too dangerous for you. I need to get you out of here."

"We both need to get out of here," she said firmly.

"Yes, but only your human body would be harmed by another explosion. If I'm mist, it would pass right through me."

"If you saw it coming. Last time, we didn't."

He hesitated, then nodded. "You're right. Another reason to depart. But first I need to know if I can learn anything from one of these shifters."

Quicker than thought, he leapt into the street and grabbed one of the enthralled marching men by the shoulders and hauled him up onto the sidewalk. The rest of the mob never even broke stride. In fact, none of them seemed to even see him do it, as if they were blind to anything but their purpose, whatever that might be.

"What are you doing?"

"Marching. Marching. Marching," the shifter said in a singsongy voice.

"Yes, I can see that. But why?" Christophe's eyes glowed hot with power and Fiona realized he was trying to break the enthrallment.

The shifter started shaking, as if caught in the throes of a fierce internal conflict, and then he slumped and fell to his knees. "Experiment," he said hoarsely, staring up at Christophe. "Telios said we were an experiment. What did he do to us? Why—where am I?"

"You're going to be all right now," Christophe said, helping the shifter lean back against the wall. "Just rest for a few minutes and try to remember what else Telios told you. Was he holding anything when he talked to you?"

The shifter clutched his head in his hands, his face screwed up with pain or effort. "A sword. He was holding a sword, and the blue stone on its hilt was glowing like it was lit up from within. But why? Why—what?" He cried out. "It hurts to try to remember. The rest is blank."

"Do you know where you were? This is important. I need to know where Telios was when he talked to you," Christophe said.

"Please," Fiona added. "We must stop him from doing this to any more of your people."

The shifter shook his head back and forth. "I don't know. I just don't know. It's like there's a big block between me and the memory." He clutched his head again. "I don't know. I don't know. I just want to go home."

"We need to get out of here," Christophe said. "He isn't going to remember any more."

"I'll call Sean." But she'd no sooner pulled her phone out of her purse than she saw Sean angling the car into a space at the next cross street.

"I swear that boy is psychic."

"Or he could have heard the sirens," Christophe pointed out, as the sound approached, shrieking its urgency.

They ran for the car.

"This is bad," Sean said, as he accelerated away. "Really bad. The radio news says Telios is claiming responsibility and that the shifters who aren't enthralled are screaming for war. The prime minister is calling in the army, and it looks like London might become a battleground. Again."

"So it's Telios," Fiona said. "The shifter was telling the truth. That answers one question."

"Does it?" Christophe shook his head. "If I'm Unseelie Court and I want to stir things up, I do something pretty awful to one side and make it look like the other side's at fault. Boom. Instant war. Then the humans call in the mobs with torches and pitchforks—"

"The army with missiles and tanks," Sean said.

"Yes, or that. The Fae retreat to the Summer Lands until

the dust settles and there you go. No more vampire or shifter problem."

"Holy hell." Sean whistled. "Pardon me, Lady F, but holy hell. That's devious. That's bloody brilliant."

"Fae aren't known for their stupidity," Christophe said dryly. "Avarice, lust, and greed, yes. Stupidity, no."

"But we'll all be caught in the cross fire," Fiona said. "Humans, and all of the shifters who don't want war. Even the vampires, and we know there are some who just want to live out their existences in peace. It's not fair to any of them."

"This war is on the ground, too. No time to put the children on trains," Christophe said, his gaze far away.

She shivered. "Were you here then? World War Two?"

He turned to look at her almost as if he'd forgotten she was there. "For part of it. We were in France a lot, helping with the Resistance. Germany used shape-shifters against farmers. It was a slaughter." His face hardened. "Never again. I will never let that happen again. We have to find that sword and stop this."

Sean switched the radio back on, and the announcer's voice rang out in the oppressive silence in the car.

"The prime minister has announced that she and other heads of state will be meeting within the next few hours by teleconference to discuss the increasingly dangerous threat from the supernatural community, with the possibility of military action on the table. The prime minister's political opponents are claiming—"

Sean shut it back off. "This is going to be really bad, isn't it?"

"Not if we can help it, Sean," Christophe said, clasping his shoulder for a moment.

Fiona appreciated that he'd used the word "we," but she held his hand tightly all the way home.

~~~~~

St. Mary's tube station

Gideon stared down at the stupid vampire who had caused him so much trouble. It was really always the same with vampires. All one needed to do was wait for daylight. This one, although old enough to be awake most of the day, certainly in the dark this far below ground, was dead to the world. Wielding the power of the Siren must have drained the vampire's energy. Even now, Telios clutched the sword in his skeletal hands.

Gideon paused to smile at his own joke. Dead to the world. And soon truly dead to the world. It was the matter of seconds to drive the wooden stake through Telios's heart, wrench Vanquish out of the vampire's clutching hands, and watch as the pathetic creature once known as Jack the Ripper dissolved into acidic slime. The curse didn't activate, of course. One could not steal an item from a dead vampire.

"Thank you," Gideon said, mocking the corpse. "Now I have much to do. I think I'll take advantage of your little ploy and build from there. The next headlines will be 'Fae prince saves the day.'"

Caressing the sword and its lovely, lovely gemstone, Gideon took a last look around the miserable place. "A fitting tomb, don't you think? And now on to the next phase of my plan. Where do you think Lady Fiona might be?"

He stepped back out of the path of the spreading slime. "Oh, my apologies. You don't have a brain left to think with." He chuckled at his own wit and then opened a doorway to his home. "I wonder if she has received my message yet?"

Chapter 35

Campbell Manor

Hopkins met them at the door before they made it out of the garage. "A note just came for you, Lady Fiona." His body practically hummed with suppressed fury. "I think we may have a problem."

He turned to Sean. "If you would please open the vault and bring out the special items I showed you once?"

"Are you sure?" Sean's face turned pale.

"Yes."

Sean wasted no more time with questions, but just took off back toward the garage.

Christophe and Fiona followed Hopkins inside and to her office. "What kind of problem? We don't need another problem. Did you read the note?" Fiona asked.

"I would not read your mail."

"I think we're a little past that. Have you listened to the news?"

Hopkins nodded grimly. "I was going to wait five more minutes for you and then read it. I think Declan's in trouble."

He handed over a thick envelope, cream parchment with

her name elegantly written on it in slanted black letters and bold black ink. She ripped it open and held the note out so they could all see it.

Lady Fiona,

As you may know, I am not precisely the man you assumed me to be. I should like to meet with both of you to discuss our future plans. Your brother has graciously accepted my hospitality, as well, and is currently enjoying a bit of light refreshment. Tell the man from the water that Declan tells me the wine is a very good vintage.

Yours,
Fairsby, Lord Summerlands

Suddenly she couldn't breathe. Her lungs absolutely refused to draw in air. She collapsed to the floor before Hopkins or Christophe could catch her.

"He has Declan. Feransel has Declan."

"We'll get him back," Christophe said, scooping her up off the floor and into his arms. "I swear to you by my oath as a Warrior of Poseidon that we *will* get him back."

"What does it mean?" She pushed away from Christophe and smoothed out the crumpled letter. "I get that 'man from the water' is you and 'Lord Summerlands' is a not very subtle way to say lord from the Summer Lands especially since that's not his title, but what does that mean about the wine?"

"It means that Declan accepted drink, maybe food, too, so they more than likely have enchanted him."

She thought about it. Thought about all the reasons why she should remain sane, and calm, and rational.

And then she threw back her head and screamed.

~~~~

Christophe understood what she was feeling. He even understood her need to howl out her rage. But it wasn't helping their current problem, and he needed for her to *think*. He figured he'd give her another minute before he tried shaking her or pouring cold water on her head, or whatever he should do to calm hysteria. One minute, and then she had to stop.

She stopped screaming thirty seconds later.

"Right," she said briskly, as if she hadn't just had a mini-meltdown. "Let's figure out what to do next."

Her cell phone rang. She pulled it out like it was a lifeline, then held it up in a shaking hand. "It's him. It's Declan."

She flipped it open and adjusted something so they could all hear.

"Declan, honey, are you okay?"

"How touching." Fairsby's voice—no, Feransel's voice—rang out.

A wave of fury hotter than molten steel forged in the fires of the nine hells swept through Christophe, searing and burning everything in its path, until all that was left was rage and determination. The Fae was going to die for hurting Fiona. He was already a dead man. He just didn't know it yet.

"You put my brother on the phone, Fairsby, at once," Fiona demanded.

The Fae laughed, and even through the phone, the sound was so chillingly evil that all three of them recoiled as if a serpent perched on the tiny electronic device instead of at its other end.

"He's a little busy at the time, with a few water nymphs. Did you know your baby brother is a virgin?" He laughed again. "Oh, too bad. I do believe *was* is the correct verb tense."

All the blood drained out of Fiona's face. Christophe took the phone out of her shaking hand.

"What a brave elf to play with little boys, na Feransel," Christophe said, mocking him. "Does your mommy still wipe your ass for you, too?"

"Call me *elf* at your own peril, Atlantean. I would think, in any case, that you had enough to concern you," the Fae said; still calm, still taunting.

Christophe had shaken that smug serenity a little bit, though, and he planned to shake it up even more. "I heard Telios stole your thunder with the Siren. Sad, that. Outwitted by a vampire. What's next? Shifters in the Summer Lands?"

"Ah, yes. Telios. I learned of his little demonstration just a bit too late. So sad that he was defenseless in his sleep this morning. One would have expected more of a fight from the celebrated Jack the Ripper. I so wanted to keep his head to decorate my wall. So tragic that they dissolve so fast."

Fiona traded a glance with Hopkins and then they both looked at Christophe. She made a "move it along" gesture.

"What, you expect us to mourn for him? Where and when do you want to meet? The boy had better be safe and intact, or you will answer to me." Christophe never raised his voice. He didn't have to. Power roared through his body and enhanced his words until they thundered through the air and into the phone.

"Interesting trick," the Fae said. "Your voice alone just killed my favorite rosebush. I'll have to take that out of someone's flesh, of course, but it was interesting. I wonder how much of that raw, rough power I have caused."

Christophe stared at the phone, but knew better than to allow the Fae to draw him into a useless argument.

"When and where?" Fiona shouted at the phone, at the Fae. "Just tell us when and where, damn you."

"The dulcet tones of my future wife. Yes, my dearest one, I know you are impatient to join with me and bear my sons. Tonight, at midnight. A bit clichéd, but for a reason. The hour holds sacred power here in the Summer Lands."

Fiona fell back against the desk, her mouth opening and closing, but no sound came out. Christophe took over, forcing himself to ignore the bit about "future wife"—for now.

"How do we get there?"

"Come to Fairsby Manor, of course," the Fae who was and was not Fairsby replied. "I'll be there to meet you. Midnight and not a minute sooner, mind, and only the two of you. Oh, and Fiona? I'll gladly trade your brother's freedom for that Atlantean's head on a plate."

The click as he hung up on them echoed in the space between the three of them.

Hopkins nodded once, decisively. "Now we go plan how to kick his arse."

"Yes," Fiona said. "Now."

An hour later

They'd cleaned up and changed from the explosion's aftermath, and now all Fiona wanted to do was take off for Lord Fairsby's family home and find her brother.

"Believe me. I'd be all for it if it had a chance in the nine hells of working, but it doesn't," Christophe said. "The entry to the Summer Lands moves around, and never at the request of non-Fae. It's like the portal to Atlantis. It has a mind of its own. If we try to storm the place early, na Feransel will make sure we *never* find your brother."

A shimmering glow was their only warning before the portal he'd just mentioned opened right before their eyes. He pulled Fiona behind him and drew his daggers, but then shoved them back in their sheaths, sighing with relief, as Brennan, Bastien, and Justice walked through, one by one.

"We hear you could use some help," Justice said, his long blue hair tied back in his customary braid and the hilt of his sword rising above his shoulder. He bowed to Fiona. "My lady."

"You all came? To help me?" Christophe couldn't quite believe it. He'd spent years shutting them all out. But then he realized what the real mission must be. "Oh, of course. The Siren."

"No, my friend," Bastien said, his voice rumbling out of the middle of his seven-foot-tall frame. "We knew you could retrieve the Siren on your own. We mostly wanted to see this woman who has finally taught you some manners, according to Princess Riley."

He, too, bowed to Fiona.

She inclined her head. "Welcome to Campbell Manor. This is my dear friend, Hopkins. The plans have changed. We need to storm the Summer Lands to fight an Unseelie Court prince who has kidnapped my brother, probably has your Siren, wants to make me his brood mare, and claims to have unfinished business with Christophe. Got it?"

A huge smile spread on Brennan's face, which still seemed

wrong, somehow. The warrior had spent more than two thousands of years with no emotion at all, thanks to a really nasty curse Poseidon had thrown at him. Now that he had regained his emotions and fallen in love, he often tried out really terrible jokes on the rest of them.

"Christophe," Brennan said, still smiling. "I really, really like this woman."

"As do we all," Hopkins said dryly, shaking hands with each of them. "Tea?"

"Guinness?" Bastien asked, hope shining on his face.

"You need a clear head," Fiona said, looking way, way up at him. Then she sighed. "I'm guessing you can metabolize a pint before midnight."

Bastien bowed again. "Atlantean metabolism, my lady. We can only very rarely become even the slightest bit drunk. It takes great effort."

"Or great stupidity," Justice added. All three of them looked at Christophe.

"Nice. With friends like you . . ."

"And the room floods with testosterone," Hopkins observed. "This way, gentlemen? I believe Lady Fiona and Christophe have some issues to discuss."

He looked back at them before following the Atlanteans out. "I have more help coming. The stockpile."

Fiona nodded, her face brightening. "Of course. Hopkins, you're brilliant."

He smiled modestly. "Just doing my job."

Christophe looked back and forth between the two of them. "What stockpile?"

"We've guns that shoot lovely iron pellets. We've swords with iron blades. All of the things that the Fae hate, in other words." She smiled fiercely, and suddenly he almost felt sorry for the Fae. "We're going to hurt him for daring to take my brother. We're going to make him pay."

Chapter 36

"If he's hurt, I've done it. I had to play ninja and my actions had repercussions. If they hurt Declan, or worse, it's just the same, you see?" She sat with her knees pulled up to her chest, aching with the need to cry, but her burning eyes were dry as death.

"You think you're like your grandfather?" Christophe shook his head. "Never, sweetheart. This is not your fault. We've been through this. If you need to blame somebody, blame me." He tried to hold her, but she pushed him away.

"No. He's mine. If he's in trouble, I'm the one. I'm just as bad as my grandfather, playing at ninja and theft, only to have the hurt fall on the innocent. My grandfather got my father killed. Now I . . . now I . . ."

She curled over into a ball, willing herself not to vomit. Sick and weak and shaky, she was no good to Declan.

Christophe paced back and forth, back and forth. "You don't even have to ask, you know. Of course I'll do it."

She could feel his sincerity and his love lighting up the

connection between them like a sun gone supernova, and she wanted to roll around in the heat and light, but she forced the door in her heart to close. It hurt too much, otherwise.

"I'll trade myself for Declan," Christophe said, spelling it out. "You don't have to ask. My head will make that plate look good."

His feeble attempt at humor died in the air between them, but she appreciated the effort. It was far more than she could do.

Flashes of memory of Declan kept shooting through her mind. Him as a baby, as a toddler who followed her everywhere, calling for his "Fee Fee." She'd hated that; thought it made her sound like a French poodle. Fifi Campbell.

School days, protecting him from the bullies who thought an orphaned pair might be fair game. They'd learned otherwise quickly enough.

"Oh, Dec," she whispered. "I'm so sorry. I'm coming for you. Your Fee Fee is coming."

Christophe lifted her clear off the chair and then sat down with her in his lap and simply held her while she finally cried. By the time the rest of the Atlanteans returned, she'd cleaned away any trace of tears and was ready to plan.

When they entered the room, Christophe stood and introduced them to her. "Lady Fiona Campbell, this is Lord Justice. He's okay in spite of the hair."

Justice faked a swat at Christophe's head and Christophe ducked and grinned. Fiona caught a flash of true fondness from Christophe's emotions and was glad for him.

"Just Fiona, please," she said, shaking hands.

"And simply Justice, for us," he said, oddly referring to himself in the plural. He was tall, dark, and gorgeous, like they all were, but with a streak of wildness in his eyes. Probably why his hair was in a braid that fell to his hips and he wore such a huge sword.

"Is there iron in that sword?" She knew she was being abrupt, but she didn't have time to waste on courtesies when Declan's life hung in the balance.

"No iron, but it has its own unique properties," he said. "It will send the Fae running."

"Brennan is the one with the sense of humor and the very

bad jokes," Christophe said, and the one who'd told Christophe he really liked her nodded.

"Bastien is the giant. Also a damn fine cook."

Bastien inclined his head. "My pleasure, Lady Fiona."

"Now what?" She looked around at each of them in turn. "You've faced them before, I have not, so I repeat, now what?"

Sean walked into the room rolling a cart. "I think I have an idea."

He opened the top of the cart and Fiona saw every type of iron weapon she could possibly have hoped for, all stacked and shining like a murderer's dream.

"Have you tried to reach Denal on the mental pathway?" Justice asked Christophe. "Do you want any of us to try?"

Christophe shrugged. "If you can, please do. Maybe you'll have better luck. I have had no success at all. Wherever he is, he either can't hear me, or he doesn't want to answer."

He refused to think of the third possibility.

Hopkins walked in and Fiona almost fell over. He wasn't wearing his suit, for perhaps the first time in her life. Instead, he was dressed all in black and he looked tough and deadly. He calmly began fastening a shoulder holster to himself.

Justice wandered over and picked up an iron sword and checked its balance. "This one is good," he told Hopkins.

"We're taking the butler?" Bastien asked. "I mean you no offense, sir, but—"

"I prefer these," Hopkins interrupted Bastien, but he was answering Justice. He chose an assortment of guns, loaded them, and holstered them in various places around his person, all in record time. "Not much for swords, but I caused some trouble with guns, back in the day." He met Fiona's gaze. "I plan to do so again tonight."

She nodded. "Thank you, Hopkins. You've always been there for us. I can't imagine surviving tonight without you."

"You don't understand, Fiona," Christophe said. "The Fae said only the two of us. The Summer Lands have a magical entrance, similar to the Atlantean portal. It will only admit the two of us, and it won't let anyone at all enter carrying weapons." He forced the words out. "None of this does us any good. Once we're in there, we're on our own."

Chapter 37

Fairsby Manor, midnight

Christophe tightened his grip on Fiona's hand and knocked on the enormous wooden door. Oak, he thought. Beautiful carving in all of the many panels. Funny how the Unseelie Fae always surrounded themselves with beauty, when they were so ugly on the inside, where it counted.

A tiny shiver passed through Fiona, but she hid any nerves behind her "lady of the manor" serenity. "Just coming to call," she said. "I've been here before."

"That's it. You can do this."

"Before I knew my best friend was a Fae princess and kidnapper," she continued relentlessly. "Before some crazy elf stole my brother and wanted to hire out my uterus."

Christophe grimaced. "I don't think he has hiring in mind. What were you talking to Justice about, by the way?"

She shrugged her shoulders under her long, heavy coat. "Nothing much. And now? I'm going to kick some elf ass," she said, smiling at the door.

"*We're* going to kick some elf butt, Partner."

She reached up to kiss him and he just barely had time to

hope it wasn't the last time he ever kissed her, and then the door opened. His jaw dropped open in shock.

"Lucinda?" Fiona leapt inside and helped support the bloody and battered shifter. "Who did this to you?"

Christophe thought, *Trap*, but it was too late, far too late, and so he followed Fiona inside and watched the door slam shut behind them.

Lucinda fell to the ground heavily. She was bleeding from so many different places that it was a wonder she was still alive.

"Why don't you shift and start healing yourself?" He crouched down next to her. "We'll stand guard."

She shook her head; a tiny movement, but even that caused her pain. "No, you don't understand. He has the Siren. He can keep us from shifting. Right now he's only playing with it and there are hundreds of us near death. If you teach him how to access its full power, we're all finished."

"No worries there," he told her. "There's not a chance in the nine hells I'll help him with anything."

The sound of boot heels ringing on marble sounded in the foyer, though there was no one there, until suddenly Gideon na Feransel stood there watching them. "Such a disappointment. Here I'd hoped it would be easy."

The Fae slowly and carefully rolled up the sleeves on his tailored shirt. "I think I need a little snack for this demonstration."

As if on command, three shifters dragged a fourth out of a doorway behind the Fae and dropped their struggling captive in front of him. The shifters, all but the captive, were enthralled. The one on the floor looked up at them, and it took Christophe a minute to recognize Evan, Lucinda's mate, in the mass of torn and tattered flesh that was all that was left of his face.

"What did you do to them?" Fiona demanded. "Gideon, how could you?"

"It's not the Gideon you think you know," Christophe reminded her. "*He* was an illusion."

"Yes, he was an illusion," the Fae repeated, mocking them. "But this isn't."

He yanked Evan up off the floor with one hand and brutally jerked the shifter's head up at a painful angle. Then he leaned forward until their faces were almost touching and he . . . inhaled.

That was all. He *inhaled*. Nothing more, and yet Evan began to scream and fight even harder than he had before, to get away. Christophe pulled his daggers, but the Fae pointed a single finger at Fiona, and the shifters attacked. The three were pure, single-minded, deadly determination in their enthralled state, and it took everything Christophe had to fight them off. By the time he'd killed the third, Gideon na Feransel was dropping the husk of Evan's drained body on the floor.

That single action caught at something in Christophe's mind and sliced away all of his years of denial in a single vicious swipe, and the memory played in full, living color.

His mother, her drained body falling to the floor. His father, only a dried-out husk remaining, thudding to the floor.

The same man the cause of all of it.

The same Unseelie Fae.

He turned blind eyes to Fiona, and she caught his arm. "What is it? What's wrong? What did he do to you?"

"He finally caught on, Lady Fiona," the Fae said mockingly. "That's all. He finally remembered that I'm the one who killed his parents."

❧～～❧

Fiona knelt on the ground, Lucinda dying in her lap, and watched the man she loved shrivel away as if the Fae had drained him instead of Evan. The agonizing memories were too much; she could feel them screaming through his brain, and she wondered how either one of them would survive it.

"That's it. Fall apart, Atlantean. I need you a bit more malleable," Gideon said. "Be a good boy and fall asleep again, like you did when you were a sniveling brat all those years ago." He laughed. "Your parents did taste so delicious. Enough life force to last me for almost a year. You Atlanteans are special. It was your fault, of course." He stalked closer, but Christophe just stood there, shuddering. "Your fault," the Fae repeated. "If you hadn't run away that day; if they hadn't wasted the time to try to find you, why, they might have escaped. You murdered your own parents, you pathetic, whining brat."

His eyes shone with a dark and evil glee, and Fiona's head nearly split with the weight of guilt and pain he was piling on Christophe with his lies and manipulation.

"No!" she screamed in Christophe's face. "It wasn't your fault. Don't let him do this to you, or he wins."

Christophe slowly raised his ravaged face to meet her gaze, and then, just as slowly, he nodded and spoke inside her mind.

He will never win while you are mine to protect, mi amara.

She could feel the Herculean effort it took as Christophe forcibly pushed his pain and terror aside and locked it into the back of his mind in a box of his own, to deal with later.

Together. We'll deal with it together, later, she promised him, sending the thought from her mind to his with all of her focus.

But Christophe fell on the ground and huddled in a ball, rocking back and forth, and only the calming feel of his thoughts kept her from believing that he had given up entirely. Hopefully, he had fooled the Fae.

"It's too late, Fiona," the Fae said, all false pity and concern. "He's no good to you. Luckily you have my offer of marriage, even though you're soiled now. All I need is to lock you in a room for at least half a year, to prove to any naysayers that none of his fucks bore fruit in your delicious body."

But then na Feransel made his first mistake. He took his eyes off Christophe, just for an instant, so he could leer at Fiona.

An instant was long enough.

Christophe leapt to his feet and shot an energy bolt through the air at the Fae. Power thundered through the room and smashed into Gideon, knocking him through the air and into the wall.

But a heartbeat later, Gideon was back on his feet and hurling his own power at Christophe. Back and forth, first one had the advantage and then the other—it was a towering magical battle between two masters, and all Fiona could do was drag Lucinda over to the wall and hope they didn't get caught in the cross fire.

It lasted forever, or it ended in mere minutes, she couldn't tell, but suddenly the door behind Gideon opened again and a shimmer of hot green light poured from it.

"That's the doorway to the Summer Lands," Lucinda whispered with the last of her strength. "He has hundreds of Fae warriors standing by in there to crush any support you brought with you."

"That's the Summer Lands? Not here?" Fiona suddenly had hope and for nearly five entire seconds she held on to the vision of Hopkins and the Atlanteans saving the day. But then her vision turned to a far different one as she saw the many dark forms crowding the doorway to the Summer Lands. In this new vision, the Fae warriors swarmed out of that door and killed them all, leaving Gideon no reason to release her brother.

She called out, and both Christophe and Gideon paused, restraining their power while they turned their attention to her.

"Willingly spoken, is that correct?"

Christophe saw it in her eyes or felt it in her soul before she even spoke the words, and he shouted a denial, but it was too late.

"I willingly go with you, Gideon na Feransel, in return for the lives of my brother and this shifter, Lucinda."

"Willingly spoken and done," Gideon said triumphantly.

Before Christophe could stop him, the Fae raised both hands and a sweep of power pushed through the room, over-powering everything and everyone it its way.

"No," Christophe said, and his anguish at what she knew he thought of as her betrayal pierced the fragments that were left of her heart.

Then the room faded to a welcoming black.

Chapter 38

Christophe woke when a massive aquamarine smashed into the side of his head.

He'd been woken up in worse ways. He closed his eyes again.

Then the reality of what had just happened caught up with his dazed and battered mind, and he changed his mind. This was the worst, ever.

Fiona had willingly given herself to the Fae. There was almost nothing he could do about it. He was tapped out of magic, trapped in the Summer Lands—and, most likely, the Unseelie Court itself, the center and source of this Fae prince's power—and the woman he loved more than his own life had just surrendered herself to the same monster who had murdered Christophe's parents.

The worst situation of his life, perhaps, but there had to be a way to win. There was always a way.

Gideon na Feransel was going to die.

All of that analysis ran through his mind in the few seconds before he opened his eyes. He then sat up and retrieved the gem that had woken him so unpleasantly. He held it up in the air and scanned the area. Rock walls. Rock floor. Light from some unknown source. A cave?

"Thank you. I've been looking for this. Telios was just a frame?"

Gideon's voice sounded in the chamber, but Christophe couldn't see him. More tricks of illusion. "Telios was a tool for me to use, who unfortunately learned secrets he should not have tried to wield. He enthralled the shifters in the Tower Guard, stole the sword, and then killed them and blamed it on the Scarlet Ninja. Our lovely Fiona will be hanging up that particular outfit from now on, by the way, unless she wants to play dress-up for me."

Christophe snarled and leapt to his feet, still clutching the Siren. "Where is she? If you've hurt her, you bastard, I'll cut your dick off and feed it to you."

"So violent. Why would I possibly hurt the mother of my future children?"

Christophe didn't understand that, either. The Fae were big on purity of the race and all that. Sort of like the Atlanteans had been before Conlan smashed right through that tradition.

"Why her? She's not Fae. Why do you want her?"

"Ah, is that what you believe? I know what you are, now, you know. Atlantean. Evidently you know less than you think you do, for a living example of an ancient race." The Fae finally appeared, roughly in the same place from which his voice had been projecting. "Fiona is a descendant of Fae royalty. Seelie Court, to be exact. She will be very happy in my . . . well, let's just call them unification efforts, shall we? Show me how to work the Siren, or I will make her life quite unpleasant, shall we say? There are many ways to harm a human without breaking her. Humans are so delightfully fragile, aren't they?"

Christophe didn't waste time or breath on more threats. "What do you want?"

"The Siren. Show me. The ancient legends tell us that it holds enormous power, and I've only been able to access a fraction of it. Your young warrior friend, the one so besotted with my dear sister, knows nothing of how to access the gem's power. But, of course, he doesn't have your magic, does he? So now you show me how to control the full spectrum of power, or else—"

"Yeah, I get it. Or else bad things happen, and so on and so forth. Show me Fiona. Now."

"Never."

"Take me to Fiona, so I can see for myself she is unharmed, or you can stuff this gem up your hairy elf ass," Christophe snarled. "I have no incentive to help you unless I know for sure she is safe and well."

Gideon's face turned red, then white again, and Christophe was sure he was finally going to die, right there on the spot.

"Yes. I will allow you to see Fiona," Gideon finally said. "After that, you will show me how to control the Siren's power. Willingly speak it to me, or I will kill you now."

Christophe inclined his head. "After I see Fiona, I will show you the full power of the Siren. Willingly spoken."

Satisfied, Gideon pointed toward a doorway that hadn't been there before. Christophe led the way out of the door.

The first chamber they entered was a deep, rich forest. The scent of green and growing things and the rich loam in the soil permeated the air and made Christophe wonder how creatures of such viciousness and hate could create and control nature's perfection so beautifully. Then he saw the unhappy faces of several wood sprites, and he knew the truth. The Unseelie Fae could harness, imprison, and control, but none of nature worked willingly in cooperation with them.

Would it be enough to lead to their downfall? He didn't know. Millennia of Fae history said the opposite.

As they neared the end of the forest chamber, Christophe heard splashing and laughter like tiny bells. Nymphs. He schooled his face to be completely expressionless, in case Fiona was there, too. Nymphs could be fairly outrageous and he'd prefer not to react.

When they rounded the final tree and came upon the pool, however, it wasn't Fiona he saw, but her brother. From the looks of him, he was in excellent spirits, too.

Not to mention stark naked.

Expressionless didn't cover this. Christophe had to force

himself not to laugh. Luckily the Fae had kept walking and was some distance ahead.

Declan saw him and turned red, making an attempt to cover himself. "Christophe! Did you come to get me out of here?"

The nymphs, three of them, all naked as the day they were born and absolutely lovely in their watery play, smiled and beckoned him to come join them.

He bowed but shook his head. "Alas, ladies, my heart is given to my one true love."

They pouted but gave up gracefully. Nymphs could overpower any man's will except for one who was truly in love. For them to have given up so easily, they must have sensed it powerfully in him.

"That's delightful," one said.

"Lovely, lovely, love," the second said, nibbling at Declan's toes. He turned an even brighter shade of red.

"We love virgins. Not that he is one, anymore," the third said, rubbing her breasts on Declan's back. His groan was heartfelt, but he splashed his way out of the pool and toward Christophe.

"Can you at least put that thing away?" Christophe tried not to laugh, but it was getting harder.

"They stole my clothes," Declan said, covering himself with his hands and hopping back and forth.

Christophe took pity on him, but they needed to get moving before the Fae changed his mind. "Compliment them and then ask about your clothes," he advised. "But they have to be really flowery compliments. Nymphs love to be flattered. Catch up to me as quickly as you can."

Christophe took off without waiting to hear what Declan came up with, and he caught up to Gideon just as the Fae was opening another doorway.

"He may come with you, since his sister needs to see that he is safe, according to our agreement," the Fae said, as if bestowing a favor upon a subject. "I will leave the doorway for him to find."

Christophe had never wanted anything as badly in his life

as he wanted to crush this murdering bastard like the monster he was. Not yet, not yet, not yet. Soon.

The next chamber was like and yet unlike the first. This, too, was woodlands, but it was *forest*; ancient and resonating with power. No nymphs would dare frolic here. This was for serious magic. Gideon led the way through the chamber, and this time a silver throne twined with living vines held center court. Seated on it, wearing nothing but a filmy gown, Maeve na Feransel kissed Denal as though her life and future depended on it.

Christophe almost wanted to turn away from the intimacy of it, but then he remembered how Denal had come to the Summer Lands.

"Denal," he called out, careful not to approach the throne. "It's Christophe. Are you still yourself?"

Denal slowly raised his head, and Christophe saw that the dark blue of his eyes contained something else. Something more. Fae magic. Intertwined with Atlantean.

He was too late.

"I spoke truly and willingly, Christophe. Go home to Atlantis. I have served Maeve as her knight for three Fae years and willingly stay longer still. My duty compels me to honor my promise to her."

"Duty? What of your duty to Atlantis?"

A wave of sadness passed over Denal's face. "They don't need me. Maeve does. I belong here, at least for now."

Then there was nothing left to say, but for one final thought.

"Be well, my friend," Christophe said, realizing as he said it that it was truth. Denal was his friend. It had been Christophe who had pushed the rest of the Seven away so he could be alone, nursing his anger and sense of betrayal. If he could finally find love, he could accept other bonds, too. "Be well."

Denal stood and bowed to Christophe. "And you, my friend."

As Denal returned to his seat, he sent a message to Christophe on the shared Atlantean mental pathway.

Beware his power, but remember that vanity is his fatal

flaw. Maeve tried her best to rescue Fiona, but Gideon is far too powerful for her to oppose right now. She has given her permission to Declan to return home, so his contract in the Summer Lands is fulfilled and he may leave. As princess, she has the power to release him even though it was Gideon who abducted him. She may pay heavily for that, so destroy Gideon if you can.

Christophe nodded.

Understood. Thank you, Denal. Until we meet again.

Gideon was still moving, striding along toward the far wall of the chamber, and Christophe followed. This time, they entered a room that, though filled with trees and flowers, was more like an enormous bedchamber than anything nature had created.

Fiona, dressed in green silk, sat in a miserable, huddled ball in the middle of the bed.

"Now. You have seen her. She is unharmed. Show me how to work the Siren. I know it enthralls shifters on a far larger scale than I have yet done. Whole countries will fall to my will with this at my command." Gideon's voice shook with excitement and greed.

Fiona stared at Christophe in shock. "You're here? You're really here? All these weeks later?"

"It was illusion, *mi amara*. I have been here the same length of time, and it has been only hours, not weeks."

She shook her head, disbelief written plainly on her face. He hated the thought that she'd been alone and afraid, and that she'd believed he hadn't come for her. Perhaps that he *wouldn't* come for her.

Yet another black mark against Gideon.

"She wouldn't eat or drink while you were unconscious, at least not anything that Maeve herself didn't give her," the Fae said sullenly. "You warned her well, Atlantean. But now that I have you and the Siren, Fiona's resistance shall soon fall, as well."

Christophe drank in the sight of her. His soul opened up all the way and invited her to be part of him for now and forever. A small stillness in her movements gave him reason to hope she had felt it.

"Willingly spoken, Atlantean. Or else I have a special treat for you." He clapped his hands and several enthralled shifters, bunched together, carried a heavy object into the room.

"A very special treat, Christophe of Atlantis. Do what I ask, or I'll put you in the box that I know you love so well."

Gideon waved his arm, and the shifters moved aside. When the last shifter had cleared his line of sight, something inside Christophe shattered and broke.

Again.

It was the exact box from his childhood. Impossible, but true. He was immediately four years old again, wanting to beg, knowing it would do no good.

Finally begging, anyway, because he was unable to do other.

He clamped his lips together against the howl that threatened to break free and forced his mind to regroup, again. Forced his will to strengthen, again. For Fiona.

Gideon threw his head back and laughed, long and loud.

Christophe vowed to kill him just for that laugh. The rest of his reasons would be merely icing on the cake of his vengeance. That laugh, in the face of his parents' murder and a little boy's torture, was judge, jury, and executioner.

"You're going to die for this," he said softly.

"I find I must have you climb in the box simply for my amusement," Gideon replied, a horrible smile spreading across his face. "*Now*, I think."

Suddenly, the Fae was standing behind Fiona and holding a silver knife to her throat. "Or I kill her."

"The mother of your future children?" Christophe was proud his voice didn't shake or waver.

Gideon shrugged. "I can find another. But you—your pain and terror is so delicious. Just like your parents' life force, all those years ago. I must have yours. Get in the box."

Fiona cried out, and a thin trail of blood trickled down her neck. "Don't do it, Christophe. Don't let him break you. He'll kill me anyway. Just get out now. Save yourself."

Christophe looked at the box, and he looked back at Gideon. And then he smiled. "I'll climb in your damn box as many times as you like. Or I'll show you how to work this pretty gem." He held up the Siren. "I won't do both, and I won't do either until you let her go."

Gideon threw Fiona on the bed. "I don't care about her. Just show me how to use the jewel. The full power, as you willingly promised, Atlantean."

"The full power, Fae," Christophe said. He held the Siren up in the air, calling on Poseidon for aid. He pushed his battered, aching mind to focus harder than it ever had before and pull more power than he had ever channeled.

"Full power," he shouted. "For Atlantis!"

He *pushed*. With everything he had and everything he was, he pushed power through the aquamarine and focused every ounce of his own magic and the magic of the gem to do exactly what it had been created to do, but with a little tweak of his own. Christophe did what he had willingly promised to do.

He used the full power of the Siren to enthrall a Fae prince.

Chapter 39

The air swirled with shadows, and suddenly Fiona leapt from the bed and raced across the room to stand between Gideon and Christophe. From the air itself, the shadows wavered and re-formed into the image of Justice's sword, which she held in arms trembling with its weight.

"Come near him and I'll kill you myself," she told the Fae, her voice quiet and deadly. "He is mine and I won't give him up so easily."

Christophe stared at the sword, wondering if the blow to his head had damaged his mind. "How did you—"

"I took a chance and shadowed it, hoping the magic door to Fae Wonderland would recognize me as part Fae and let me in carrying it," Fiona said. "Remember when I talked to Justice? I borrowed it and hid it under my coat."

"I can't believe he let you touch his precious sword."

"I can't believe we're talking about this now," she snapped.

She was right. He called to power every element he could touch, and sent fire and water and earth and air soaring through his body, through his magic, toward the Fae. Right now, he needed to verify that he really had enthralled Gideon.

Atlantean power met Fae power and question met answer. Christophe had succeeded in wielding the Siren correctly. Gideon na Feransel, prince of the Unseelie Court, was firmly in Christophe's power.

"Maybe I should make him dance," Christophe muttered.

"Maybe you should get on with it, so I can put this sword down."

Christophe marveled at her courage and strength and was so humbled by her love that again, just for an instant, he felt that he could never deserve her. Then he looked at the hated box and back at Fiona, and he realized that they deserved each other.

"We're better together than apart," he said. "Isn't that what love truly means?"

She almost dropped the sword. "I'm a little busy here for philosophical discussions. Come on, we have to get out of here before he hits us with some kind of Fae super whammy."

Christophe carefully took the sword, placed it on the edge of the bed, and then pulled his protesting love into his arms and kissed her thoroughly.

"There will be no whammy, super or otherwise. I have enthralled him with the gem he sought so hard to control."

He watched the realization dawn on her face. "Willingly spoken. But all you promised was to show him the full power. Which you did, by ramming it down his throat."

"Exactly."

"Have I told you how much I love you?"

"You can spend an eternity telling me," he said seriously. "It will never be enough."

"Will you do me a favor?"

"Anything."

She pointed to the box. "Destroy that damn thing."

"Gladly." He sent ball after ball of pure blue energy smashing into the hated box until it exploded into tiny shards of wood. Fiona and he watched from behind his energy shield as it burned and, after ensnaring the Fae in a web of glittering strands of power, he turned to his woman and kissed her senseless.

Declan burst into the room. "Hey, cut out the mushy stuff. Let's get out of here. I feel waterlogged."

Fiona rushed over to hug her brother, who hugged her back for a minute then squirmed out of her embrace.

"Are you safe? Maeve told me you were, but I didn't believe her," Fiona said, tears streaming down her face. "She—I can't ever trust her again. They wouldn't let me see you and I was so afraid."

"I'm fine, Fee," Declan said, blushing. "Tip-top. Let's go, already. I marked the way out."

"What a good idea," a new voice said.

"Maeve. Where is Denal? Are you okay?" Fiona hesitated, but then started to go to her friend. Christophe held her back. Here, in this place, Maeve was not the woman Fiona had loved.

And yet the Fae princess's face softened and she smiled. Maybe Christophe was wrong, but he still wasn't taking the chance. Not with Fiona, not ever again.

"Only you would worry over my well-being, Fiona," Maeve said. "So I will grant you another boon, neither repayment nor debt owed."

With that, she waved a hand and Justice's sword flew through the air and neatly beheaded Gideon. Fiona buried her face in Christophe's shoulder in horror, but he inclined his head toward Maeve. "My thanks, my lady. That boon is one I happily accept, although I would have enjoyed doing it myself. Both for Fiona and for my parents."

"Perhaps, for once, you do not have to be the dealer of death," Maeve said. "Had you not rescued Fiona, he never would have given her up, and she is my friend, not a whore to be held captive as a sex slave," she said, and the ice and thunder in her voice made him glad that he had not made her an enemy. On the floor, Gideon's body and head dissolved into a fine sparkling dust and then vanished.

"He was rogue, my wicked, scheming brother," she continued. "Running rampant, working out of the hierarchy in the Unseelie Court. A mere upstart trying to take over my line and curry favor with our queen, my lady mother."

"So this is a family squabble," Fiona said, raising her head. "All of this for that? I don't believe it."

"The world is in a state of unbalance since Anubisa, the vampire goddess, has been missing," Maeve said. "The vampires are working on their own agendas. The gods are unhappy. *Ragnarok* is coming. Can't you feel it, Atlantean? Do you really choose for your land to rise at a time so similar to the one that drove you beneath the waters?"

Christophe took a deep breath. "I hear the truth in your words. I may even agree with you in some part. But I have sworn an oath, and I must honor it. The Siren must be returned to Atlantis."

"We of the Unseelie Court are not in opposition to your plans, Atlantean. We are fine allies to have, you will learn—or dangerous enemies. The Seelie Court will soon learn this, we hope, and our alliance will be completed. Now that Gideon is dead, that time may come sooner."

"*That* I believe."

Fiona shuddered. "I am so sorry, Maeve. I know your people are different, but to have to kill your own brother . . . I am so sorry."

Maeve's eyes glistened with something as she regarded her friend. Christophe would almost have sworn they were unshed tears. But she didn't respond.

"Now what?" Christophe asked.

"I will study you and your methods through your warrior representative Denal for some while. Then we shall meet and determine what to do next. Strategy is like breath to the Fae, and we are more well-versed in . . . *breathing* . . . than most."

Christophe bowed deeply. He could hear between her words to the truth beneath. Maeve would almost certainly be the next queen of the Unseelie Court. Now would be as good a time as any to begin an ambassadorial relationship.

Fiona took a few steps toward her old friend. "I don't even know what to call you anymore, Your Highness."

Maeve's face lit up. "Call me your friend. That's all I have ever asked."

"I'm your friend, too. Always," Fiona promised.

"And possibly a distant cousin," Christophe murmured.

"Seelie Court Fae. I wonder what Rhys na Garanwyn will have to say about that."

"If he says anything unpleasant, please leave him to me," Maeve said, her smile turning to something glittering and fearful.

"I will clear the Scarlet Ninja's name," Maeve continued. "Perhaps even make an extra donation to a few of your causes. Before the week is done, all shall know that the Scarlet Ninja saved England from a war."

"Thank you, but I could only do that with a lot of help from Atlantis and from a Fae princess who used to borrow my lipstick," Fiona said, smiling, but then she turned solemn. "The shifters he enthralled?"

"Already released. Please extend my apologies to the families of the ones he killed. We will extend monetary reparation, for what little that does to help. Lucinda, the alpha you rescued with your sacrifice, will heal."

"How do you know—"

"I have my ways." Maeve said. "How do you think I always knew where to find the hot guys in school?"

"The hot guys found you," Fiona said, smiling a little. "Thank you for what you said about the shifters. I'll tell Lucinda."

Maeve laughed. "Never thank a Fae, or you will become beholden. You can send me more Chanel for a solstice gift to pay this small debt."

With that, Maeve led them to the way out of the Summer Lands. In a short time, Fiona, Christophe, and Declan were standing on the steps outside of Fairsby Manor, dazed, as Hopkins and the Atlanteans rushed toward them. The sun shone brightly overhead. Christophe gave Justice his sword and the two exchanged nods.

"What in the name of all the gods happened to you?" Bastien demanded. "You were in there for more than two weeks."

Declan blushed a fiery red. "Um—"

The Atlanteans stared at him, fascinated.

"Nymphs," Christophe said dryly.

"Ohhhh. Nymphs," Brennan said. "So will we be going

back in around nine months from now on another rescue mission?"

"What?" Fiona rounded on her brother, but then her cheeks flamed red as she realized. "Oh. Ohhhhh."

Declan hung his head, his cheeks as hot as his sister's. "Trust me, sis. You don't want to know the details."

Justice bowed to Fiona. "My sword, my lady? Did it help?"

"Yes, Just holding it made me braver."

"I doubt that's even possible," Christophe said.

"Can we go home now?" Declan asked. "I really need to go home now."

"How about we go home now?" Christophe opened a portal, and this time it flared to brilliant life as soon as he called. Interesting, that.

"And never say the word nymph again?" Declan pleaded.

Christophe always claimed, later, that it was one of the others who started laughing first.

Chapter 40

Campbell Manor

When all the tales had been told, the experiences recounted, and the promises made to Declan that he would never, ever, tell anybody else, especially Hopkins or Fiona, the exact details about finding Declan with the nymphs, Christophe knew it was time to go. His friends had gone through a portal hours earlier, but he had been content to sit, holding Fiona as dusk's shadows claimed the corners of the room.

"I need to return to Atlantis and report in," he finally said, unable to put it off any longer. He opened his hand and they both looked at the Siren, so innocent and quiet in his hand. "This must be restored to the Trident immediately."

"You didn't give it to the others to return," Fiona said softly. "Why?"

"It's something I need to do. This mission, from beginning to end. Does that make any sense?"

She kissed him, hard. "It makes a great deal of sense. So call the portal and get it over with, and then come back to me."

"I've never made love to you in your office," he said, putting the Siren on her desk and filling his hands with her breasts, which were infinitely more pleasant to hold.

"Oh, that is a terrible oversight," she agreed. She wiggled out of his arms and crossed to the door, locked it, and then turned around to face him.

"What exactly are you going to do about it?"

He leapt across the space separating them and pinned her to the door with his body. "I believe there was a debt owed," he said solemnly.

"A debt?"

"A spanking."

Her mouth fell open. "Oh, no, you're not going to spank me."

He nodded, trying to keep a straight face. "Oh, yes. Naked."

She tried to answer, but her mouth got tangled up trying to tell him all the ways he was not going to spank her. He finally gave in and started laughing and she glared at him.

"Oh, you're going to pay for that, partner," she threatened him.

"Gladly." He bent his head and kissed her as if his very life depended on taking her mouth right that moment. Perhaps it did. All he knew was he had to have her. Now.

"On your desk?" he suggested, his voice raspy with desire and a primal need. "On the sofa?"

"How about in the air? On swirling water?" She flashed a wicked smile. "I'm always up for something different."

He started laughing, and then he called to water. "Yes, my naughty love. Let's play."

In seconds, she was naked, her body gleaming in the sunlight pouring through the windows. It was a matter of a thought for him to dispense with his own clothes, and then he lifted her into the air and sent ribbons of water playing around her luscious body. She gasped at the chill and then cried out when he concentrated harder and directed tiny fingers of cool water to toy with every inch of her skin.

"That's not fair," she said, gasping.

"Neither is this," he said, and he let go of her—with his hands. The ribbons of water held her, trapped, in the air, with her arms and legs spread out at her sides. He stepped in closer to her body and licked droplets of water from each tight nipple and then licked his way down her body. Just when he reached the pale blond curls between her thighs, he stopped and straightened before walking around behind her.

"A spanking, naked," he repeated. He rubbed her lovely, lovely ass with one hand.

"You wouldn't dare," she said, turning to glare at him over her shoulder.

"Ask me not to," he challenged.

She tightened her mouth, refusing to speak the words. But a delicious gleam in her eyes told him she might not be as reluctant as she pretended.

"You only have to say one tiny word, my princess. Just say no."

She stuck her tongue out at him but said nothing.

He grinned, and drawing his hand back just a little, lightly smacked her gloriously round ass. Fiona made a noise but it definitely wasn't a *no*.

"A lady doesn't enjoy having her bum smacked," she said primly.

His heart sank to his feet. Now she would hate him. "*Mi amara,* I'm so sorry. I was just playing—"

"Lucky for you, I'm not a lady; I'm a ninja," she said, cutting him off, that deliciously seductive smile back on her face. "Stop with the water. I want you inside me. Now."

He did as she commanded and in seconds she was flat on her back on the sofa and he drove his cock so far inside her they both cried out. "You belong to me, forever and ever," he said, barely able to speak through the knot in his throat.

"Yes," she said. "Yes. Always."

"And I to you," he added, plunging into her warm wet heat, over and over, until her body arched up into his and she screamed his name. Then, and only then, he gave in to his own release and collapsed on the sofa next to her. "Forever."

Some time later, they managed to sit up and he pulled her on his lap and grinned. "So you like spankings?"

She glanced demurely up at him through her lashes. "How about I try it on you this time?" His cock jumped a little against her hip and she laughed. "You naughty, naughty man."

"Oh, you have no idea the naughty ideas I have for you, Lady Fiona."

"A true warrior would demonstrate," she said primly.

And so he did.

It was nearly two hours later before he called the portal.

"I'll return as soon as I can," he told her.

"I know."

He hugged her again, put the Siren in his pocket, and stepped through the portal, knowing that nothing would keep him from her.

~~~

"It's still open, Lady Fiona," Hopkins observed. "Seems like a sign to me."

"When will you call me Fiona?"

"When you gather your nerve and go after him," he said, handing her paint box and a parcel to her. "I'll handle everything here. Please give this to the Atlantean, if you will."

"You always do handle everything. I love you, you know. I'll bring you to visit as soon as I can." She hugged him tight, and then, gathering her courage in one hand and her paints in the other, she stepped through to Atlantis and landed right on top of the love of her life, knocking him to the grass.

One of the guards, choking suspiciously, held out a hand, and pulled her up when she took it. Christophe just lay there, sprawled in the grass, staring up at her with his mouth hanging open. Through their bond, she could feel his exquisite joy that she'd chosen to follow him.

"Thank you, Marcus," she said.

"I really think I'm going to like you."

"You know," she said, puzzled, "when I'm around Atlanteans, I get that a lot."

On the ground, Christophe started laughing. "Does this make me Lord Christophe?"

"In your dreams," Marcus advised.

"Oh, no," Christophe said, grinning that seductive, wicked smile. "My dreams are far more exciting than that."

"Here," she said, holding the package out to him. "This is for you. From Hopkins."

Christophe opened it, still sitting on the ground, and then stared up at Fiona in astonishment. "Why on earth would Hopkins give me pajamas with barnyard animals on them?"

～～～

As they explored the gardens together later that day, Christophe suddenly lifted Fiona in the air and swung her around.

"Wait till our sons take up their first training swords," he said, eyes gleaming with anticipation. "They will make us so proud. With magic plus might, they'll be the toughest warriors ever to set foot—"

"Oh, no. My sons are not going to go around sword fighting. They're going to be doctors. Or teachers. Or—"

"Daughters," he said, wrapping a long strand of her hair around his fingers. "Beautiful, charming daughters, just like their mother. And the boys will be after them—wait. Damn boys. I'll kill them. I'll kill any boy who so much as—"

"Ouch! That hair is attached," Fiona said, extracting it from his fingers. "Maybe before you get your pants in a twist over our future children, you could tell me more about just how we're going to go about getting all of these sons or daughters?"

He bent down and lifted her into the air, then shouted out his joy and swung her around. "Maybe I could show you," he said, bending to kiss her as she wrapped her arms and legs around him, right there on the path to the palace, in front of anybody who might care to pass by.

When they could finally breathe again, he pulled her a little ways off the path, into the palace gardens, and dropped to one knee. "I know this is the way they do things in your world," he said, every ounce of the love he felt for her naked on his face. Exposed and vulnerable, just like his heart.

"Lady Fiona Campbell, will you spend the rest of your life with me?"

Her answer shone like the bright Atlantean sun on her face and in her heart. "Oh, yes. Most definitely yes."

Turn the page for
a special preview of Daniel's Story
in the Warriors of Poseidon Series

VAMPIRES IN ATLANTIS

By Alyssa Day

Coming soon from Berkley Sensation!

Chapter 1

Daniel looked out at the sea of red eyes glaring back at him in the vast chamber of the Primus and wondered, not for the first time, why the hell he'd ever wanted to be the ruler of the North American vampires. Also, he wondered how long it would be until the vampire goddess Anubisa discovered his ongoing betrayal and slowly tortured him to death.

The goddess of Chaos and Night was really, really good at torture. It was her specialty, in fact.

"So, shall we call you Daniel, then?" the vampire from South Carolina called out from behind the false safety of the rich mahogany wooden semicircular desk. His voice was a bizarre hissing drawl; Deep South meets bloodsucker. "Or Drakos? Maybe Devon? You have so many identities; we wouldn't want to use the wrong one."

"You may call me Primator, Ruler of the Primus, the third house of the United States Congress. Or Sir. Or even Master, if you adhere to the old ways," Daniel said, smiling. It wasn't a nice smile. He made sure to show some fang.

"Or you can call me the one who delivers you to the true and final death, if you continue to be an obstacle to these negotiations," he continued, still polite. No longer smiling. "If we cannot work amicably and peacefully with the humans, we will find ourselves back to the days of angry mobs and wooden stakes and flaming torches. Except this time, the mobs have missiles instead of pitchforks."

The South Carolinian sat down abruptly and clamped his mouth shut, with not even a hint of fang showing. Daniel's sense of victory was as fleeting as it was futile. They'd never agree. Humans were sheep to them, especially to the oldest ones. Predators couldn't become politicians, and he had no wish to continue in the role of trying to lead them. It was, as his Atlantean friend Ven would say, like herding seahorses: a task that would always fail and usually leave the herder with a severe case of insanity. Daniel's sanity was precarious enough already.

A flash of memory tugged at him: Quinn's face when he'd forced the blood bond on her to save her life.

Another: Deirdre's face as she lay dying in his arms.

It was the only thing he was really good at—failing to protect the women he cared about. He'd started that tradition more than eleven thousand years ago, after all.

Serai.

Daniel's assistant shuffled some papers on his desk and glanced up at him. "Shall we adjourn then, Primator?"

Daniel snapped out of his dark thoughts and looked out at the members of the Primus. Still glaring at him, for the most part. Undoubtedly planning a coup or some other evil manipulation. After all, they *were* vampires.

He recognized the irony.

"Adjourned." He struck the gavel once on its sound block, but they were already up and streaming out the vaulted double doors. Not a single one stopped to speak to him or even looked back. Plotting, always plotting.

After eleven thousand years, he was tired of all of it. Tired of the loneliness, the constant despair. The futility of hope. He'd had enough. He'd *done* enough. It was time for one last glimpse of the sun, before it incinerated him.

He stood in one fluid motion and tossed the gavel on his assistant's desk. "Adjourned and done. I'm resigning the title and job of Primator and getting out of Washington, DC. Good luck with my successor."

Before the poor man could form a single word, Daniel leapt into the air and flew through the room and out the doors—right into the waiting ambush. Four ready to hurt him. None ready to help.

The pundits were right. DC *was* a dangerous town.

"Are you ready to die, *Master*?"

It was South Carolina again. Daniel didn't recognize the trio of flunkies with him. Hired muscle, maybe, or members of South Carolina's blood pride. Didn't matter.

They wouldn't be around long.

"Actually, I am ready to die," Daniel said, enjoying the look of shock that widened the other vampire's eyes. "But not at your hand."

He hit the first two flunkies with a flying kick so powerful it crushed the first one's head and left the other one unconscious on the ground. The third he dispatched with a blow from his dagger that removed the vamp's head from its body, both of which began to disintegrate into the characteristic acidic slime of a decomposing vampire.

Then Daniel turned to South Carolina, who was backing away from him and trembling.

"I'm sorry. They made me do it," he cried out, trembling and whimpering like the coward he was.

"Then die with them," Daniel replied, realizing he didn't care enough to even ask who "they" was. He caught South Carolina's head between his hands and, with one powerful twist of his arms, wrenched it off the vampire's neck. The body fell to the ground, already decaying, before Daniel realized he still held the head. He flung it away from himself in disgust and scrubbed his hands against his pants.

The voice from behind him was uncharacteristically serious. "You didn't get anything on your hands."

Daniel whirled around. "Ven? What are you doing here? Or, more to the point, why didn't you help?"

The tall Atlantean prince rolled his eyes and shrugged. "Seriously? Against only four of them? Are you a girl, now?"

"Better not let Quinn hear you say that," Daniel said, before the pain of her name caught up to him. She'd been his friend, he'd thought. Until the forced blood bond. Now she was—if not an enemy—no longer a friend. Wary. Not afraid, not Quinn, but she'd never trust him again. He knew, because he could still sometimes feel her inside him. Whispers of her resonance touched his mind at times. The blood bond.

He'd saved her life and killed her trust. He'd thought it a fair trade, at the time.

"Quinn's not a girl. She's a rebel leader. Now are we going for a beer or what?" Ven gestured toward Daniel's hands. "Also, quit going all Lady Macbeth. You don't need to 'out, damned spot,' when you didn't get slime on them."

"Quoting Shakespeare? I expected something from the *Rocky Horror Picture Show*." Daniel tried to grin but couldn't sustain the effort. "Lady Macbeth. Interesting you say that. I feel like I've gotten slime on my hands every day since I took this job." Daniel forced himself to quit rubbing his hands on his pants and took a deep breath. "I'm not a politician."

Ven threw back his head and laughed. "Nobody sane is. You're a warrior, my friend, like me. Now let's go get that beer and talk about how we're going to keep you bloodsuckers from taking over the world. No offense."

"Not tonight. I'm not a politician anymore, anyway. I just resigned." Daniel looked up at the stone front of the Primus, built only a few years ago to look like it had existed for millennia. The vampire aristocracy was big on pretense. Like the idea that they *were* aristocracy. Daniel's own mother had been a peasant who owned a single mule.

Ven whistled long and low. "Conlan is not going to be happy to hear that."

"With all due respect to your brother, whether or not the high prince of Atlantis is happy with my career choices is not high on my list of concerns. Good-bye."

Ven's hand grasped Daniel's arm with almost vampire-like speed. Damn Atlanteans.

"Remove your hand, or I'll do it for you," Daniel snarled. "You presume too much."

"I've been told that before," Ven said, but he released Daniel's arm. "You saved my life. I'm not going to stand idly by while you sacrifice your own."

"How did you—"

"You said good-bye," Ven said roughly. "You never say good-bye. Ever. It doesn't take a genius to guess that a vampire who has lived for thousands of years might get tired of putting up with life every once in a while. Especially when every day brings a new battle."

Daniel stared steadily into his friend's eyes and lied. "I'm not there yet."

Ven stared back at him, hard, but finally nodded. "Fine. Take a rain check on that beer?"

"Another night," Daniel said in agreement. He watched as the prince of Atlantis, one of the few men Daniel had ever called friend, leapt into the air and dissolved into a sparkling cloud of iridescent mist. The Atlantean powers over water were both beautiful and deadly. Daniel had seen both.

He waited until the last droplet of mist had long since vanished from his sight before he spoke, repeating the words that had given away his intent. "Good-bye, my friend."

And then he went to face the dawn.

The fate of Atlantis is on the line—
and the world is at stake . . .

FROM *NEW YORK TIMES* BESTSELLING AUTHOR

ALYSSA DAY

ATLANTIS REDEEMED

The Warriors of Poseidon

Poseidon's warriors have learned that the battle to protect humanity produces unexpected enemies— and alliances. But none can be more unexpected than the bond between a cursed Atlantean warrior and a woman whose sight exposes any lie.

penguin.com

The WARRIORS OF POSEIDON
series by *New York Times* bestselling author

ALYSSA DAY

Atlantis Rising

Atlantis Awakening

Atlantis Unleashed

Atlantis Unmasked

Atlantis Redeemed

Atlantis Betrayed

Penguin Group (USA) Online

What will you be reading tomorrow?

Patricia Cornwell, Nora Roberts, Catherine Coulter,
Ken Follett, John Sandford, Clive Cussler,
Tom Clancy, Laurell K. Hamilton, Charlaine Harris,
J. R. Ward, W.E.B. Griffin, William Gibson,
Robin Cook, Brian Jacques, Stephen King,
Dean Koontz, Eric Jerome Dickey, Terry McMillan,
Sue Monk Kidd, Amy Tan, Jayne Ann Krentz,
Daniel Silva, Kate Jacobs…

You'll find them all at
penguin.com

*Read excerpts and newsletters,
find tour schedules and reading group guides,
and enter contests.*

Subscribe to Penguin Group (USA) newsletters
and get an exclusive inside look
at exciting new titles and the authors you love
long before everyone else does.

PENGUIN GROUP (USA)
penguin.com